MARVEL
www.marvel.com

ULTIMATE STICKER COLLECTION

AVENGERS ASSEMBLE!

How to use this book

Read the captions in the booklet, then turn to the sticker pages and
choose the picture that best fits in the space available.
(Hint: check the sticker labels for clues!)

•

Don't forget that your stickers can be stuck down and peeled off again.

•

There are lots of fantastic extra stickers too!

LONDON, NEW YORK, MUNICH,
MELBOURNE, AND DELHI

Written by Julia March
Edited by Samira Sood
Designed by Rajnish Kashyap, Akanksha Gupta, and Manish Chandra Upreti
Jacket designed by Robert Perry

First published in the United States in 2012 by
DK Publishing
375 Hudson Street,
New York, New York 10014

10 9 8 7 6 5 4 3 2 1
001–182970–Jan/12

TM & © 2012 Marvel & Subs.

Page design copyright © 2012 Dorling Kindersley Limited

A catalog record for this book is available from the Library of Congress.

ISBN: 978-0-7566-8997-1

Color reproduction by Media Development & Printing Ltd, UK
Printed and bound in China by L. Rex Printing Co. Ltd.

Discover more at
www.dk.com
www.marvel.com

Avengers Assemble!

"Avengers Assemble!" When this battle cry rings out, it means that the world faces a threat too huge for any Super Hero to take on alone. Only the combined powers of Earth's mightiest Super Heroes can save the day. Meet the Avengers!

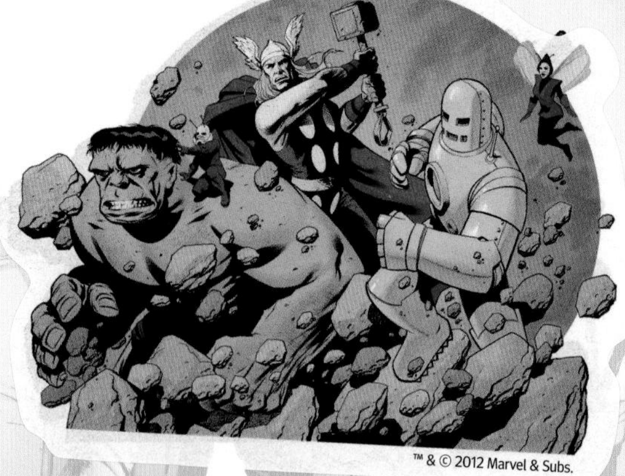

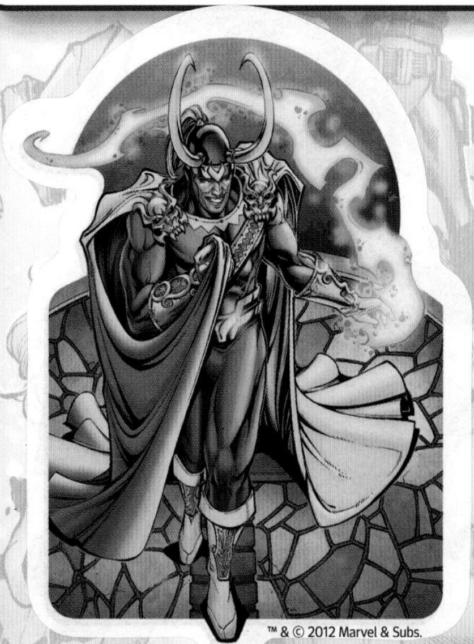

The beginning

The Avengers were formed when Loki, the god of mischief, tried to start a fight between Hulk and Thor.

First Avengers

Thor, Hulk, Iron Man, Ant-Man, and the Wasp joined forces to defeat Loki. They worked so well together that they decided to stay as a team. The Avengers were born!

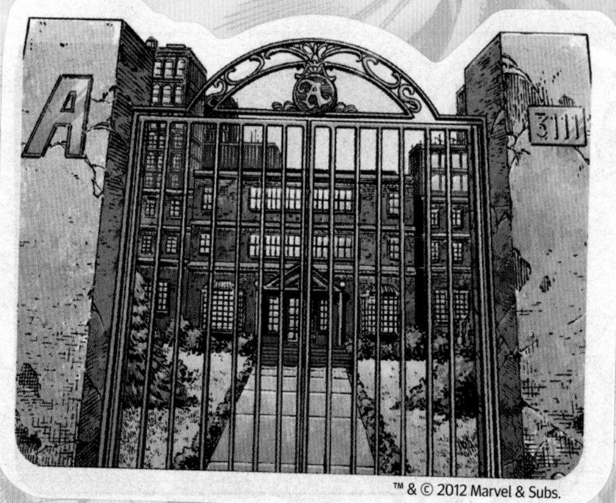
A
3111

Captain America

Captain America didn't join the Avengers until later, but he fitted in so well that the others made him their leader.

Avengers Mansion

Avengers Mansion was once the residence of Iron Man's wealthy family. Now it's home to the Avengers.

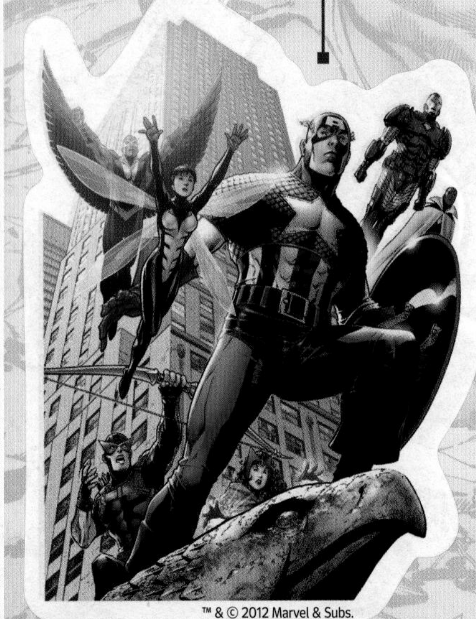

Jarvis

Even Super Heroes can use help around the house. Jarvis the butler looks after Avengers Mansion, and often gets mixed up in the team's adventures!

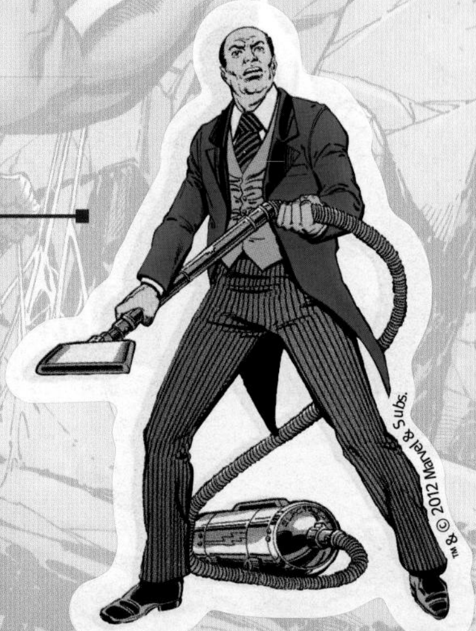

Quinjets

Special planes called Quinjets take the Avengers wherever they need to go. Quinjets can also adapt to deep-sea or space travel.

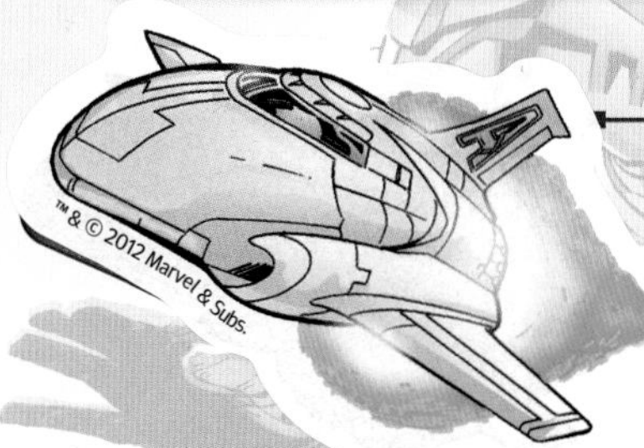
™ & © 2012 Marvel & Subs.

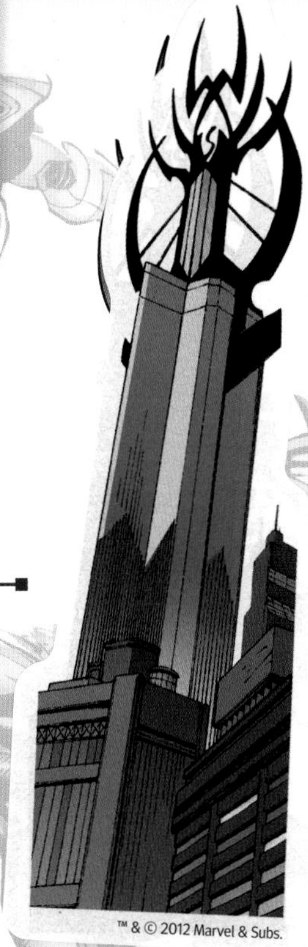
™ & © 2012 Marvel & Subs.

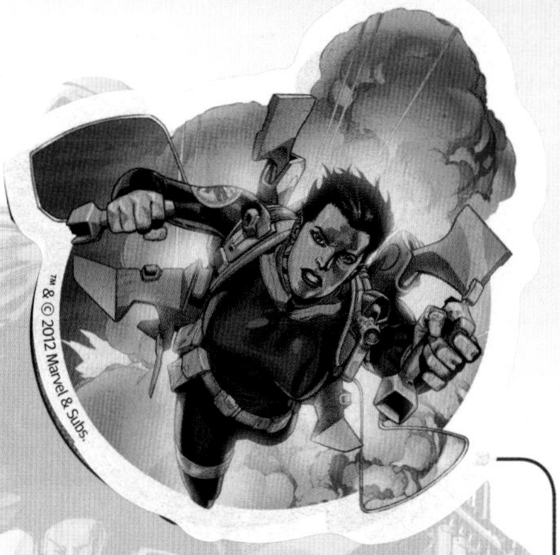
™ & © 2012 Marvel & Subs.

Maria Hill

Maria Hill is the current leader of the team—Captain America himself chose her for the job. She is an ex-member of the law enforcement agency SHIELD.

Avengers Tower

The Avengers' headquarters are in Avengers Tower, a 93-story building in Manhattan, New York City.

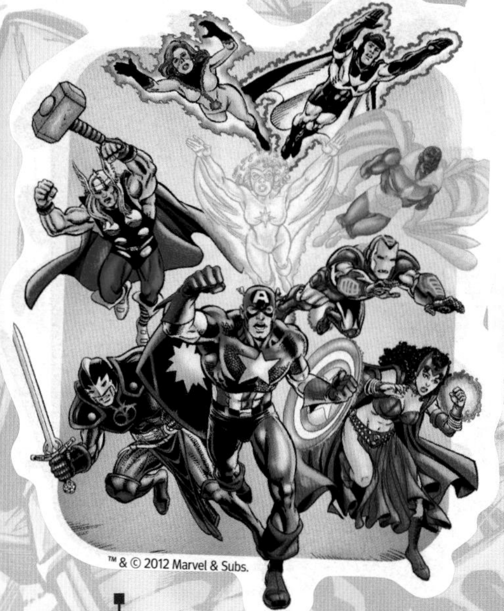
™ & © 2012 Marvel & Subs.

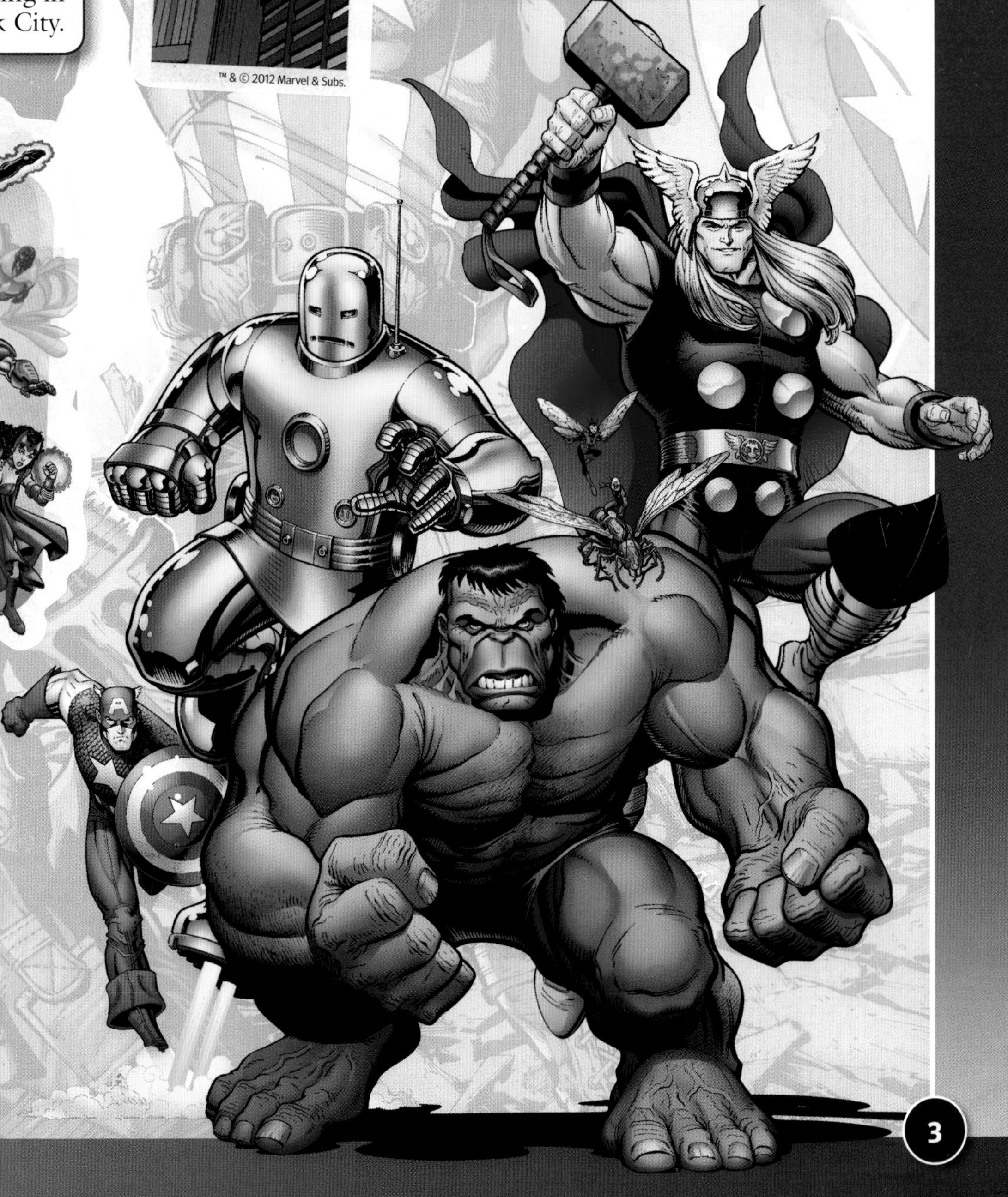

Changing roster

The Avengers' roster constantly changes, but there will always be heroes ready and waiting to heed the call—"Avengers Assemble!"

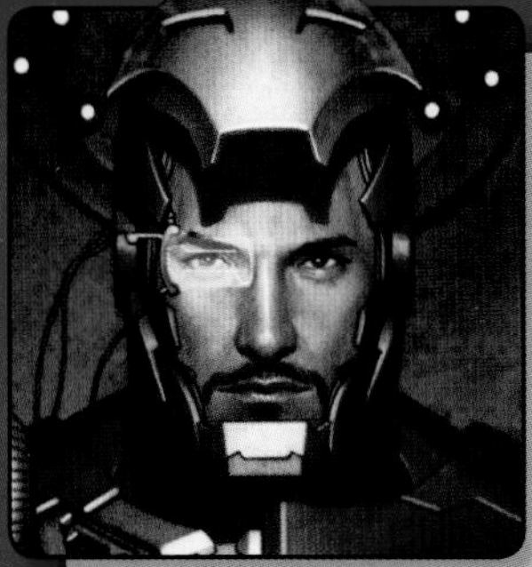

Iron Man

Nicknamed the Armored Avenger, Iron Man is known for his gleaming red and gold suit. It is a beacon to his teammates in battle and to anyone in peril. Bold, brave, and brainy, Iron Man is always working on new gadgets and weapons to add to his armor.

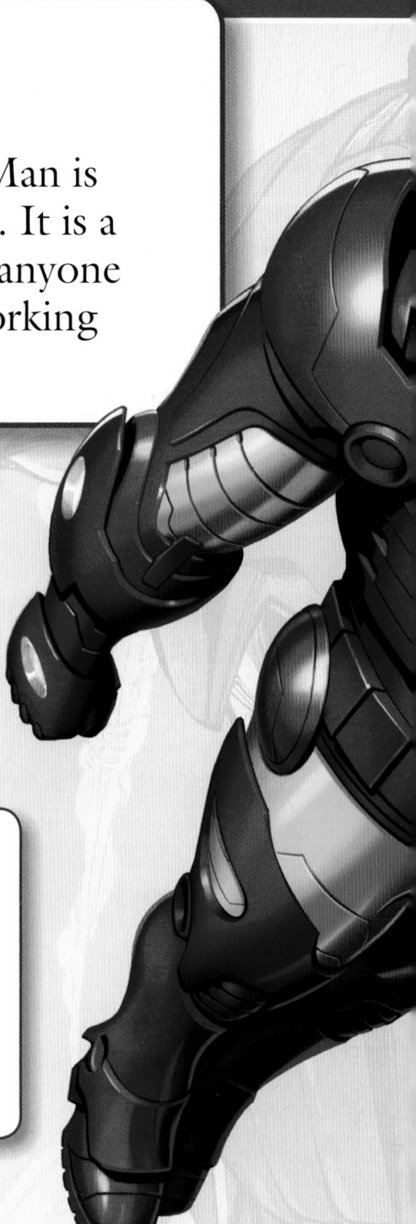

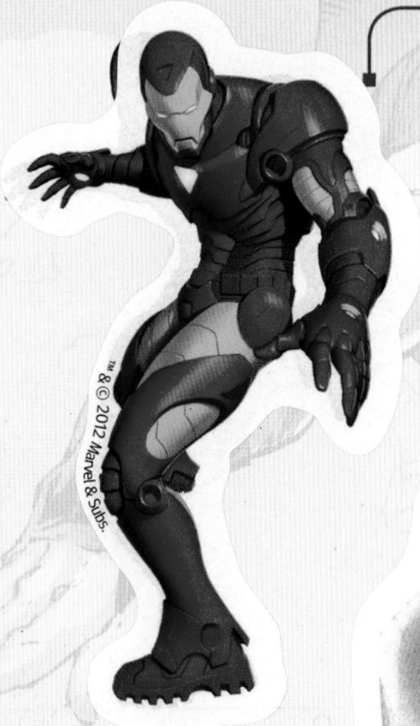
™ & © 2012 Marvel & Subs.

Man of metal
He has no superpowers, but Iron Man can do amazing things. It's all thanks to the technology in his metal suit!

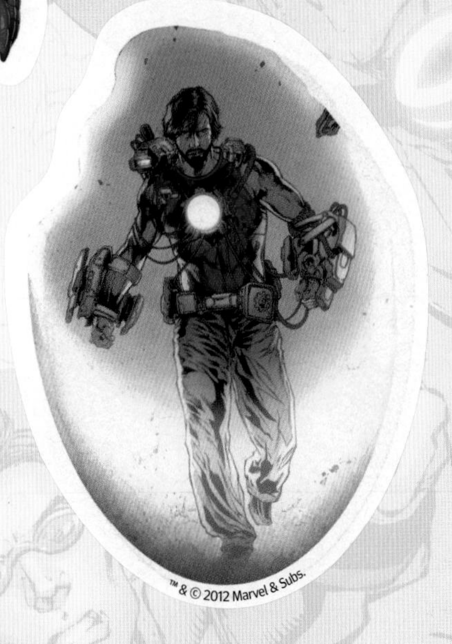
™ & © 2012 Marvel & Subs.

Tony Stark
Rich businessman Tony Stark's life changed when he was injured in a bomb blast. He had to build an iron suit to keep his heart beating.

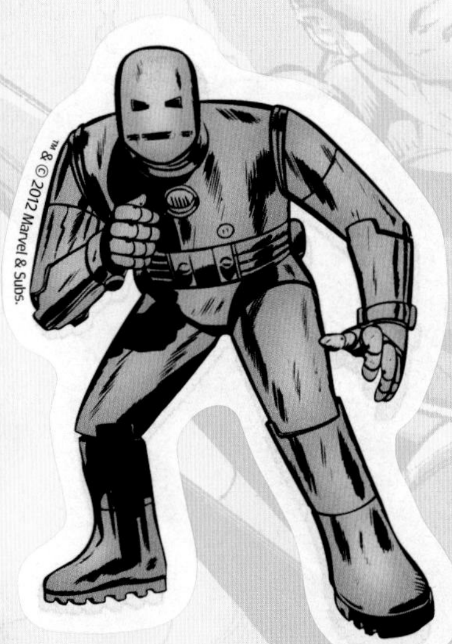
™ & © 2012 Marvel & Subs.

Armor
Tony began to upgrade his armor, and found he could use it to fight crime. He just needed a Super Hero name. How about "Iron Man"?

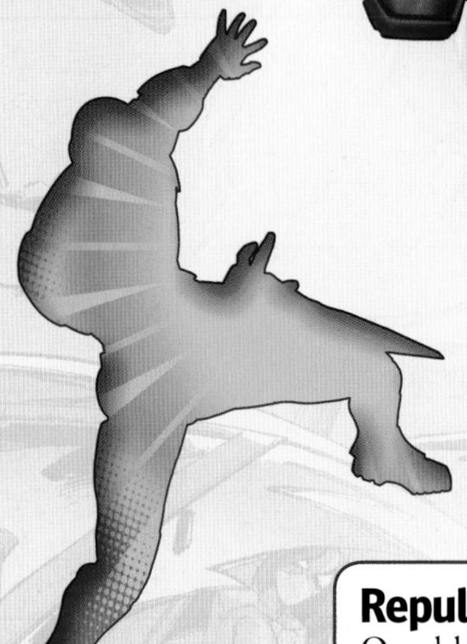

Repulsor rays
One blast from the repulsor beams on Iron Man's gloves can send his enemies hurtling into oblivion!

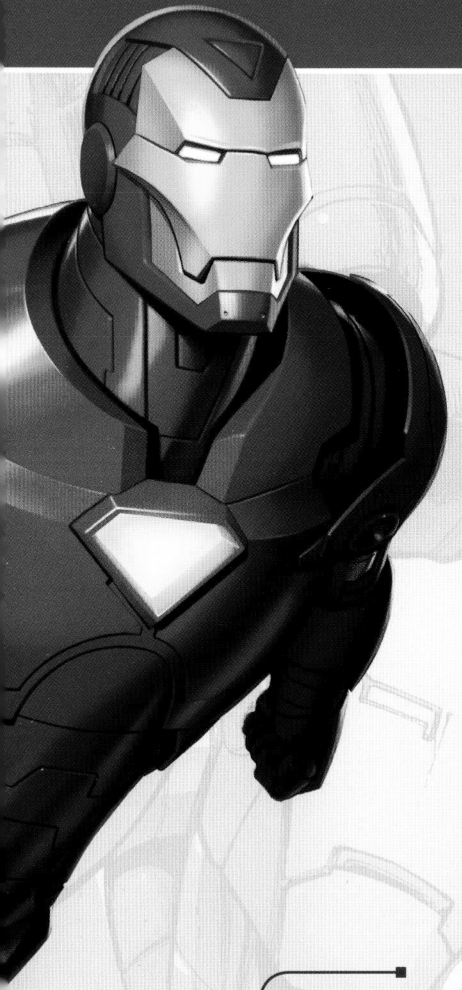

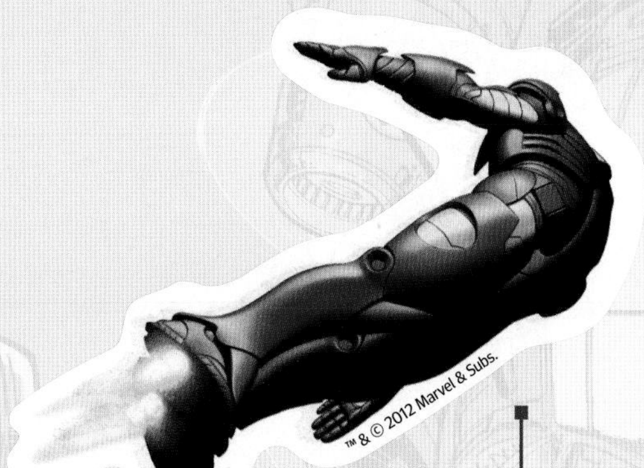
™ & © 2012 Marvel & Subs.

Ice breaker
When turned up to full strength, Iron Man's glove repulsors can knock holes in almost any object or break the thickest ice.

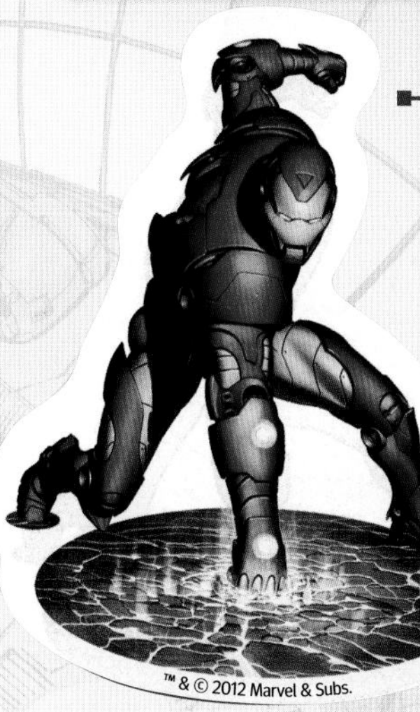
™ & © 2012 Marvel & Subs.

Jet boots
Jets in the soles of Iron Man's boots enable him to fly faster than the speed of sound.

Deep-sea armor
Iron Man has many suits of armor, including deep-sea armor. This suit can mimic the defence mechanisms of sea animals, such as the shocks of electric eels.

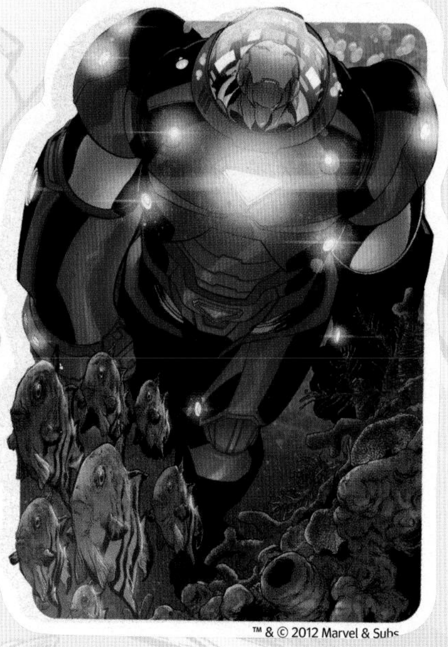
™ & © 2012 Marvel & Subs

Dr. Doom
Iron Man and his enemy Dr. Doom are well matched. Doom's armored power suit has advanced weaponry just as powerful as Iron Man's.

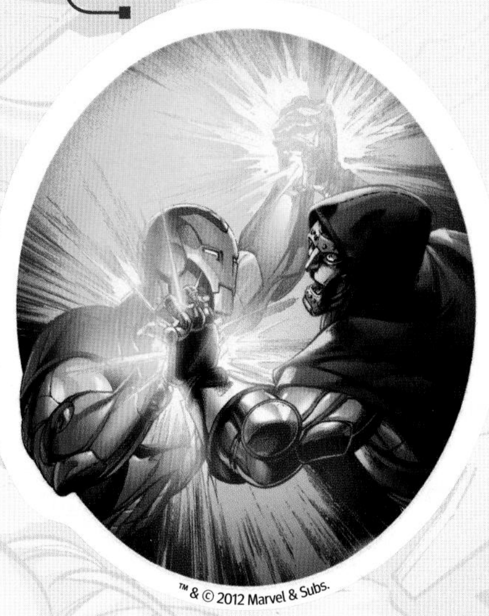
™ & © 2012 Marvel & Subs.

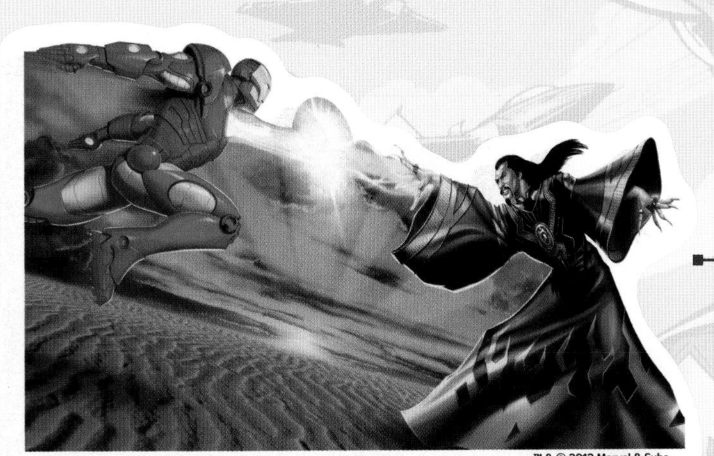
™ & © 2012 Marvel & Subs.

The Mandarin
The sinister Mandarin is Iron Man's archenemy. He has attacked the Avengers many times.

The Incredible Hulk

Hulk Smash! With his bulging muscles, towering height, and tireless energy, Hulk is immensely powerful—and he gets even stronger when he's angry. No wonder they call him the Incredible Hulk, and no wonder the Avengers are glad to have him on their side!

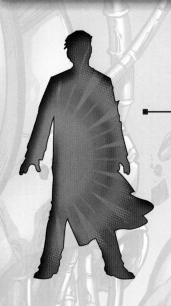

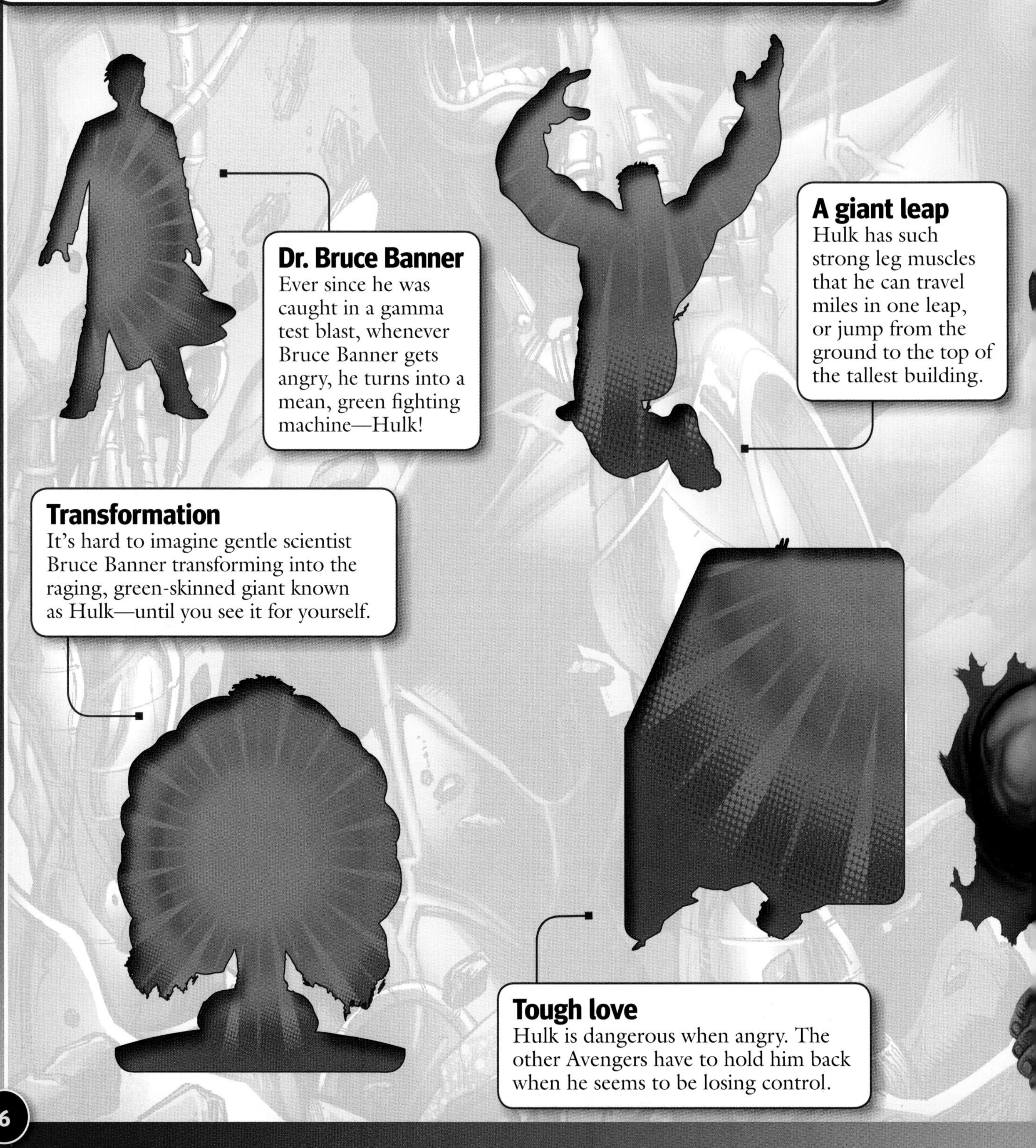

Dr. Bruce Banner
Ever since he was caught in a gamma test blast, whenever Bruce Banner gets angry, he turns into a mean, green fighting machine—Hulk!

A giant leap
Hulk has such strong leg muscles that he can travel miles in one leap, or jump from the ground to the top of the tallest building.

Transformation
It's hard to imagine gentle scientist Bruce Banner transforming into the raging, green-skinned giant known as Hulk—until you see it for yourself.

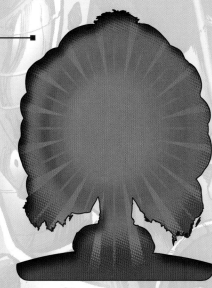

Tough love
Hulk is dangerous when angry. The other Avengers have to hold him back when he seems to be losing control.

Mean and green

Hulk has superhuman speed and stamina, and rapid healing, but his main power is his strength. When calm, Hulk can lift 100 tons (89 tonnes), and when he's angry, his strength is almost limitless.

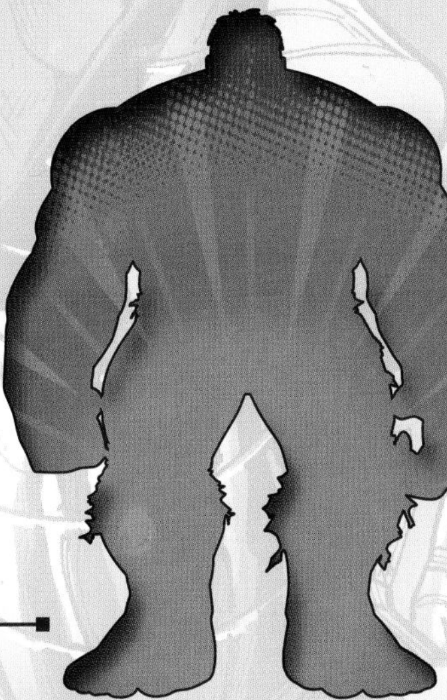

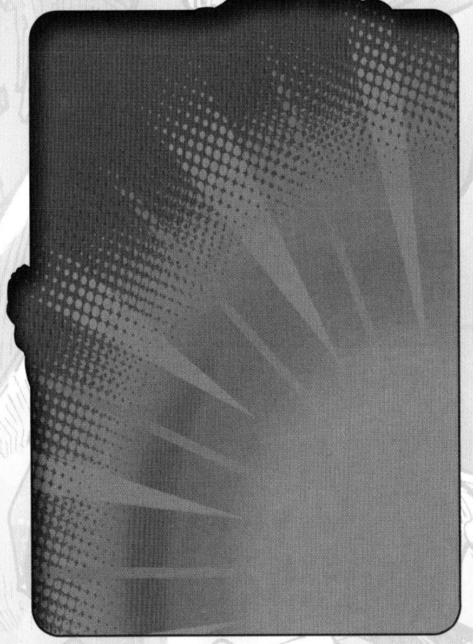

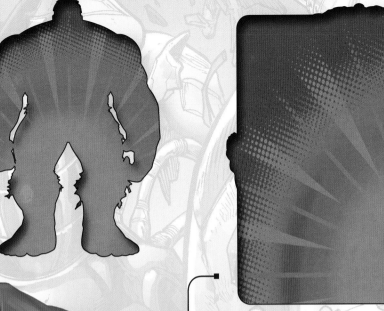

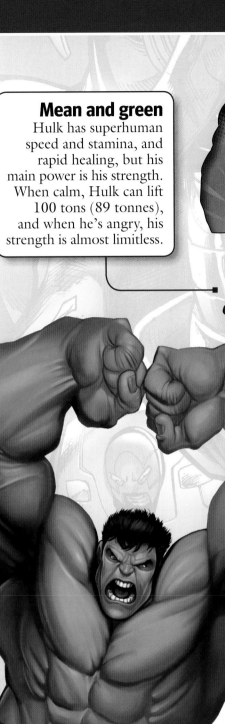

Team player

Hulk has served with other Super Hero teams too, including the Defenders, alongside Namor, Silver Surfer, and Doctor Strange. However, he always returns to the Avengers in the end!

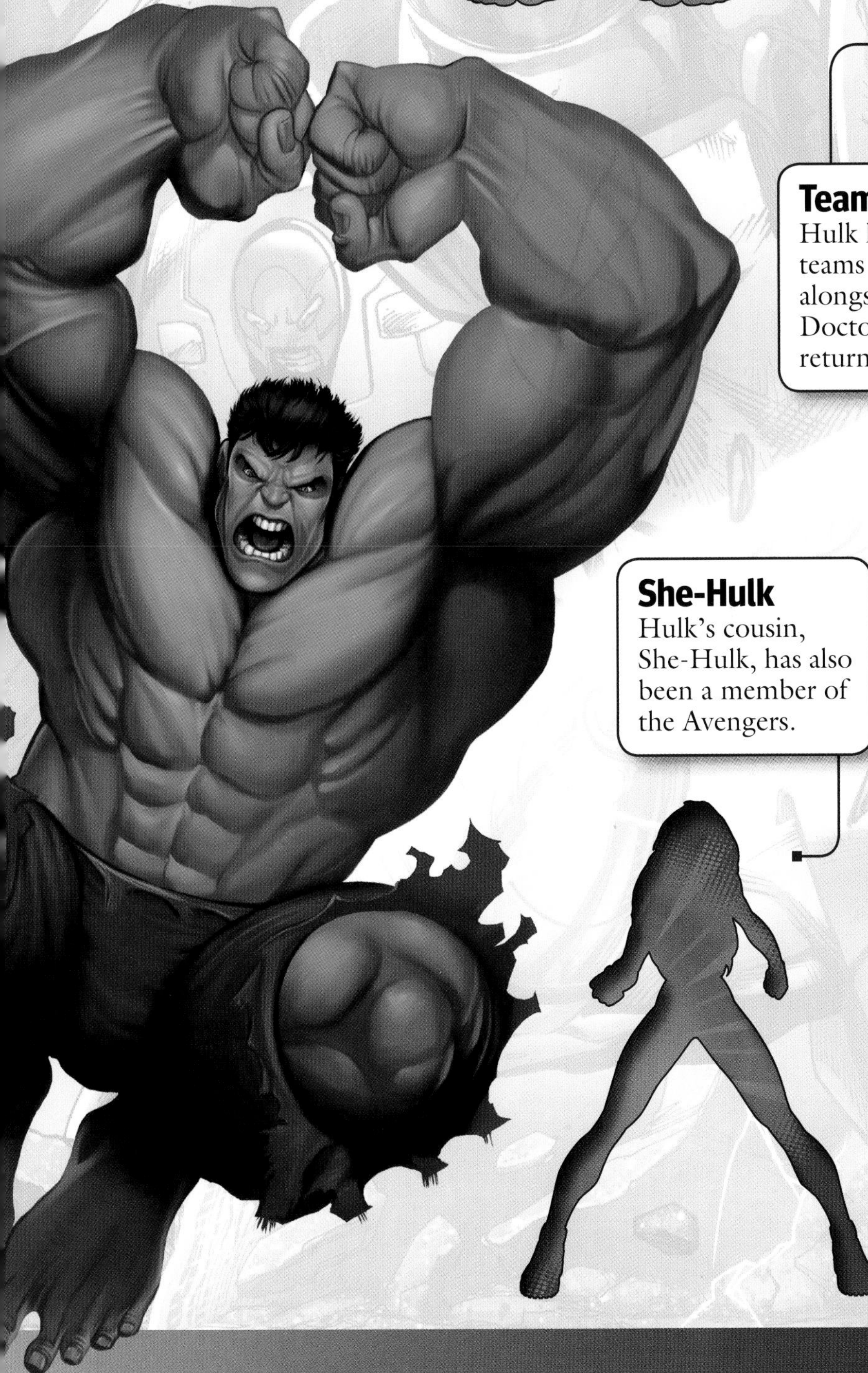

She-Hulk

Hulk's cousin, She-Hulk, has also been a member of the Avengers.

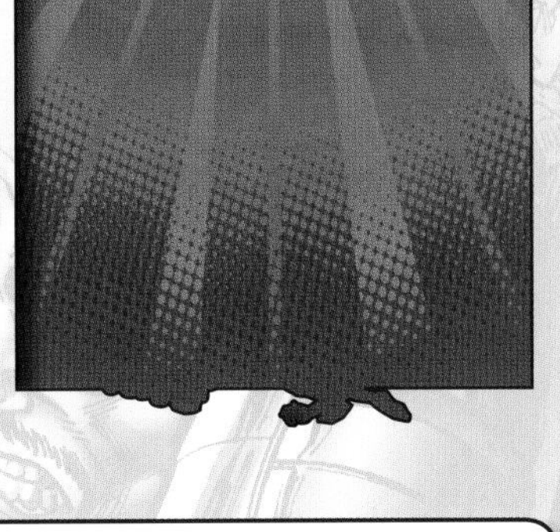

The Leader

One of Hulk's fiercest foes is the Leader. Like Hulk, he was also exposed to gamma radiation, but it was his brain and not his body that gained immense power.

Thor

Norse god Thor can make the Earth tremble with one smash of his hammer, but he prefers to make the enemies of the Earth tremble. He is one of the founding members of the Avengers, and never forgets that he is there to serve those weaker than himself.

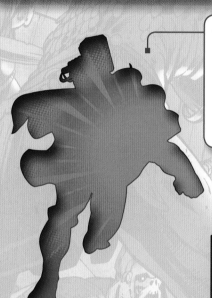

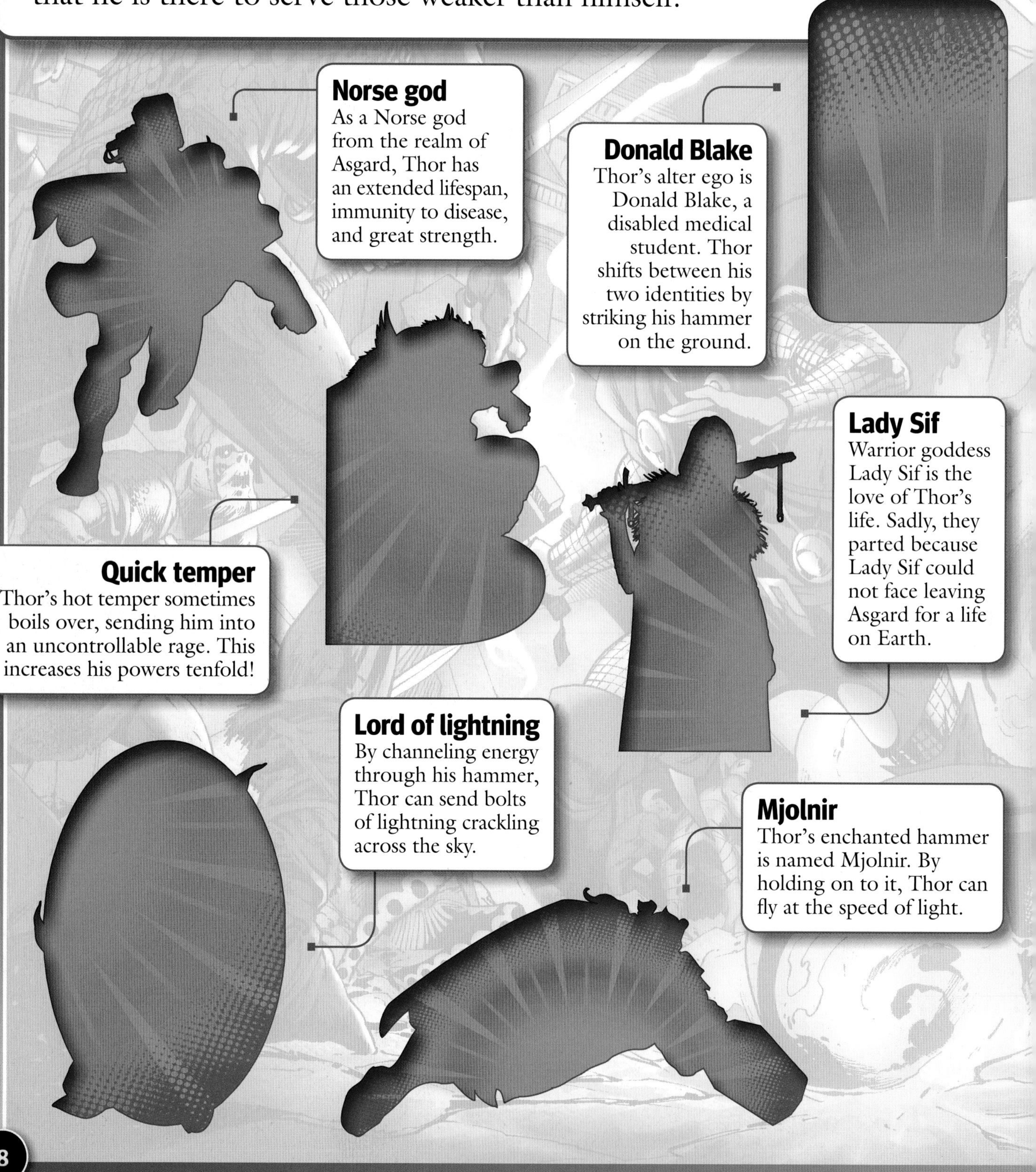

Norse god
As a Norse god from the realm of Asgard, Thor has an extended lifespan, immunity to disease, and great strength.

Donald Blake
Thor's alter ego is Donald Blake, a disabled medical student. Thor shifts between his two identities by striking his hammer on the ground.

Lady Sif
Warrior goddess Lady Sif is the love of Thor's life. Sadly, they parted because Lady Sif could not face leaving Asgard for a life on Earth.

Quick temper
Thor's hot temper sometimes boils over, sending him into an uncontrollable rage. This increases his powers tenfold!

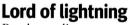

Lord of lightning
By channeling energy through his hammer, Thor can send bolts of lightning crackling across the sky.

Mjolnir
Thor's enchanted hammer is named Mjolnir. By holding on to it, Thor can fly at the speed of light.

Such power

Through serving with the Avengers, Thor has learned to control his arrogance and hot temper—at least most of the time!

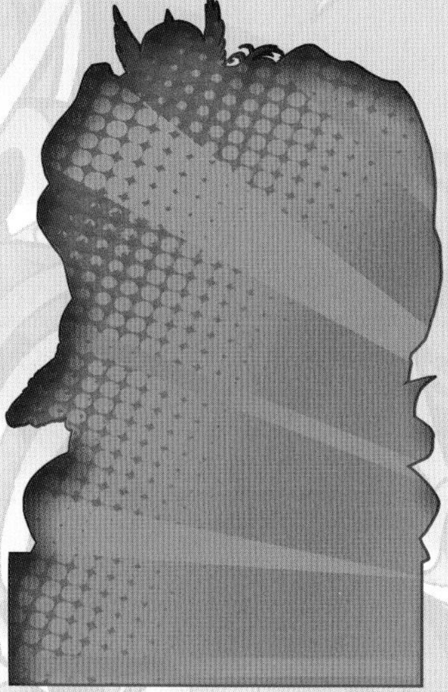

Moondragon

When a new Avenger, Moondragon, showed signs of arrogance, Thor had her removed from the team as he saw his own weakness in her.

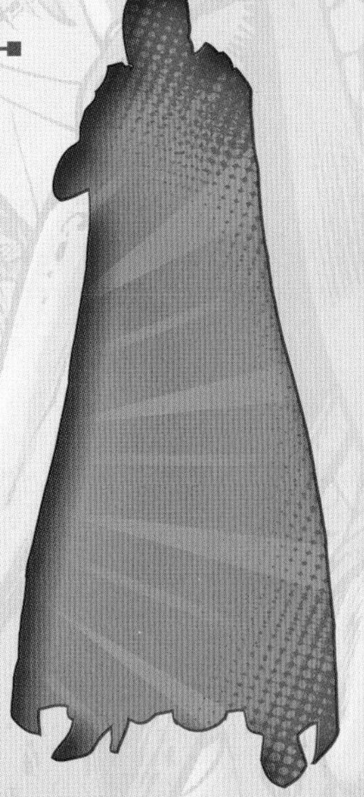

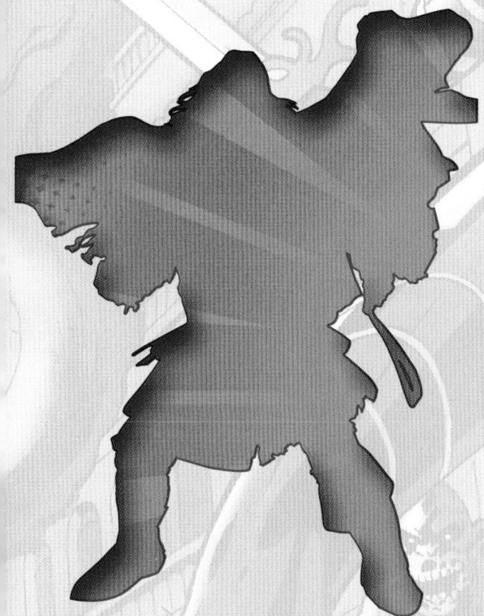

Odin

It was Thor's wise old father, the god Odin, who first sent him to Earth. He hoped Thor would learn humility by living among mortals.

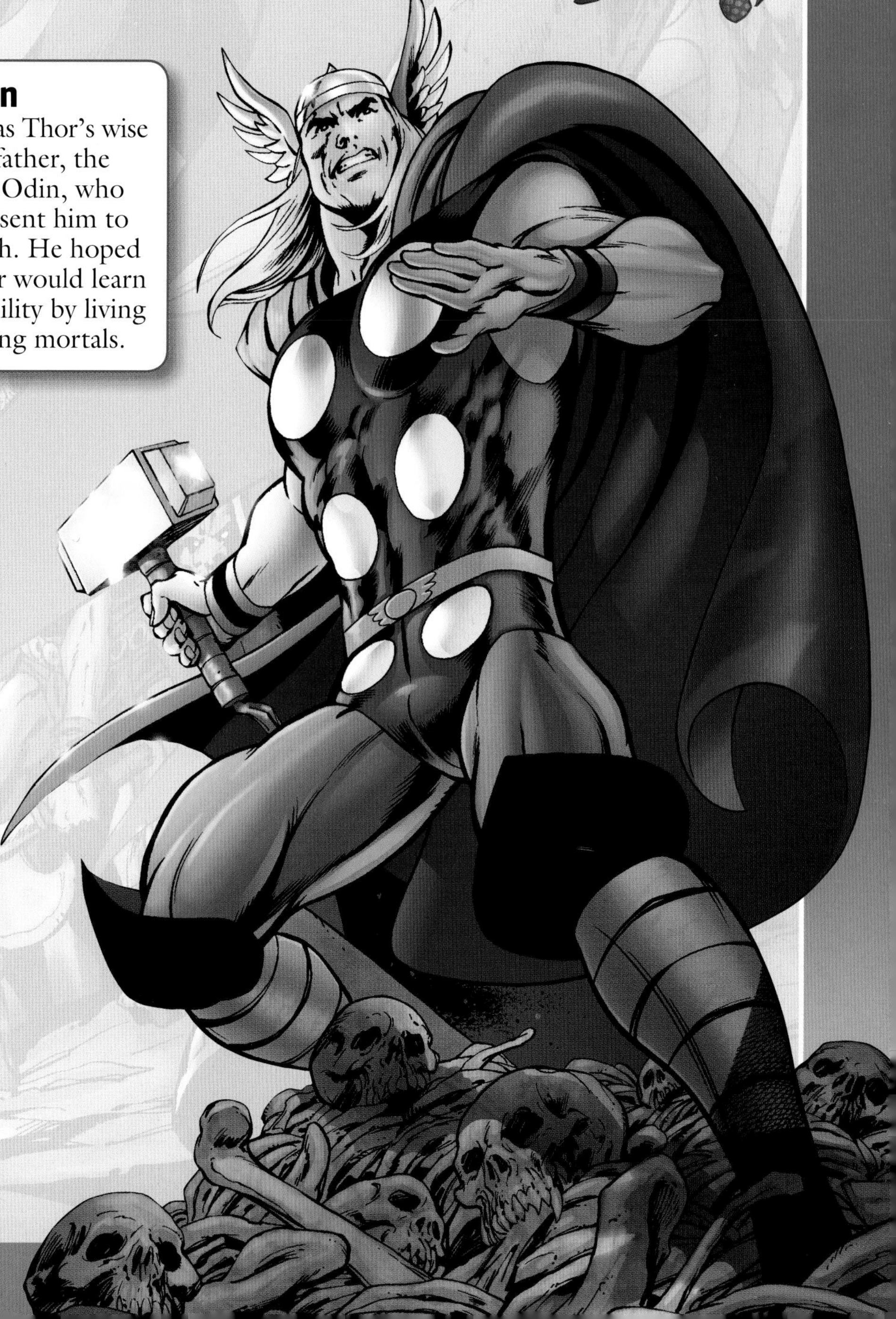

Battling brothers

Thor's adoptive brother Loki, the god of mischief, has never got along with Thor. His jealousy has led to clashes with Thor and the Avengers.

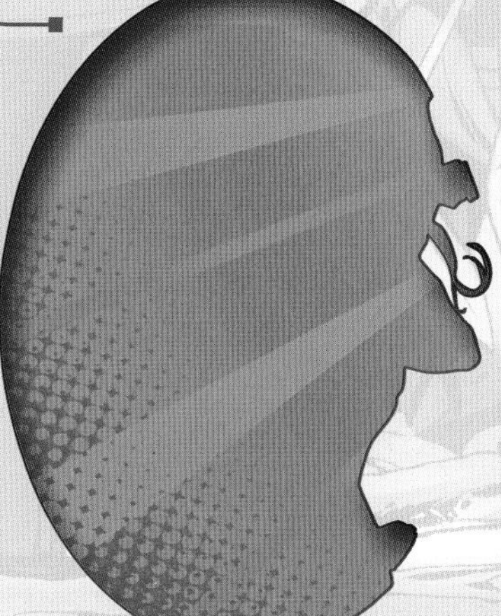

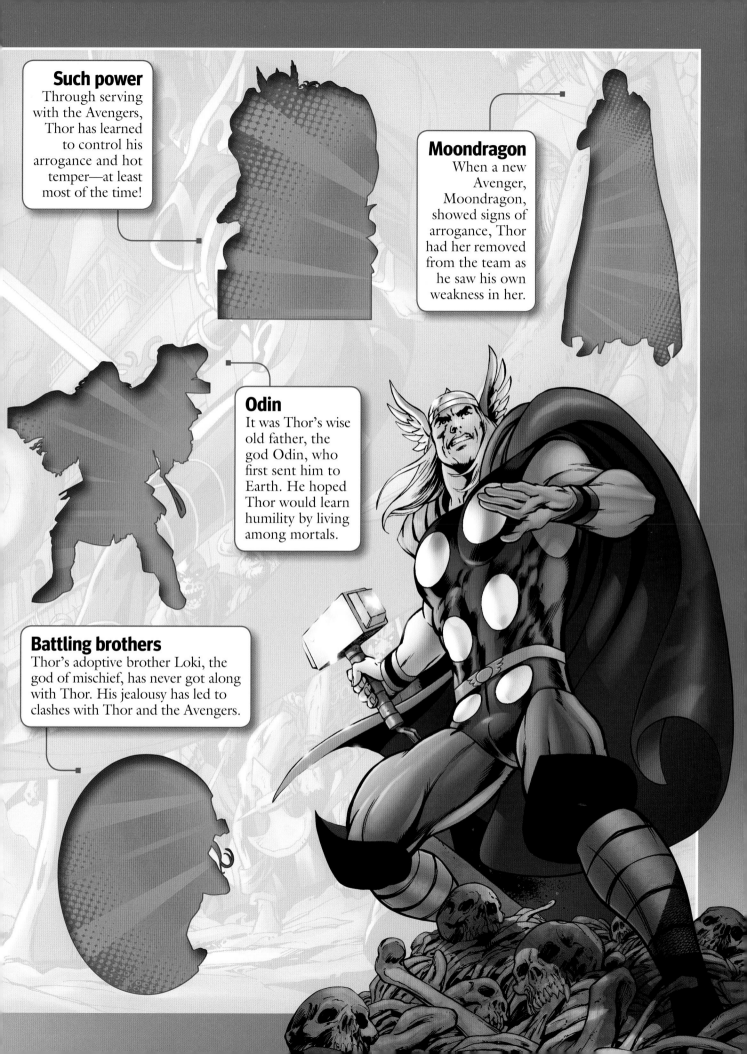

Captain America

Captain America is his name—but you can call him Cap. He's a living symbol of freedom, and with his red, white, and blue costume and star-spangled shield, he is American through and through. However, Cap is a hero to the whole world, and most of all, to his teammates.

The Avengers' leader
When it comes to fighting evil, Cap never compromises! That's why the Avengers have so often looked to him as their leader.

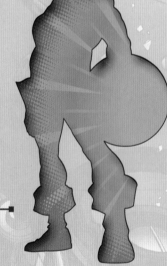

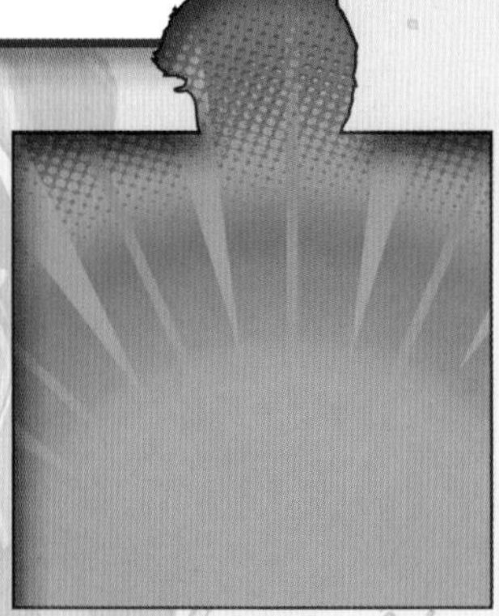

Zero to hero
Weedy Steve Rogers took part in US government experiments with a Super Soldier Serum. His body quickly changed from puny to powerful.

Super Cap
Cap has superhuman strength, speed, agility, and reflexes. Yet he was once an ordinary guy named Steve Rogers.

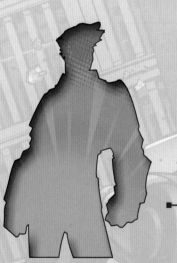

Bucky Barnes
Cap's faithful sidekick, Bucky Barnes, was hand-picked for the job when he was just a kid growing up in a US army camp.

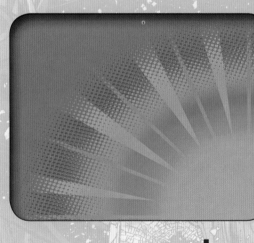

Ice Cap
When the Avengers first met Cap, he was frozen in a block of ice floating in the sea. After a warm welcome from the team, he soon thawed out.

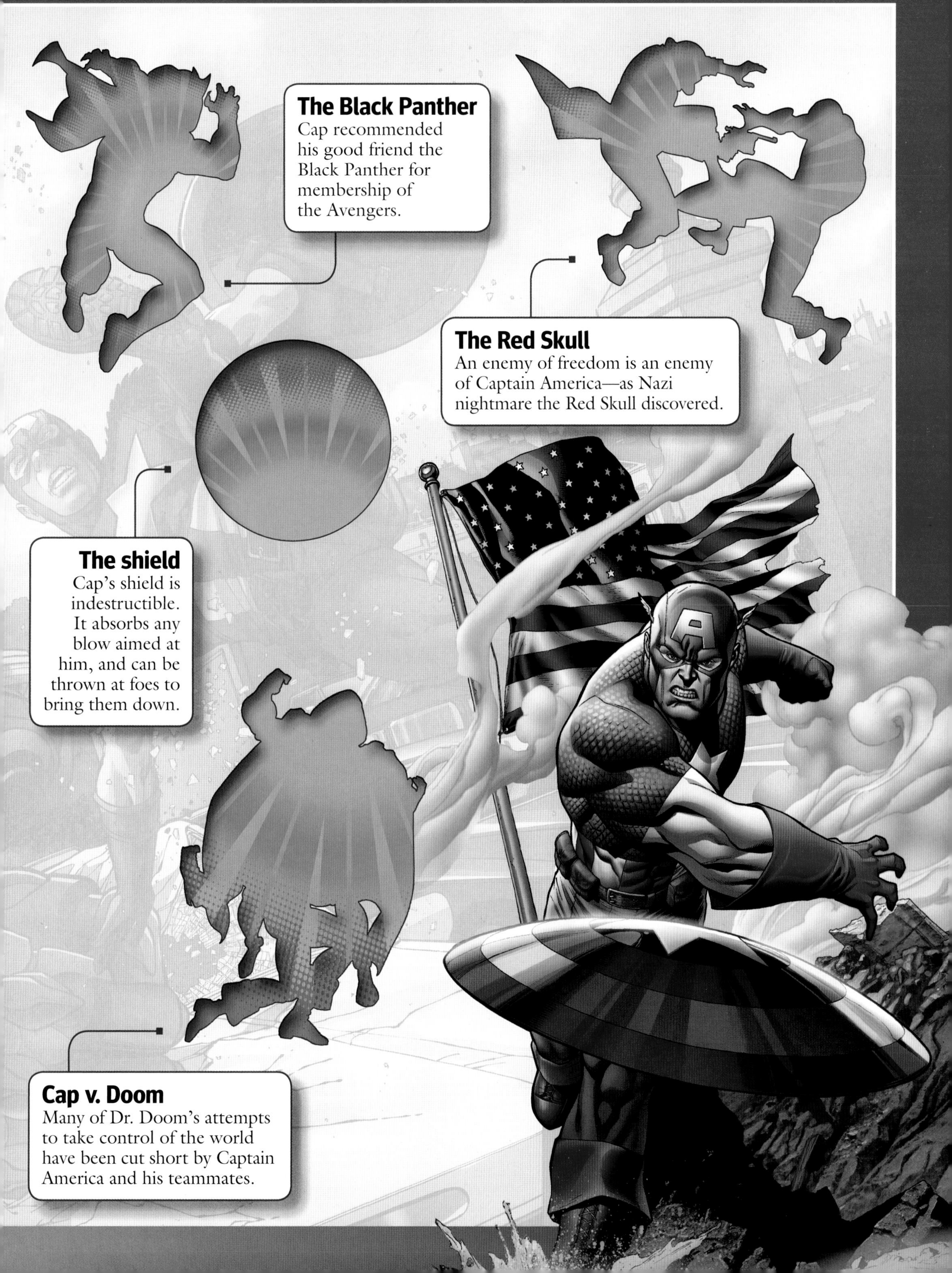

The Black Panther
Cap recommended his good friend the Black Panther for membership of the Avengers.

The Red Skull
An enemy of freedom is an enemy of Captain America—as Nazi nightmare the Red Skull discovered.

The shield
Cap's shield is indestructible. It absorbs any blow aimed at him, and can be thrown at foes to bring them down.

Cap v. Doom
Many of Dr. Doom's attempts to take control of the world have been cut short by Captain America and his teammates.

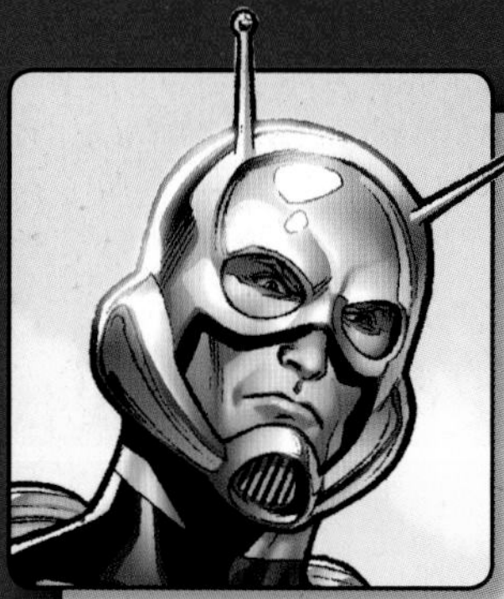

Ant-Man

Who says you must be big to be a Super Hero? Ant-Man can shrink to the size of an ant but he still packs a full-size punch. He is super smart too, and has created much of the Avengers' special equipment. Plus he has an army of ants at his command!

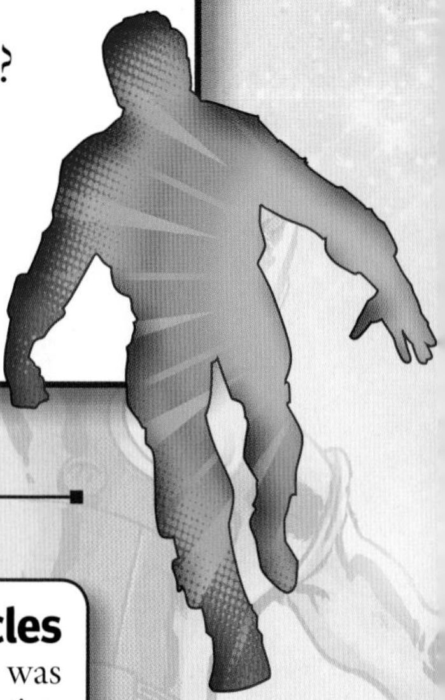

Ant Avenger
Two heroes have taken on the Ant-Man identity: Henry Pym and Scott Lang. Both have been loyal members of the Avengers.

Pym particles
Dr. Henry Pym was a brilliant scientist. He discovered subatomic particles that could make people shrink or grow.

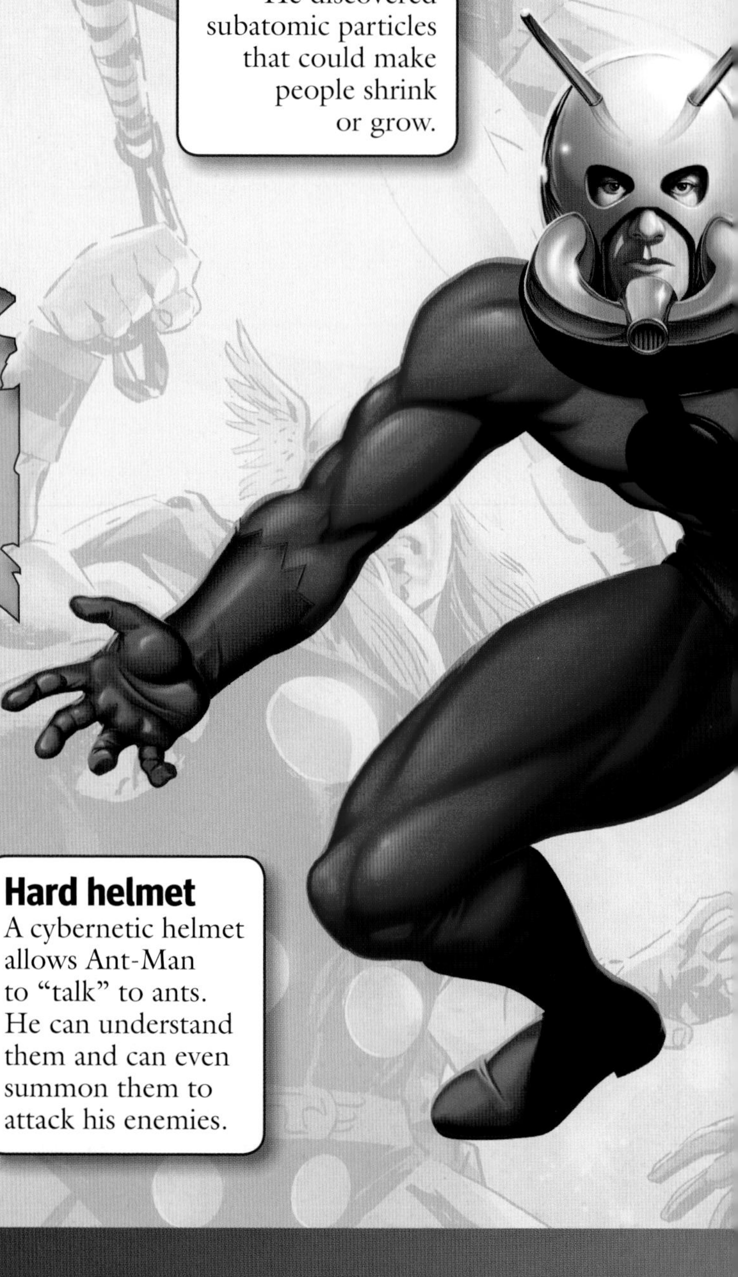

Sizing up
Pym found that he could grow to giant size or shrink to ant size in an instant, while keeping his full strength. A career as a Super Hero beckoned!

Hard helmet
A cybernetic helmet allows Ant-Man to "talk" to ants. He can understand them and can even summon them to attack his enemies.

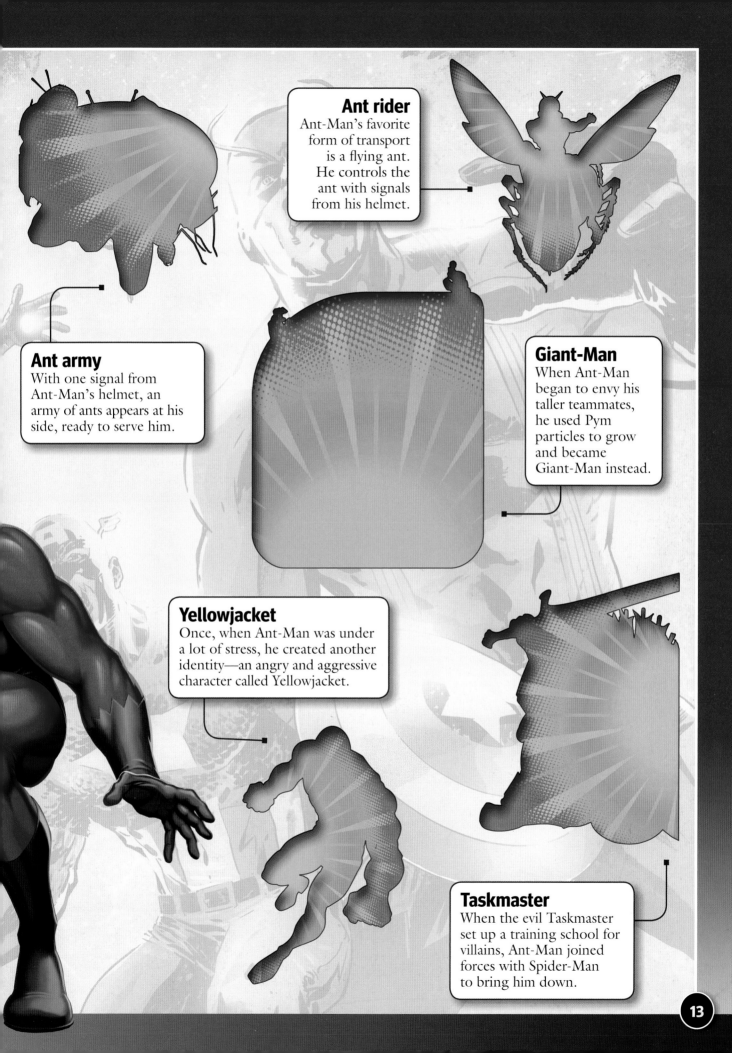

Ant rider
Ant-Man's favorite form of transport is a flying ant. He controls the ant with signals from his helmet.

Ant army
With one signal from Ant-Man's helmet, an army of ants appears at his side, ready to serve him.

Giant-Man
When Ant-Man began to envy his taller teammates, he used Pym particles to grow and became Giant-Man instead.

Yellowjacket
Once, when Ant-Man was under a lot of stress, he created another identity—an angry and aggressive character called Yellowjacket.

Taskmaster
When the evil Taskmaster set up a training school for villains, Ant-Man joined forces with Spider-Man to bring him down.

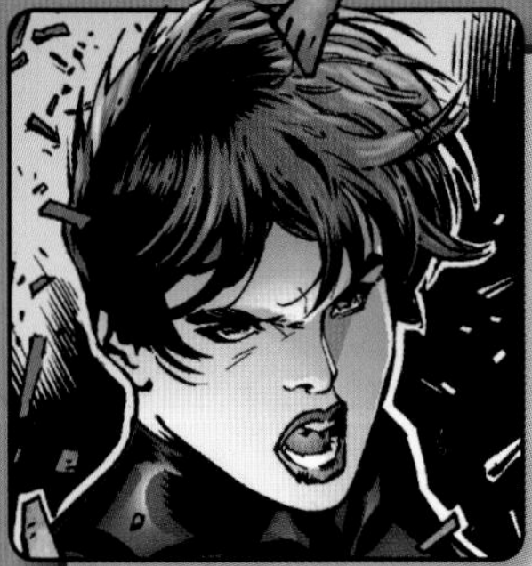

The Wasp

When the Wasp takes flight, villains had better look out! Any foe buzzed by the Wasp is likely to feel a nasty sting—and with a top speed of 40 miles (64 kilometers) per hour, she'll be gone before they have a chance to swat her.

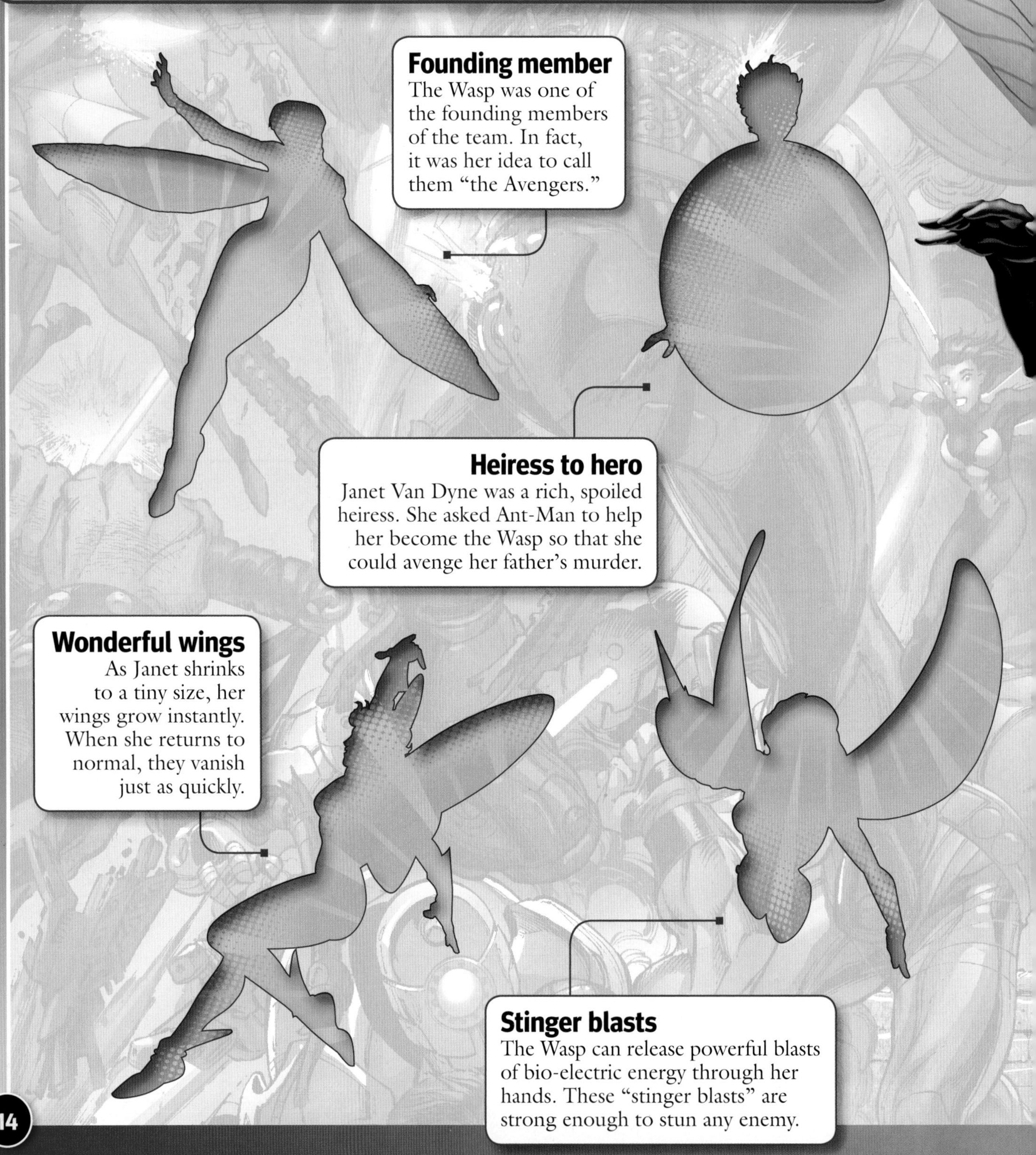

Founding member

The Wasp was one of the founding members of the team. In fact, it was her idea to call them "the Avengers."

Heiress to hero

Janet Van Dyne was a rich, spoiled heiress. She asked Ant-Man to help her become the Wasp so that she could avenge her father's murder.

Wonderful wings

As Janet shrinks to a tiny size, her wings grow instantly. When she returns to normal, they vanish just as quickly.

Stinger blasts

The Wasp can release powerful blasts of bio-electric energy through her hands. These "stinger blasts" are strong enough to stun any enemy.

Giant Wasp
The Wasp is known for her costume changes, but she once made the ultimate change when she grew to giant size!

Ant fan
The Wasp and Ant-Man have always had a close, but stormy relationship. They've been through tough times together.

Jocasta
The villain Ultron once stole the Wasp's personality and emotions. He implanted them into his creation, a robot called Jocasta.

Girl power
The Wasp and Black Widow are two of the best-known female Avengers. They are well matched in agility, and often work together.

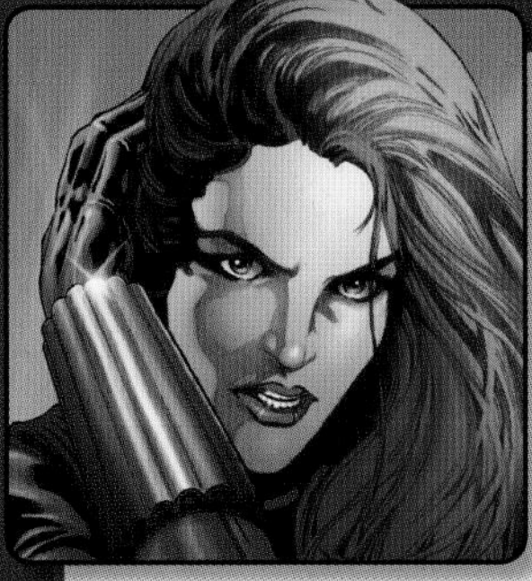

Black Widow

Like her spider namesake, Black Widow is both agile and deadly. She was once a Russian spy, brainwashed into fighting the Avengers, but later switched sides and joined them. Now Black Widow focuses on trapping villains rather than hunting heroes.

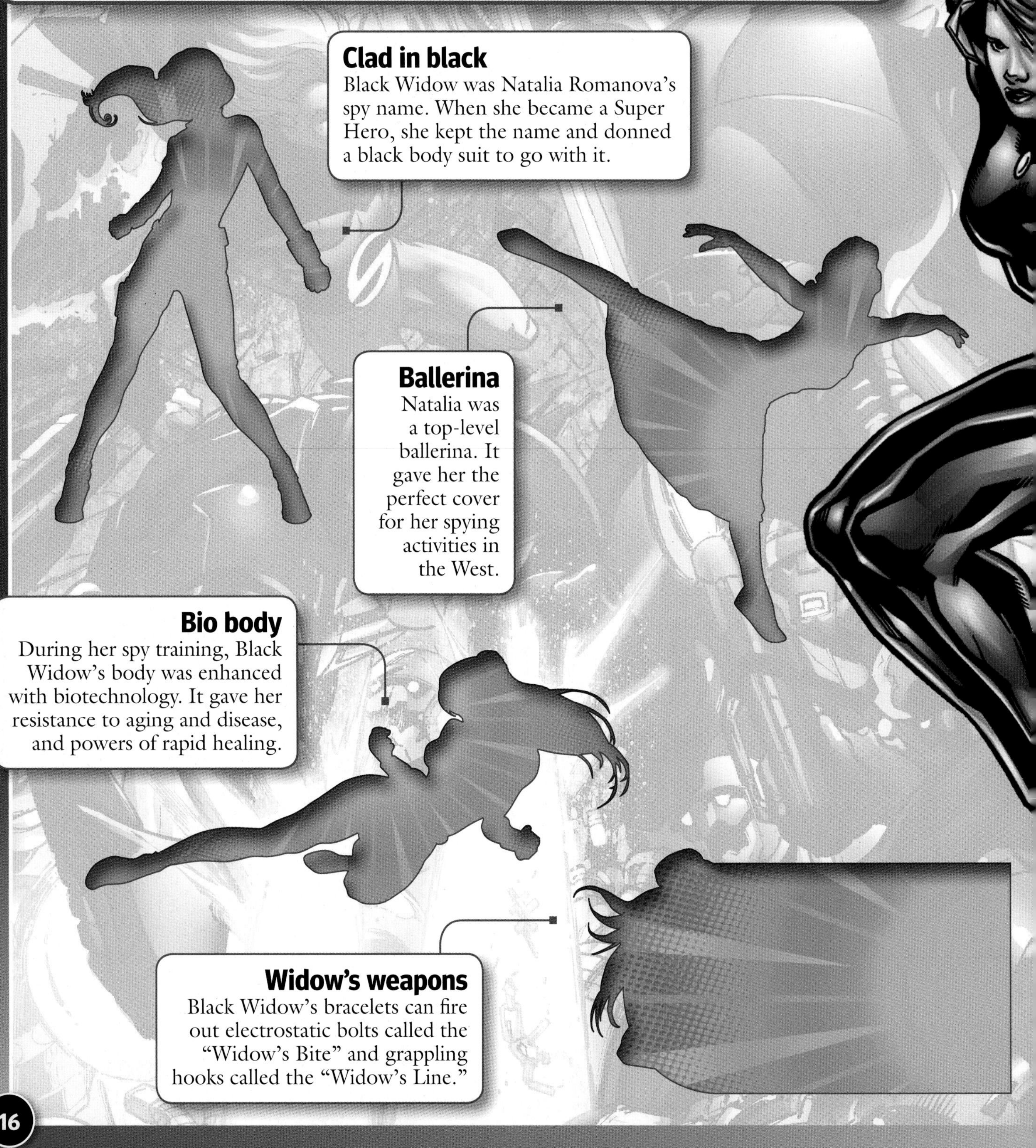

Clad in black
Black Widow was Natalia Romanova's spy name. When she became a Super Hero, she kept the name and donned a black body suit to go with it.

Ballerina
Natalia was a top-level ballerina. It gave her the perfect cover for her spying activities in the West.

Bio body
During her spy training, Black Widow's body was enhanced with biotechnology. It gave her resistance to aging and disease, and powers of rapid healing.

Widow's weapons
Black Widow's bracelets can fire out electrostatic bolts called the "Widow's Bite" and grappling hooks called the "Widow's Line."

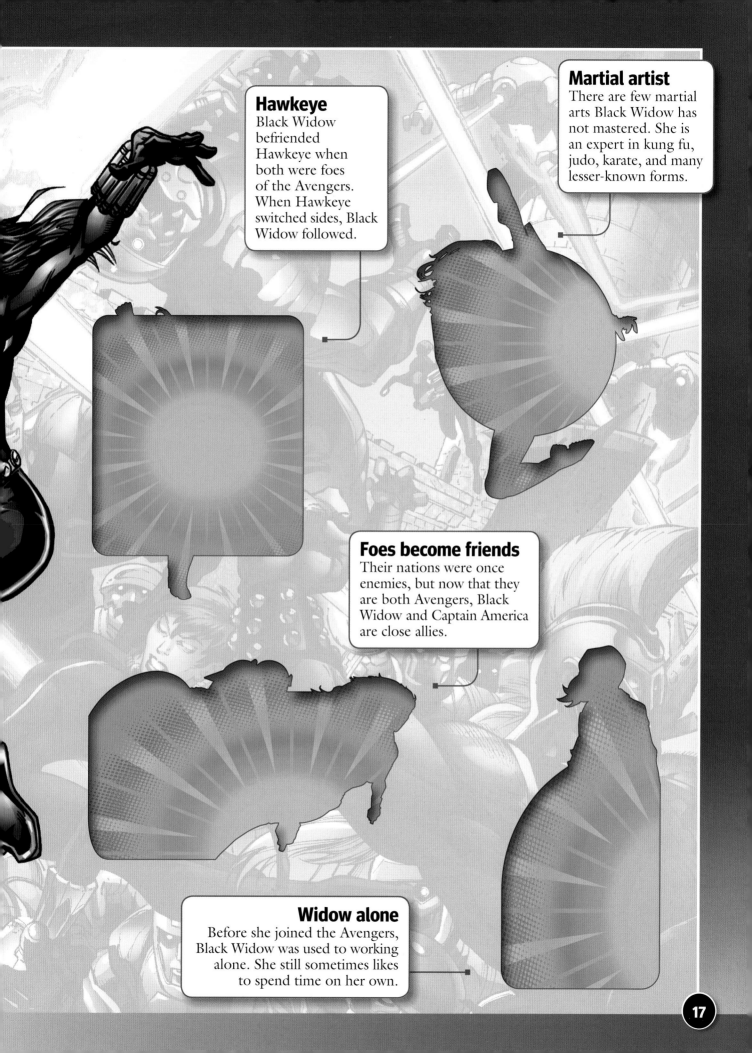

Hawkeye
Black Widow befriended Hawkeye when both were foes of the Avengers. When Hawkeye switched sides, Black Widow followed.

Martial artist
There are few martial arts Black Widow has not mastered. She is an expert in kung fu, judo, karate, and many lesser-known forms.

Foes become friends
Their nations were once enemies, but now that they are both Avengers, Black Widow and Captain America are close allies.

Widow alone
Before she joined the Avengers, Black Widow was used to working alone. She still sometimes likes to spend time on her own.

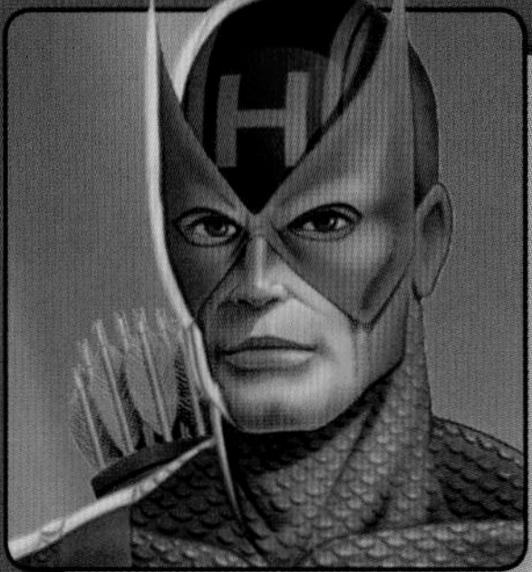

Hawkeye

If there is an enemy to bring down or a crisis to crush, Hawkeye always gives it his best shot. His skills with the bow and arrow more than make up for his lack of superpowers. Hawkeye is one of the most loyal Avengers—and he aims to keep it that way.

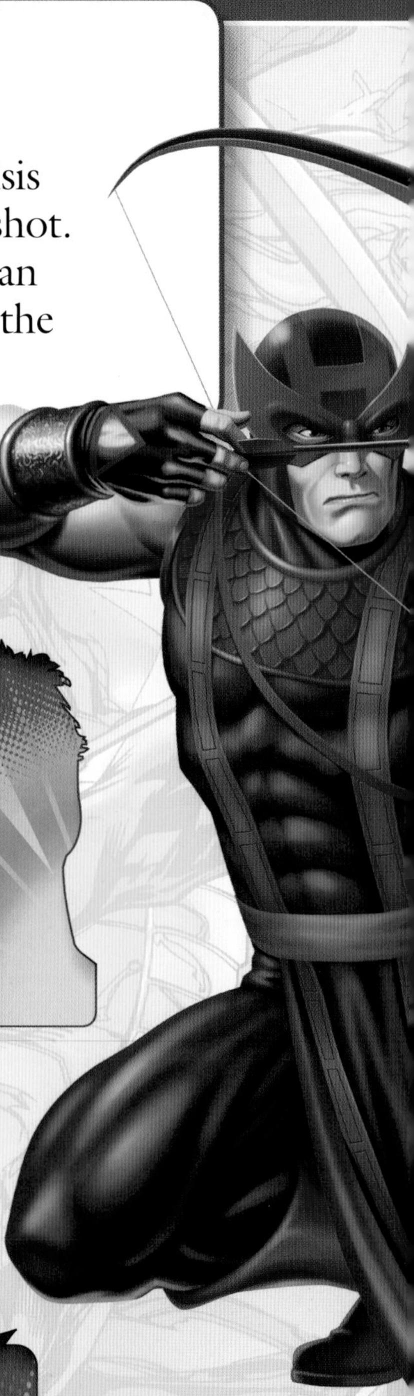

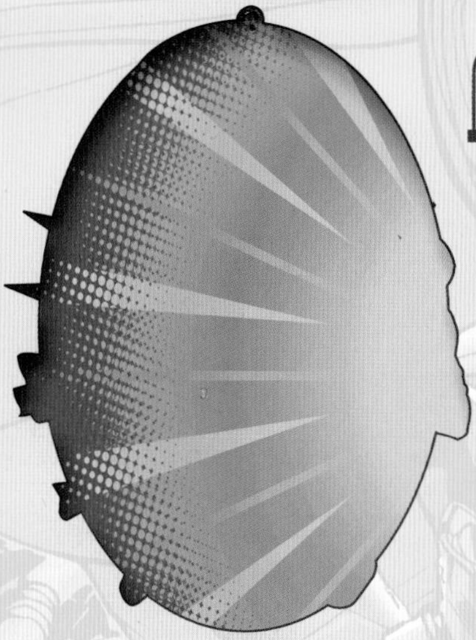

On target
Hawkeye got his name because like a hawk, he zooms in on his target with unerring accuracy.

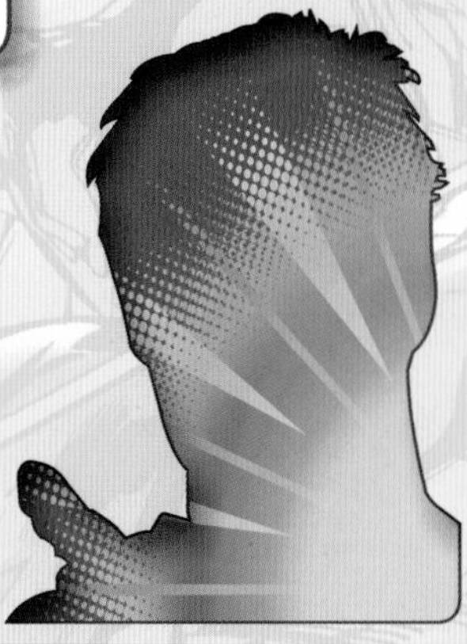

Clint Barton
Ex-circus performer Clint Barton once used his skills with trick arrows to pursue a criminal career.

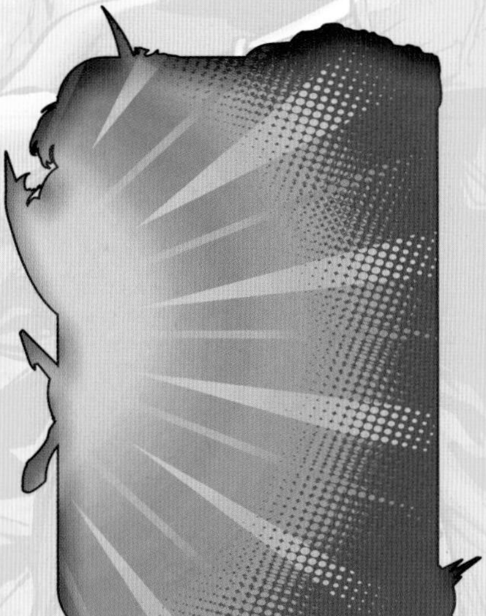

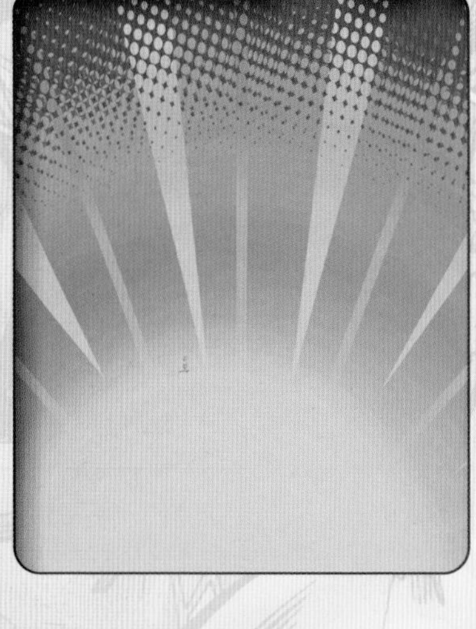

Hotshot hero
Now that he is the Avenger Hawkeye, Clint uses his skills strictly for fighting villains.

A dream come true
It was admiration for Iron Man that made Hawkeye want to be an Avenger. His dream came true when he was accepted as one of the team.

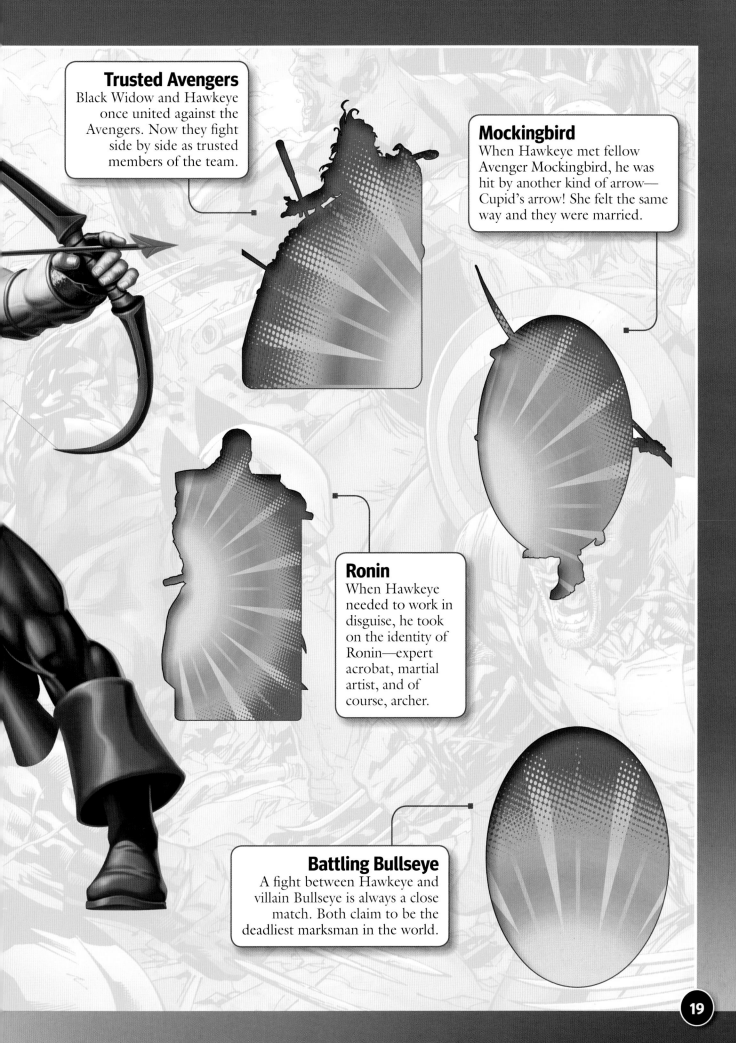

Trusted Avengers
Black Widow and Hawkeye once united against the Avengers. Now they fight side by side as trusted members of the team.

Mockingbird
When Hawkeye met fellow Avenger Mockingbird, he was hit by another kind of arrow—Cupid's arrow! She felt the same way and they were married.

Ronin
When Hawkeye needed to work in disguise, he took on the identity of Ronin—expert acrobat, martial artist, and of course, archer.

Battling Bullseye
A fight between Hawkeye and villain Bullseye is always a close match. Both claim to be the deadliest marksman in the world.

19

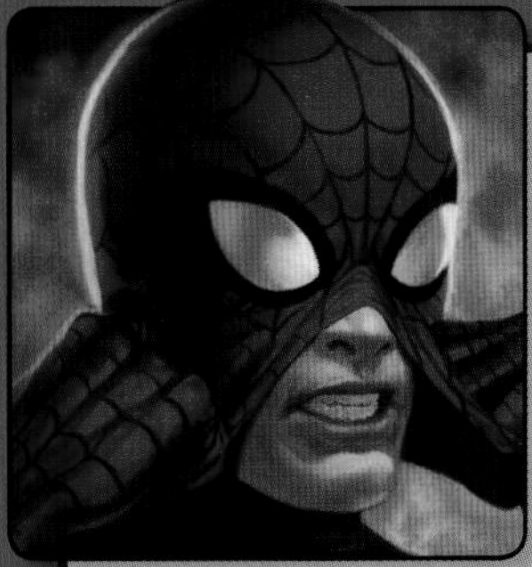

Spider-Man

For years, the Avengers tried to convince their friend Spider-Man to join the team. Finally they caught their spider, and he agreed to become an official member. Since then, loyal Spidey has stuck with the Avengers as firmly as he sticks to walls and ceilings.

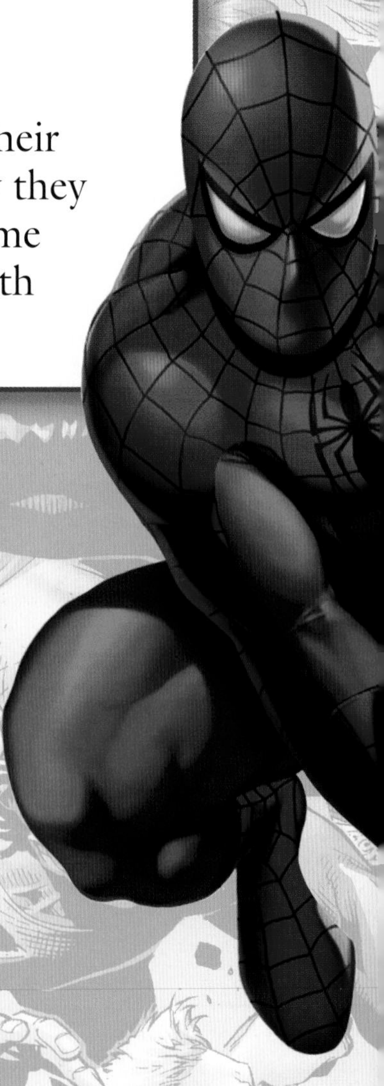

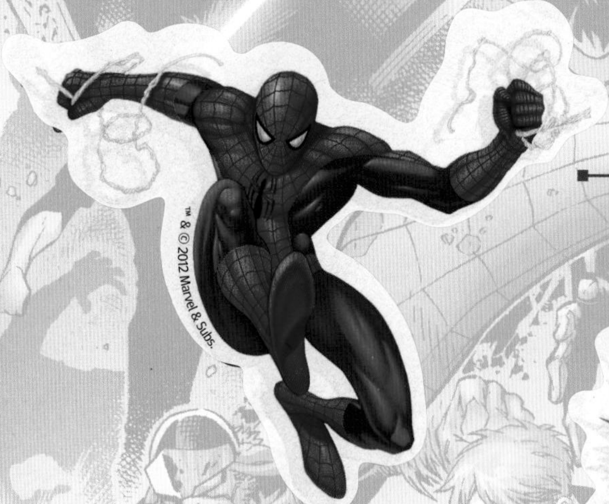
™ & © 2012 Marvel & Subs.

Web-slinger

When chasing criminals, Spidey swings into action on weblines fired from his wrists and anchored to tall buildings.

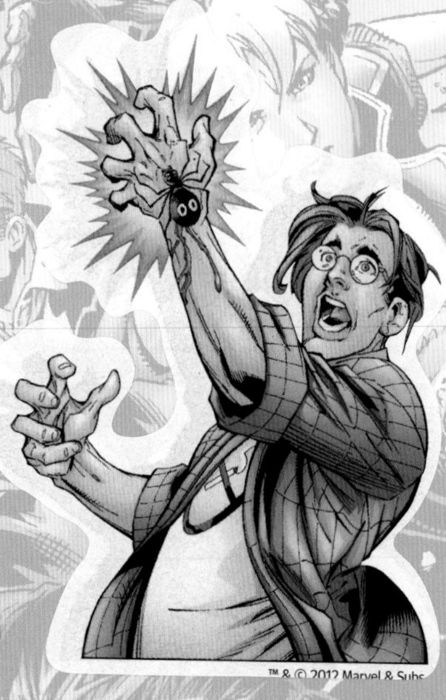
™ & © 2012 Marvel & Subs.

Peter Parker

Teenager Peter Parker became Spider-Man when a bite from a radioactive spider gave him spider-like powers.

Spider-sense

A tingling at the base of his skull lets Spider-Man know when danger is near. This early warning system is known as his "spider-sense."

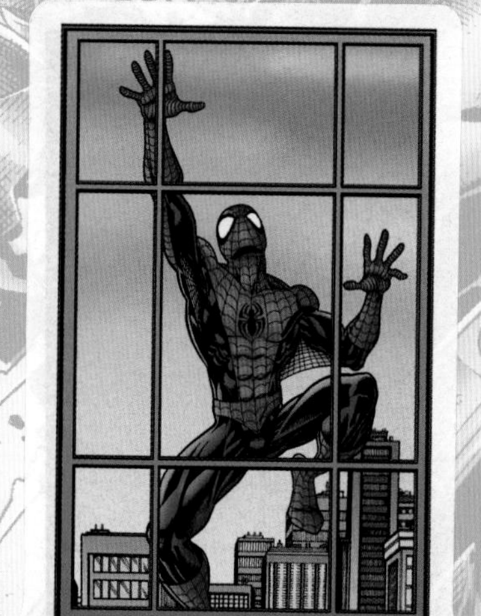
™ & © 2012 Marvel & Subs.

Wall-crawler

Spidey is able to stick to smooth surfaces such as walls, ceilings, and windows. That's why he's often called "the Wall-Crawler."

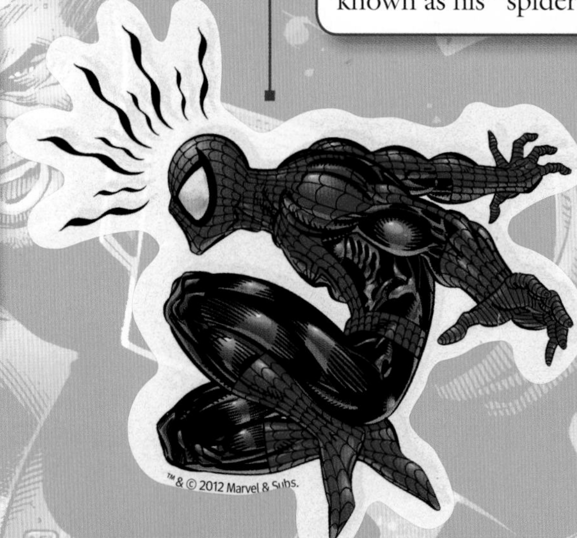
™ & © 2012 Marvel & Subs.

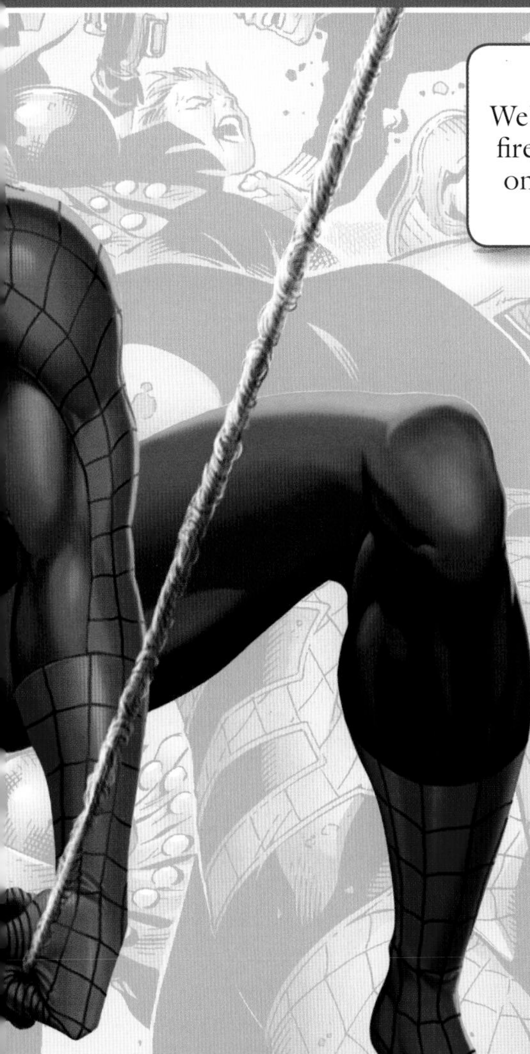

Web-shooters
Web-shooters on Spidey's wrists fire out strands of web to swing on or thicker webs that he uses as nets to capture criminals.

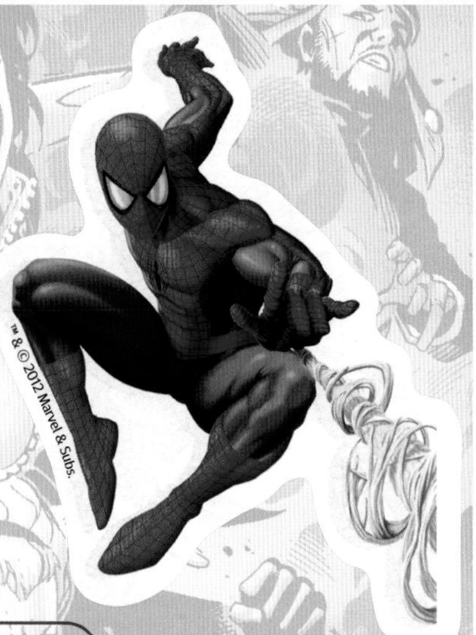
™ & © 2012 Marvel & Subs.

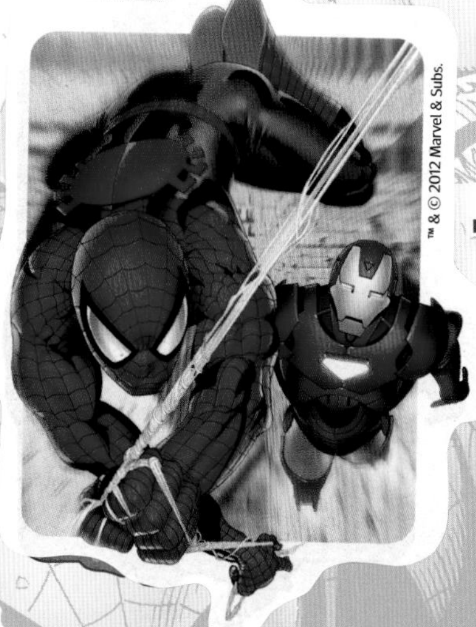
™ & © 2012 Marvel & Subs.

Super pals
Spider-Man and Iron Man are great friends. Iron Man once even designed an armored suit for Spidey.

Spidey v. Spidey
Spidey once had to save the Avengers from an evil, robotic clone created by the villain Kang.

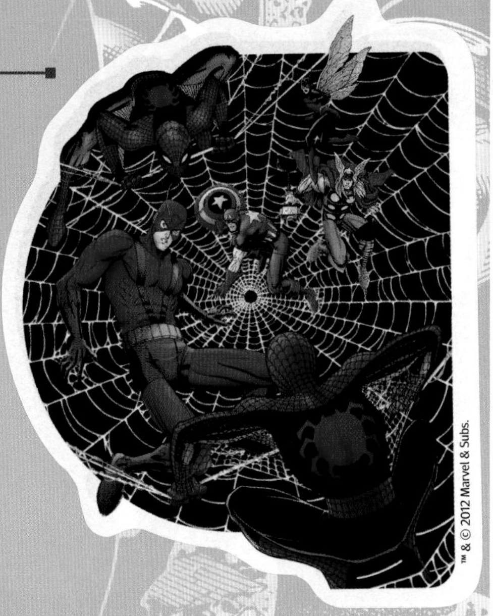
™ & © 2012 Marvel & Subs.

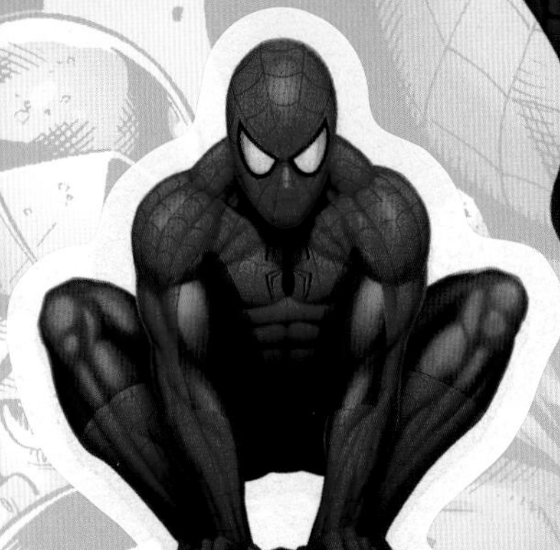
™ & © 2012 Marvel & Subs.

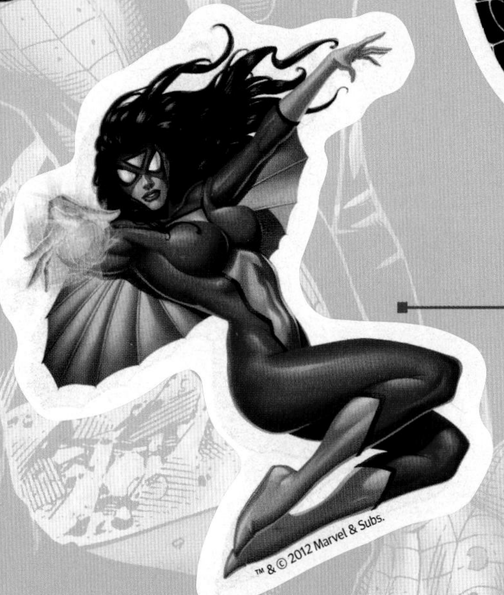
™ & © 2012 Marvel & Subs.

Spider's eye view
Spider-Man can often be seen perched at the top of a tall building. From there, he watches for signs of trouble in the city below.

Spider-Woman
Spidey helped Spider-Woman to develop her own powers. Like him, she eventually joined the Avengers.

Alternative Avengers

The Avengers are the most famous and respected team of Super Heroes in the world. It's no wonder so many other teams have wanted that special word "Avengers" as part of their name. Some are offshoots of the main team, others are keen newcomers—there are even a few imposters!

West Coast Avengers
When the original Avengers felt that they needed to expand their influence, they set up a second team on the West Coast of America.

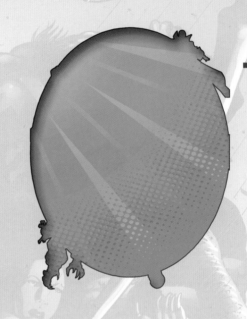

Great Lakes Avengers
A new team of Super Heroes called themselves the Great Lakes Avengers. They got into trouble for using the name "Avengers" without permission.

Dark Avengers
The Dark Avengers were a team of villains who impersonated the real Avengers. Both the government and the public were completely fooled!

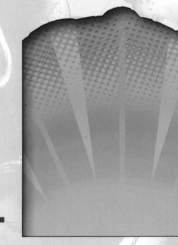

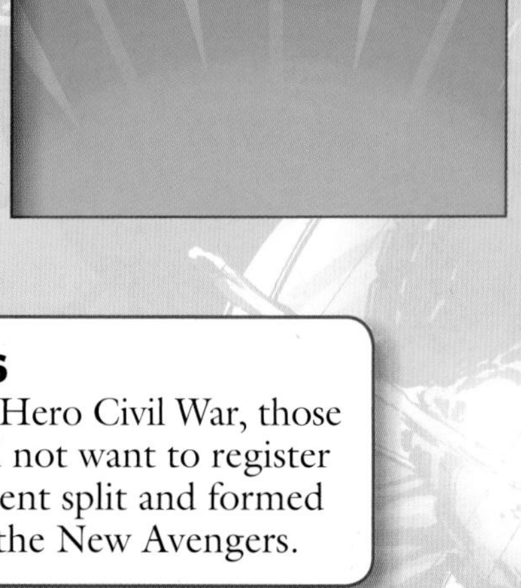

New Avengers
During the Super Hero Civil War, those Avengers who did not want to register with the government split and formed their own team—the New Avengers.

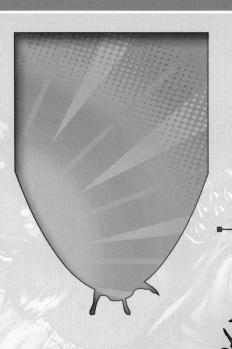

Young Avengers
The Young Avengers ignored warnings from Iron Man and Captain America, who did not think the teenagers were quite ready to be Super Heroes.

Mighty Avengers
When the Dark Avengers fooled the government into granting them official status, Ant-Man set up a rival team called the Mighty Avengers.

Secret Avengers
The Secret Avengers are a shadowy team working alongside the main Avengers. Their work demands complete secrecy.

Fake Avenger
The New Avengers were once infiltrated by Skrull queen Veranke disguised as Spider-Woman. She was unmasked before she could do too much harm.

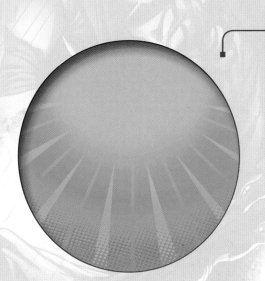

Young Avengers v. Dark Avengers
When the Young Avengers fought the Dark Avengers, the result was an unexpected victory for the youngsters.

Avengers All

The Avengers have been around for a long time, and in that time, dozens of heroes have served in their ranks. Some have stayed, some have gone solo, some are now with other teams, but all remain Avengers at heart. Here are just a few of them.

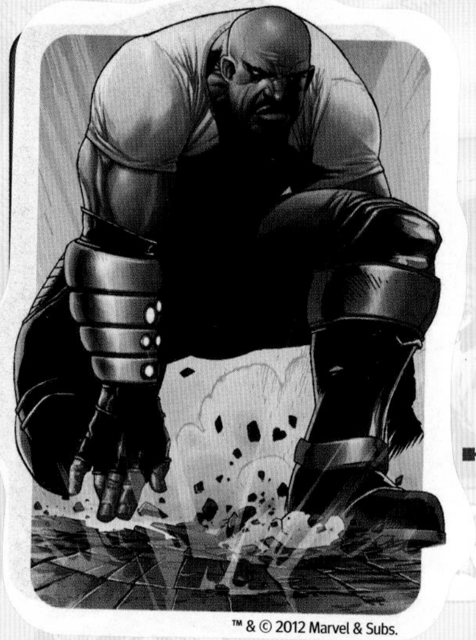
™ & © 2012 Marvel & Subs.

Power Man
With skin as hard as steel and nerves to match, Power Man is a tough street-fighter who doesn't pull his punches.

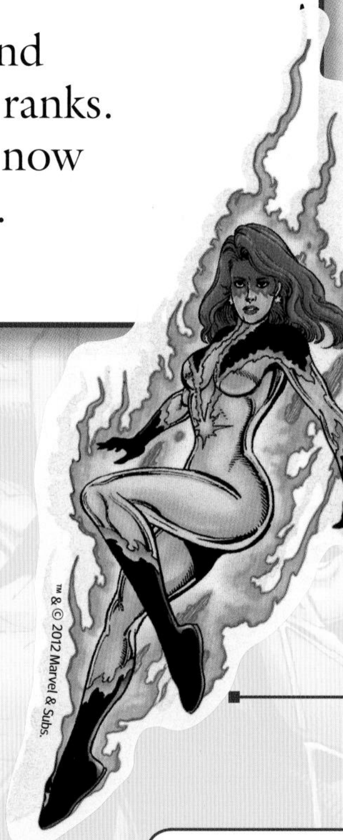
™ & © 2012 Marvel & Subs.

Firestar
Things certainly heat up when Firestar joins the battle! This fiery female can manipulate microwaves to cook up a world of trouble for the Avengers' foes.

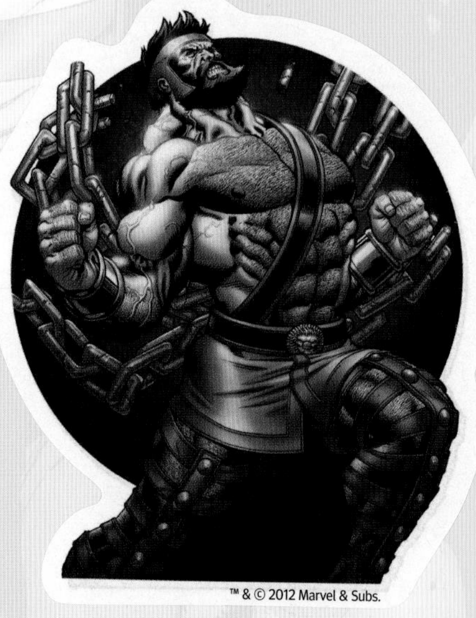
™ & © 2012 Marvel & Subs.

Hercules
The son of Greek god Zeus, Hercules was born with super strength that allows him to lift more than 100 tons (89 tonnes) with ease.

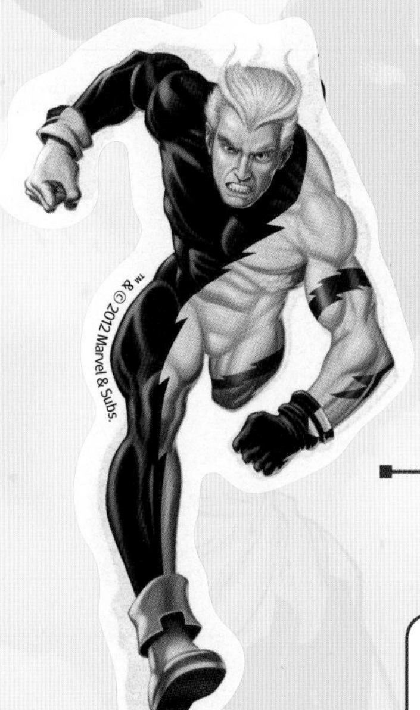
™ & © 2012 Marvel & Subs.

Quicksilver
Quicksilver can run faster than the speed of sound. He builds up such momentum that he is able to run across water or up walls.

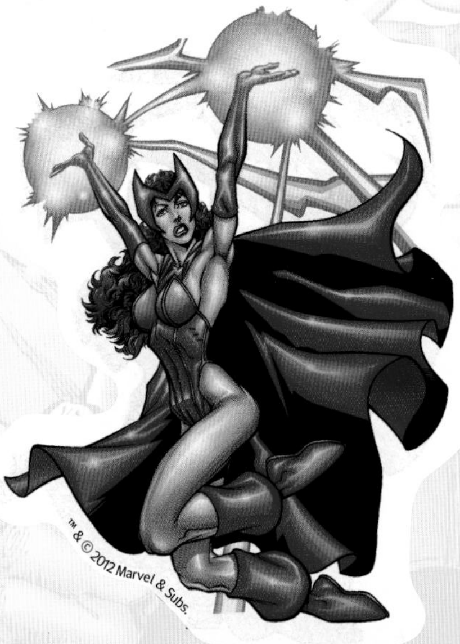
™ & © 2012 Marvel & Subs.

The Scarlet Witch
The Scarlet Witch can throw hexes that make objects explode, missiles stop in midair, and doors fly open.

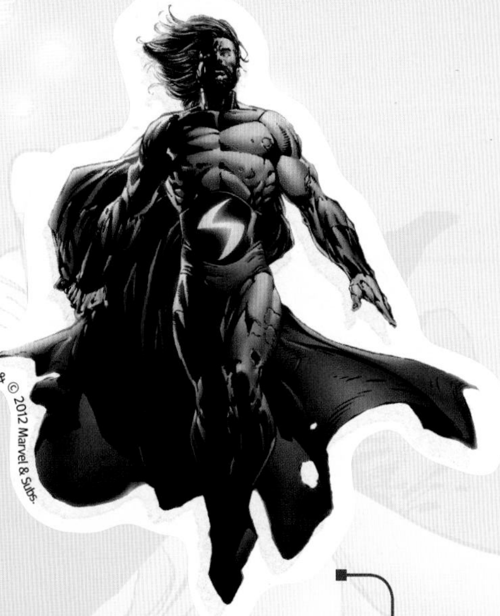
™ & © 2012 Marvel & Subs.

Beast
With his blue fur, fangs, and claws, Beast looks like a real brute. Yet this mutant has the brains of a genius and the heart of a hero.

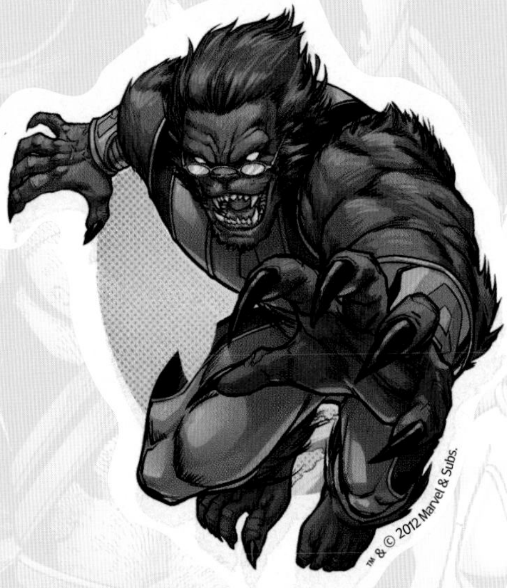
™ & © 2012 Marvel & Subs.

Sentry
Sentry was set to become one of the greatest Avengers ever. However, he could not control his destructive alter ego, the Void.

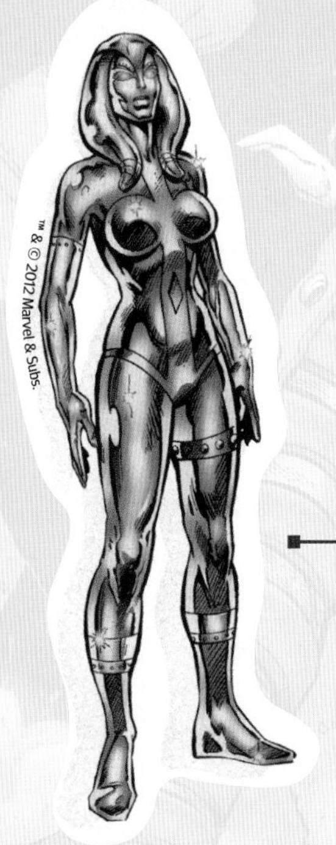
™ & © 2012 Marvel & Subs.

Jocasta
Evil Ultron created the robot Jocasta to be an enemy of the Avengers. To his dismay, she turned against him and joined the team.

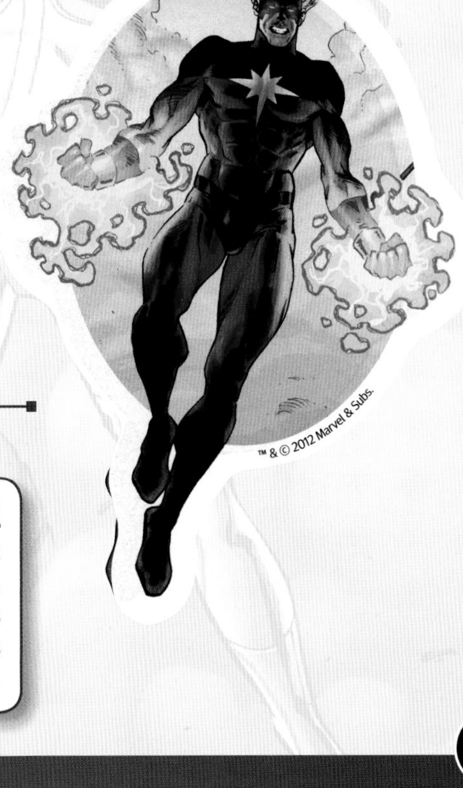
™ & © 2012 Marvel & Subs.

Captain Marvel
The alien Kree race sent Captain Marvel to spy on planet Earth. However, Captain Marvel was so impressed by the Avengers that he ended up joining them.

More Avengers

The Avengers are the Earth's mightiest Super Heroes, and a place in the team is the highest honor for any Super Hero. Naturally, there is no shortage of eager new recruits! Meet some more of the humans, mutants, aliens, and others who have been proud to call themselves Avengers.

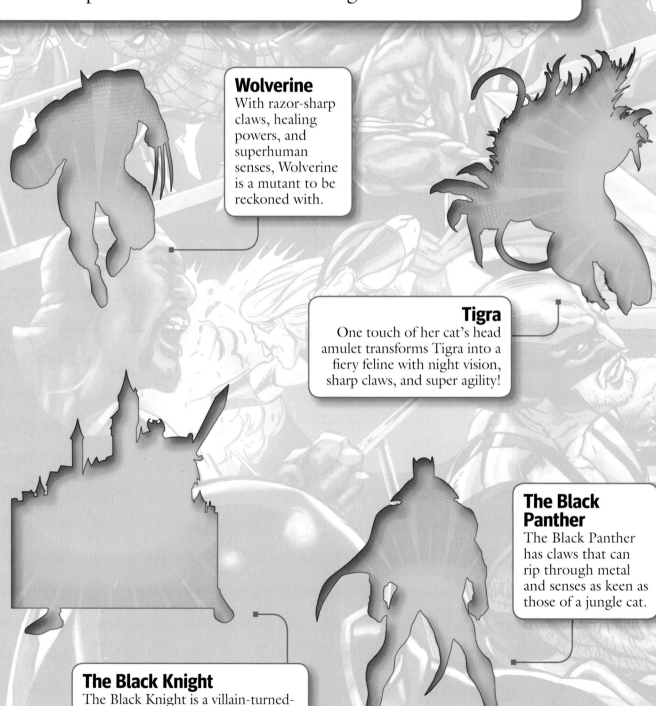

Wolverine
With razor-sharp claws, healing powers, and superhuman senses, Wolverine is a mutant to be reckoned with.

Tigra
One touch of her cat's head amulet transforms Tigra into a fiery feline with night vision, sharp claws, and super agility!

The Black Panther
The Black Panther has claws that can rip through metal and senses as keen as those of a jungle cat.

The Black Knight
The Black Knight is a villain-turned-hero. His enchanted sword, the Ebony Blade, was created from a piece of fallen meteorite.

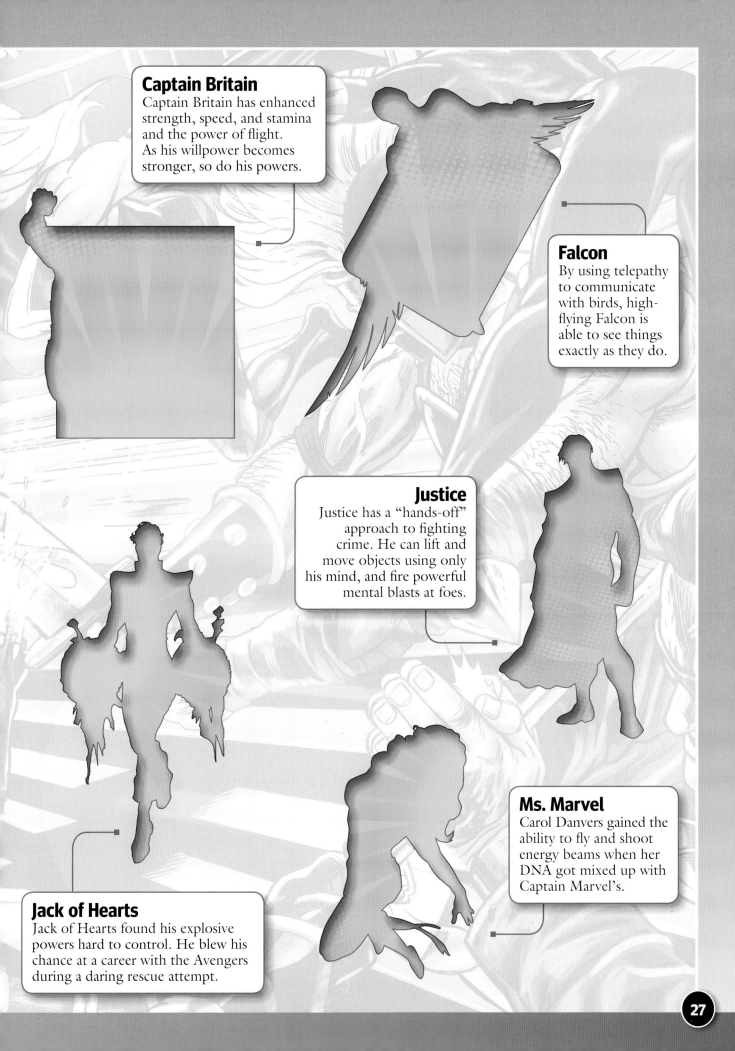

Captain Britain
Captain Britain has enhanced strength, speed, and stamina and the power of flight. As his willpower becomes stronger, so do his powers.

Falcon
By using telepathy to communicate with birds, high-flying Falcon is able to see things exactly as they do.

Justice
Justice has a "hands-off" approach to fighting crime. He can lift and move objects using only his mind, and fire powerful mental blasts at foes.

Ms. Marvel
Carol Danvers gained the ability to fly and shoot energy beams when her DNA got mixed up with Captain Marvel's.

Jack of Hearts
Jack of Hearts found his explosive powers hard to control. He blew his chance at a career with the Avengers during a daring rescue attempt.

Avenger Adversaries

Who are these beings who dare to take on the Avengers?
What kinds of villain are so dangerous that only
Earth's mightiest heroes can stop them? Here are
just a few of the evildoers who are the very reason
for the Avengers' existence.

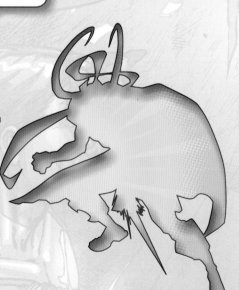

Ares
The Olympian god of war, Ares,
relishes battle for battle's sake.
He has a special hatred for his
Avenger half-brother, Hercules.

The Enchantress
The beautiful
Enchantress was
furious when she
could not make Thor
fall in love with her.
Now, she uses her evil
magic to attack Thor
and the Avengers.

Kang the Conqueror
Kang rides through time in his
time-ship, gathering technology
for use in his never-ending
quest to conquer worlds.

Loki
Mischievous Loki
loves to confuse
his enemies by
shape-shifting—
taking on the
appearance of
another being.

Dr. Doom
World domination is Dr. Doom's
dream. His armor hides an arsenal
of weapons and enables him to
fly and travel in space.

The Mandarin

The Mandarin has ten power rings, each emitting a different kind of beam or blast. He uses them mercilessly in his attempts to take over the world.

The Collector

The Collector once tried to capture the Avengers to add to the other life forms he had trapped in his museum-world.

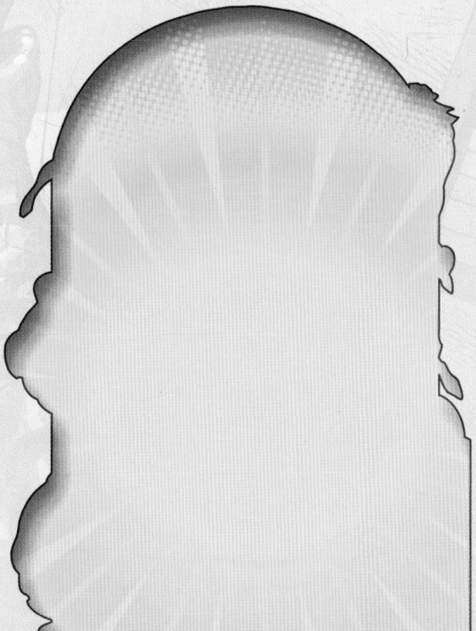

Egghead

Egghead is a mad scientist consumed by jealousy of Ant-Man. He has tried to destroy his rival many times.

Morgan le Fay

Sorceress Morgan le Fay is half human and half faerie. She once cast a spell that enslaved the Avengers, making them her soldiers.

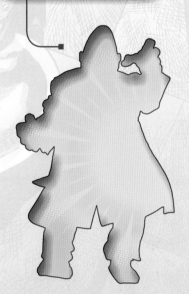

Juggernaut

When the Avengers tried to halt one of Juggernaut's charges, they found out exactly why he is known as "the Unstoppable"!

More Adversaries

Even as one enemy is defeated by the Avengers, another waits to take his or her place. Many return again and again, with more and more devious plans. That's why we will never stop needing the Avengers—and why they will never stop being there for us.

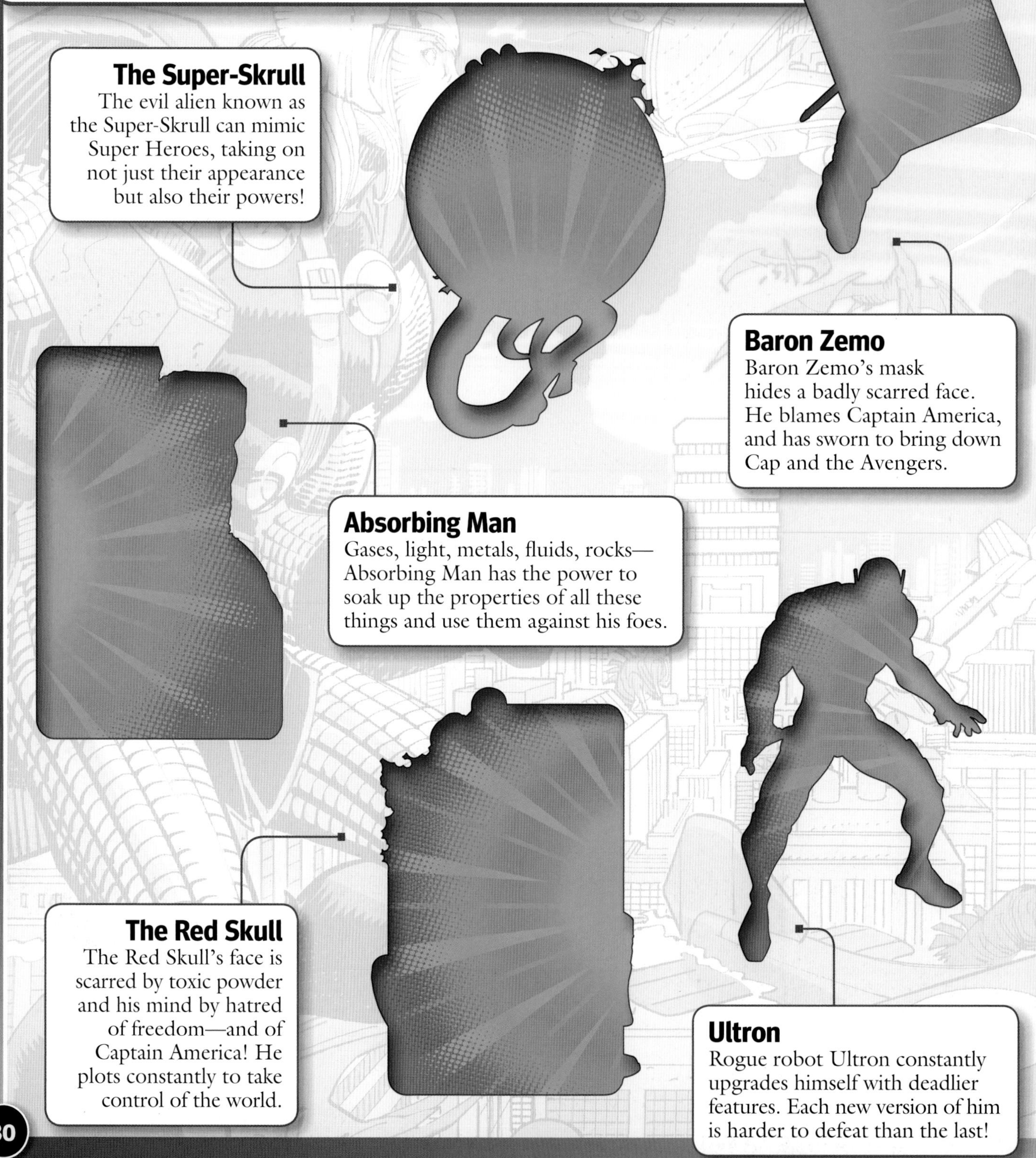

The Super-Skrull

The evil alien known as the Super-Skrull can mimic Super Heroes, taking on not just their appearance but also their powers!

Baron Zemo

Baron Zemo's mask hides a badly scarred face. He blames Captain America, and has sworn to bring down Cap and the Avengers.

Absorbing Man

Gases, light, metals, fluids, rocks—Absorbing Man has the power to soak up the properties of all these things and use them against his foes.

The Red Skull

The Red Skull's face is scarred by toxic powder and his mind by hatred of freedom—and of Captain America! He plots constantly to take control of the world.

Ultron

Rogue robot Ultron constantly upgrades himself with deadlier features. Each new version of him is harder to defeat than the last!

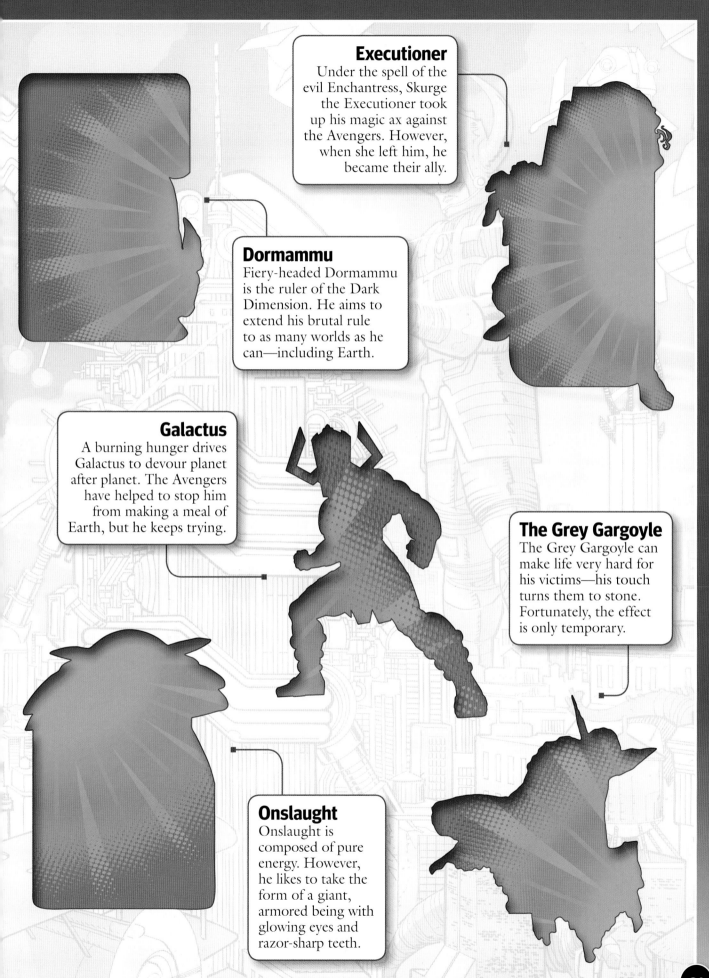

Executioner
Under the spell of the evil Enchantress, Skurge the Executioner took up his magic ax against the Avengers. However, when she left him, he became their ally.

Dormammu
Fiery-headed Dormammu is the ruler of the Dark Dimension. He aims to extend his brutal rule to as many worlds as he can—including Earth.

Galactus
A burning hunger drives Galactus to devour planet after planet. The Avengers have helped to stop him from making a meal of Earth, but he keeps trying.

The Grey Gargoyle
The Grey Gargoyle can make life very hard for his victims—his touch turns them to stone. Fortunately, the effect is only temporary.

Onslaught
Onslaught is composed of pure energy. However, he likes to take the form of a giant, armored being with glowing eyes and razor-sharp teeth.

Enemy Teams

Everyone knows there is strength in numbers—after all, that's why the Avengers got together. Maybe it's not so surprising then, that many Super Villains have had the same idea. Here are some of the terrifying teams that have tried to defeat the Avengers.

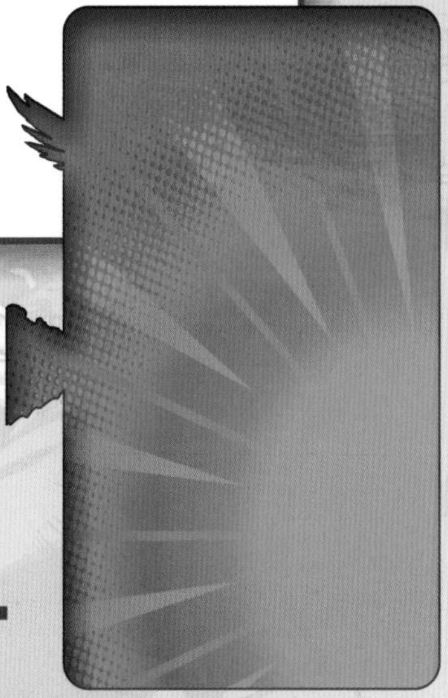

Masters of Evil
Baron Zemo sought out villains with the most horrifying powers to form his Masters of Evil team.

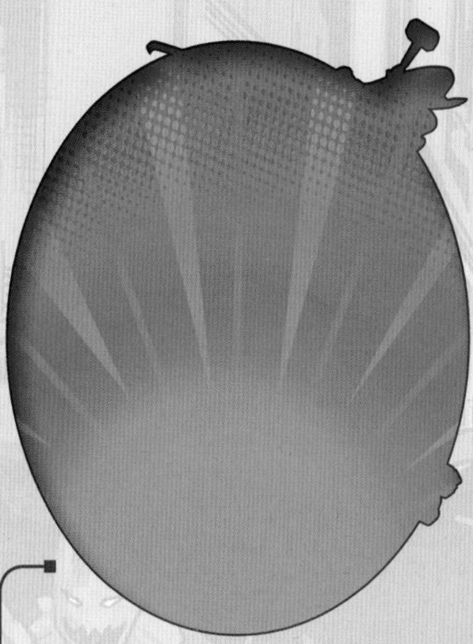

Wrecking Crew
Escaped convicts Wrecker, Thunderball, Piledriver, and Bulldozer were the crashing, crushing villains known as the Wrecking Crew.

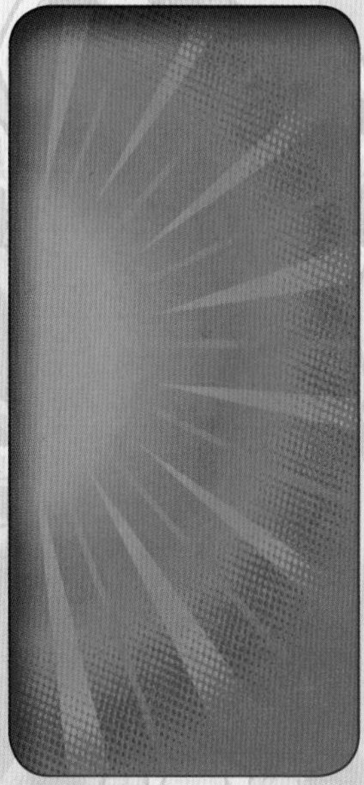

Serpent Society
The Serpent Society is a group of snake-themed mercenaries who hate the Avengers. They have especially directed their venom at Captain America.

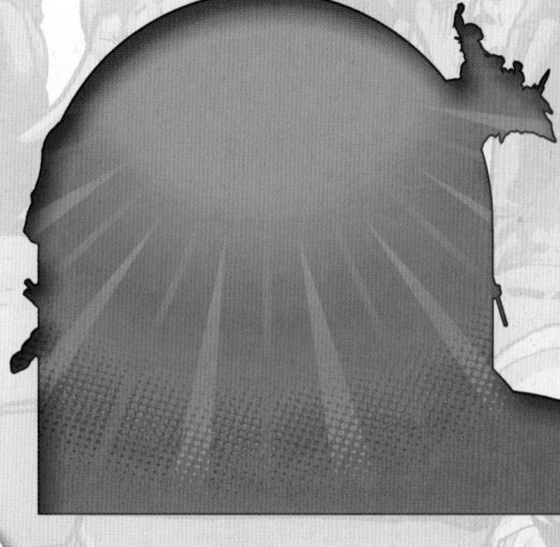

Thunderbolts
The world welcomed the Thunderbolts as a bold new Super Hero team. Nobody knew that they were really the Masters of Evil in disguise.

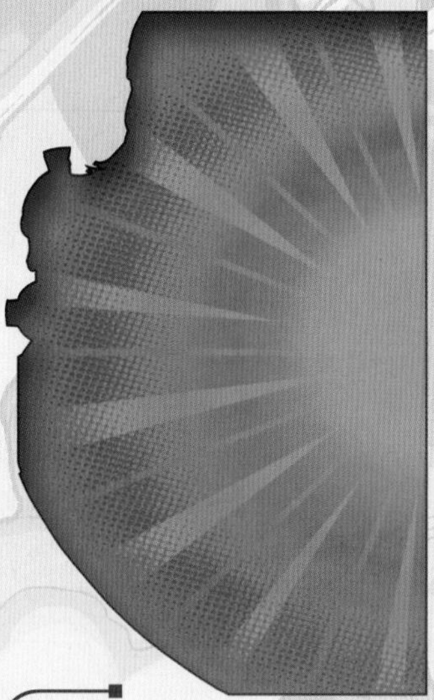

Lethal Legion
The Lethal Legion might have stood more of a chance against the Avengers if only they had stopped fighting amongst themselves!

STICKERS

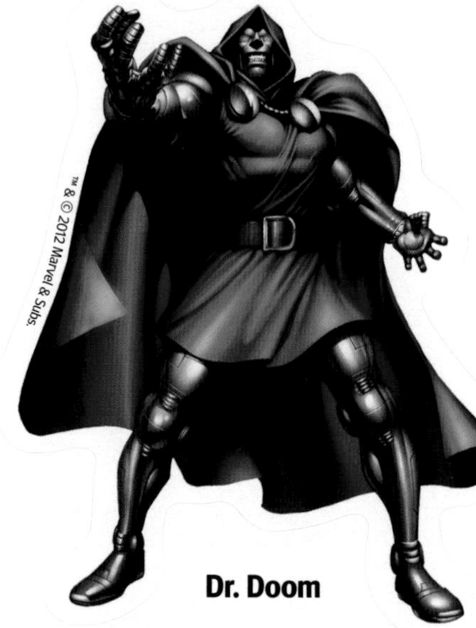
™ & © 2012 Marvel & Subs.

Dr. Doom

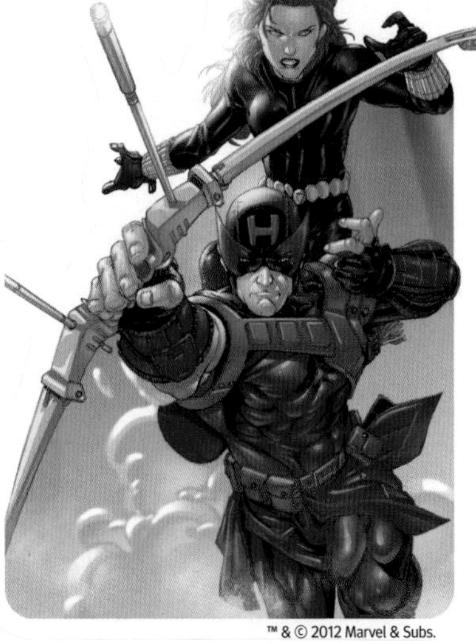
™ & © 2012 Marvel & Subs.

Trusted Avengers

Changing roster

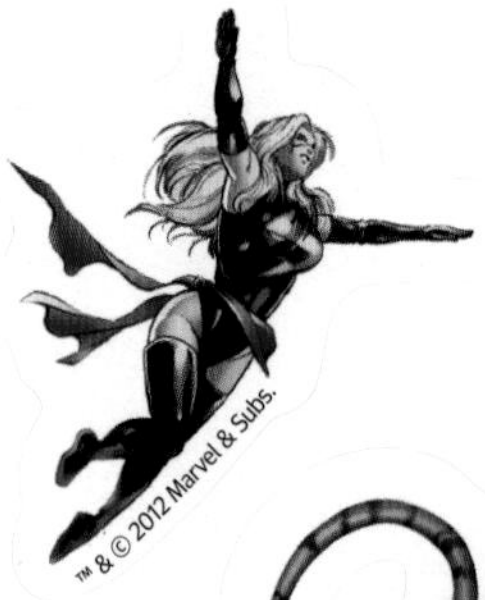
™ & © 2012 Marvel & Subs.

Ms. Marvel

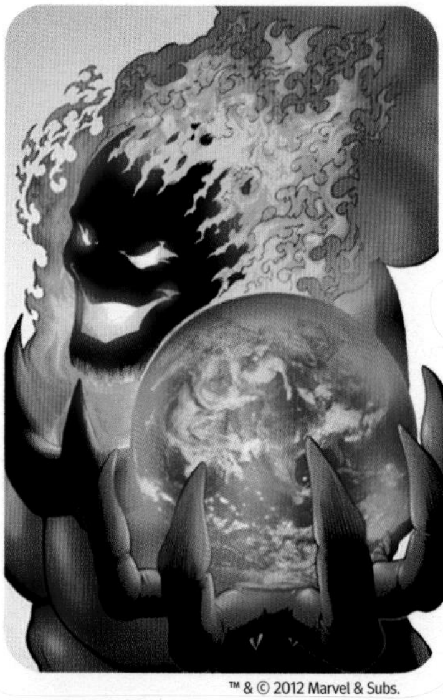
™ & © 2012 Marvel & Subs.

Dormammu

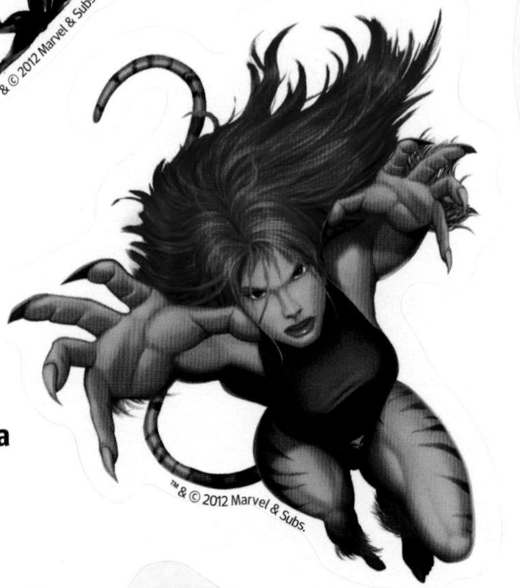
™ & © 2012 Marvel & Subs.

Spidey v. Spidey

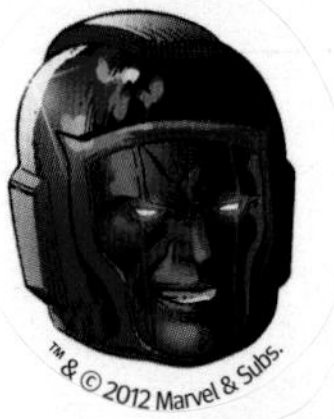
™ & © 2012 Marvel & Subs.

Kang the Conqueror

Tigra

Loki

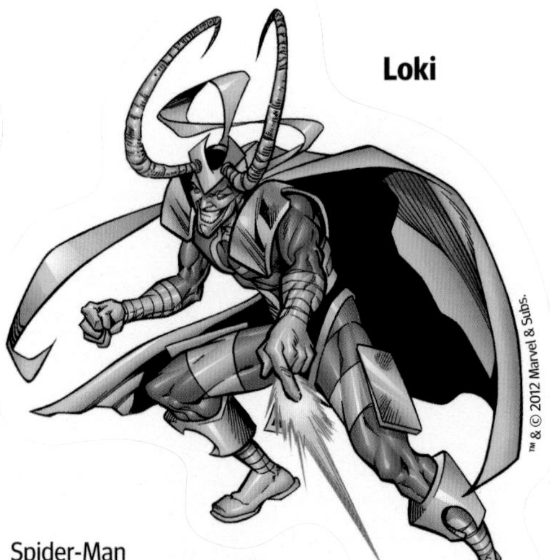
™ & © 2012 Marvel & Subs.

Spider-Woman

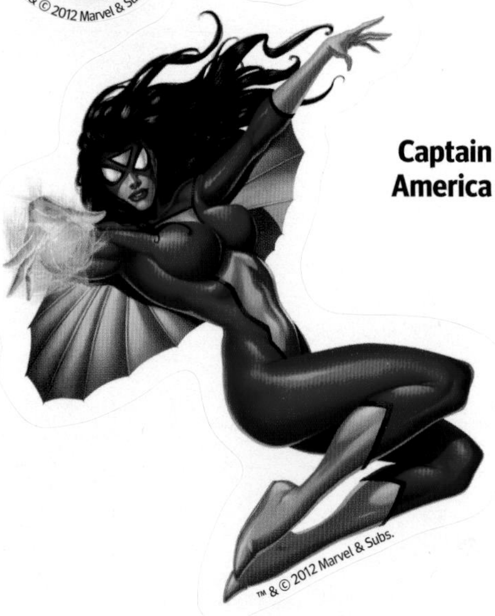
™ & © 2012 Marvel & Subs.

Captain America

Spider-Man

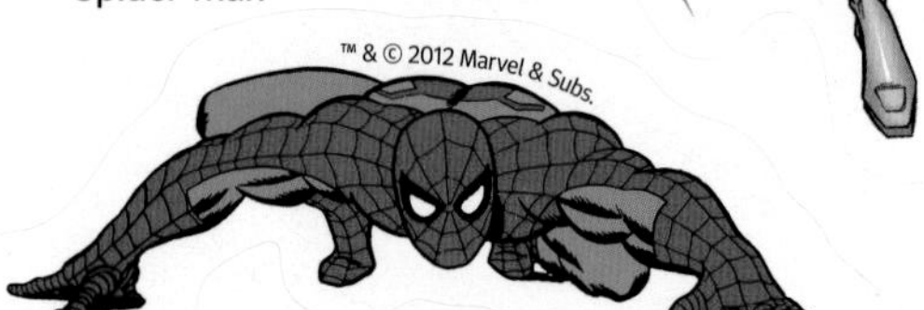
™ & © 2012 Marvel & Subs.

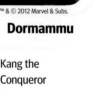

STICKERS

Galactus

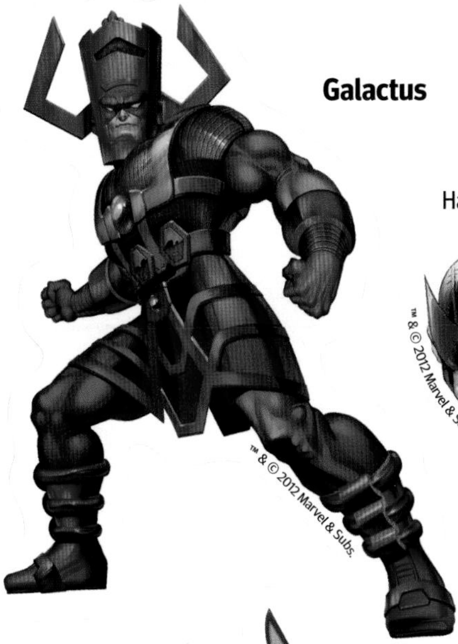
™ & © 2012 Marvel & Subs.

Hawkeye

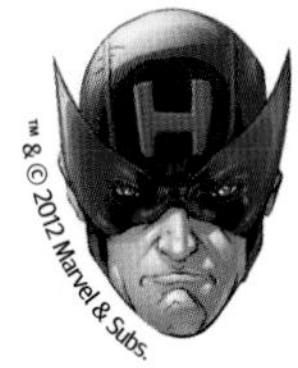
™ & © 2012 Marvel & Subs.

Captain Britain

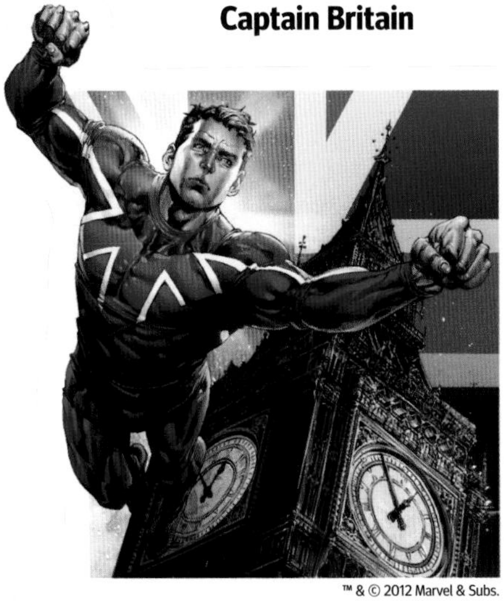
™ & © 2012 Marvel & Subs.

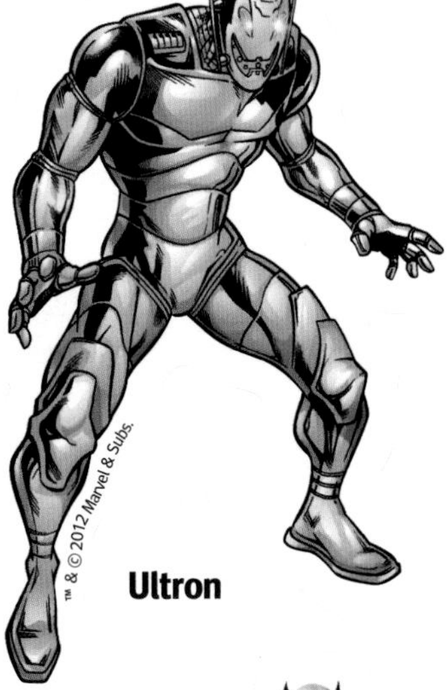
™ & © 2012 Marvel & Subs.

Ultron

Falcon

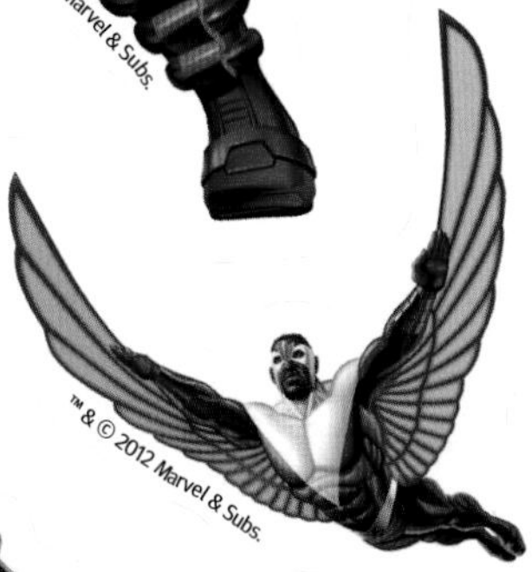
™ & © 2012 Marvel & Subs.

Wolverine

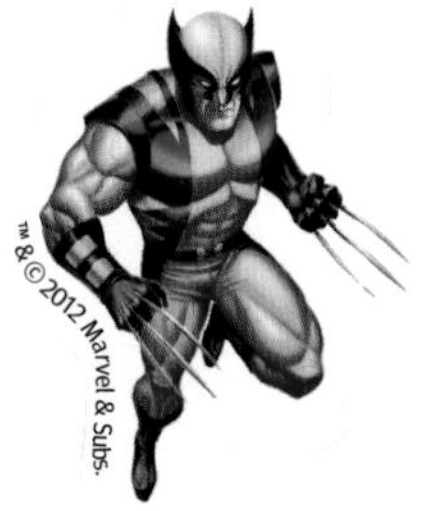
™ & © 2012 Marvel & Subs.

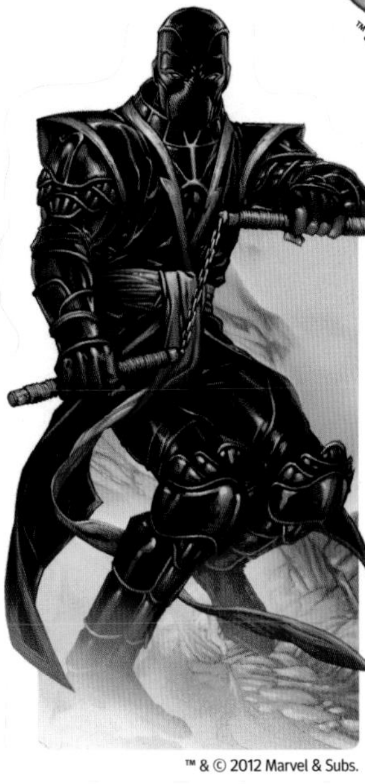
™ & © 2012 Marvel & Subs.

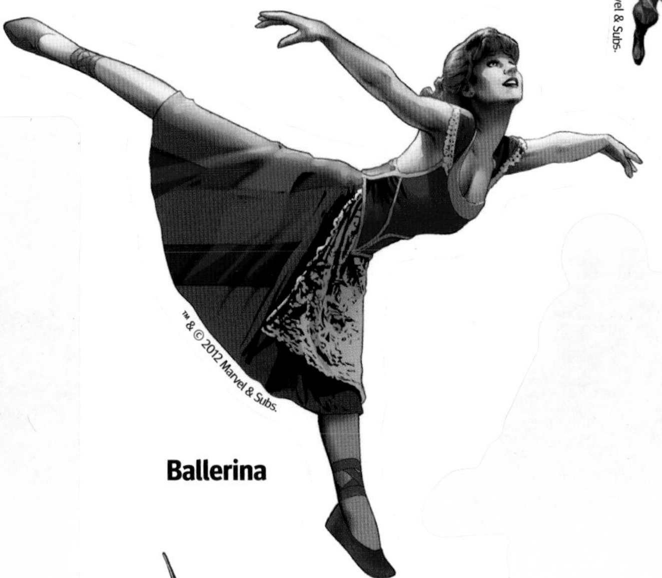
™ & © 2012 Marvel & Subs.

Ballerina

Ronin

The Red Skull

Wall-crawler

Jarvis

Mockingbird

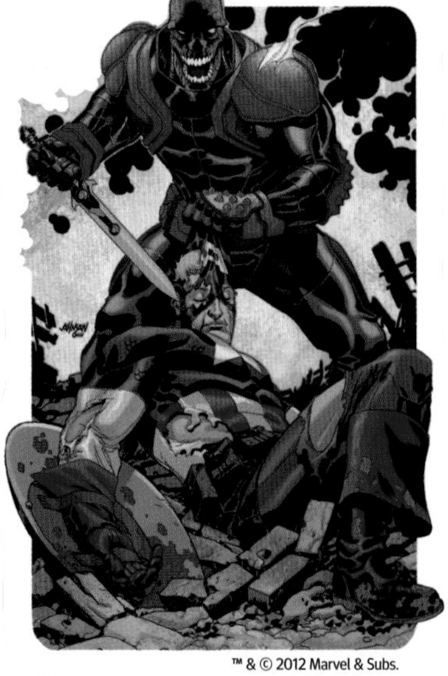
™ & © 2012 Marvel & Subs.

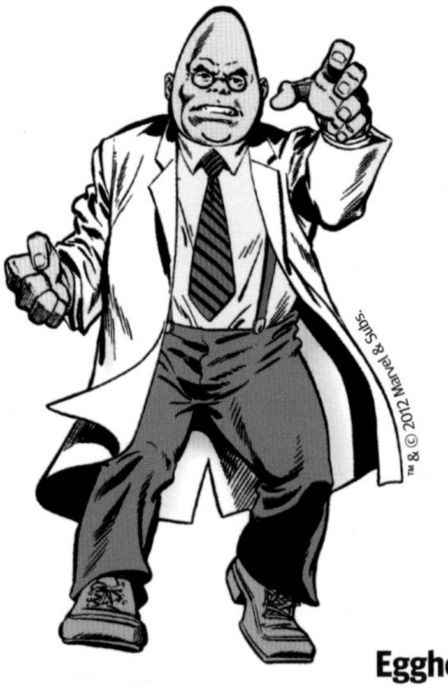
™ & © 2012 Marvel & Subs.

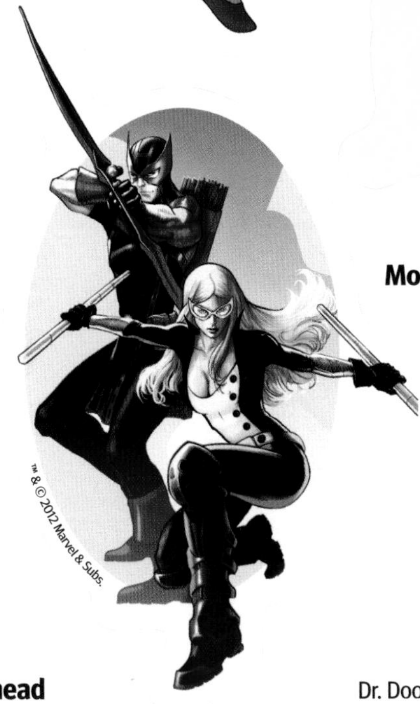
™ & © 2012 Marvel & Subs.

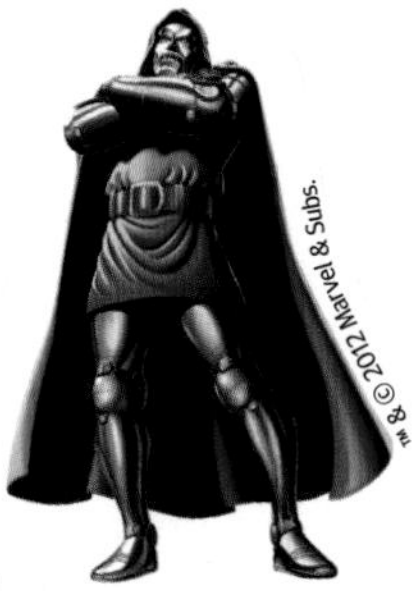
™ & © 2012 Marvel & Subs.

Egghead

Dr. Doom

STICKERS

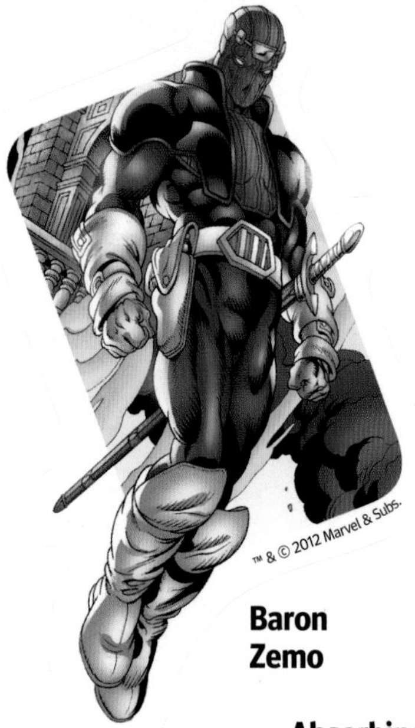
™ & © 2012 Marvel & Subs.

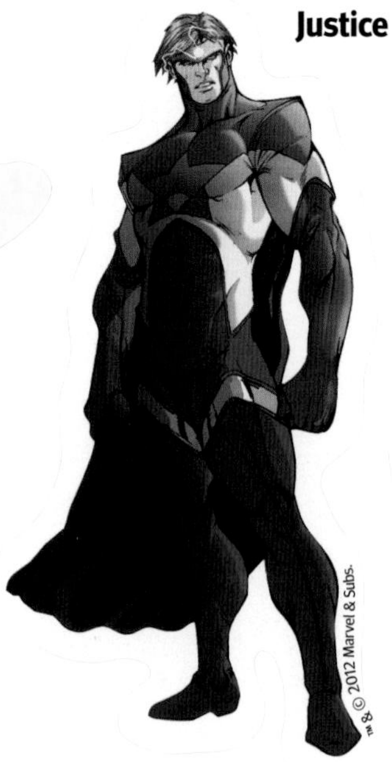
™ & © 2012 Marvel & Subs.

Justice

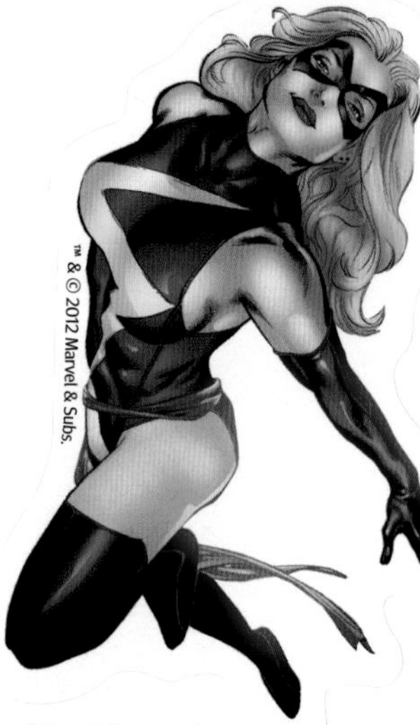
™ & © 2012 Marvel & Subs.

Quinjets

Baron Zemo

Ms. Marvel

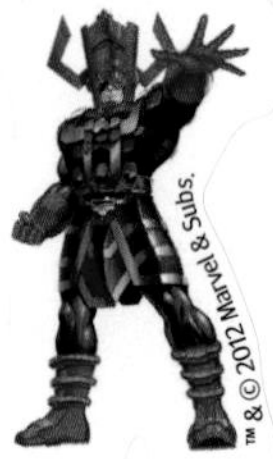
™ & © 2012 Marvel & Subs.

Galactus

Absorbing Man

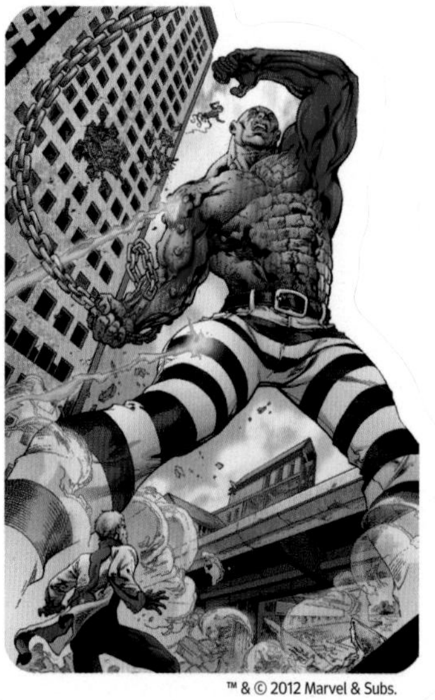
™ & © 2012 Marvel & Subs.

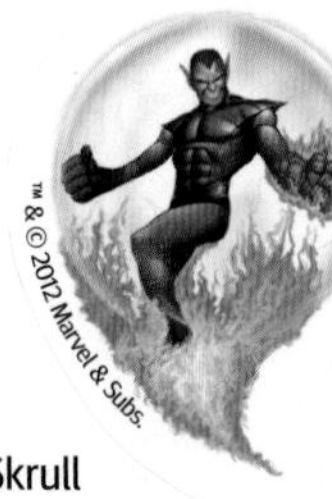
™ & © 2012 Marvel & Subs.

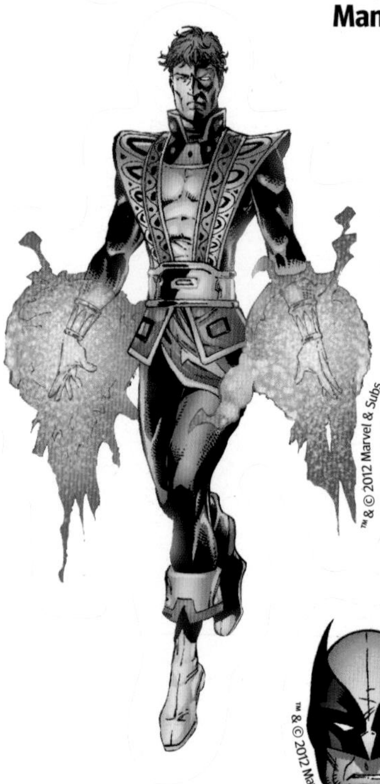
™ & © 2012 Marvel & Subs.

Jack of Hearts

The Super-Skrull

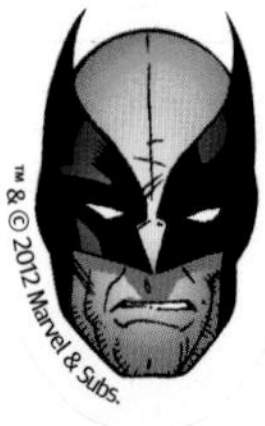
™ & © 2012 Marvel & Subs.

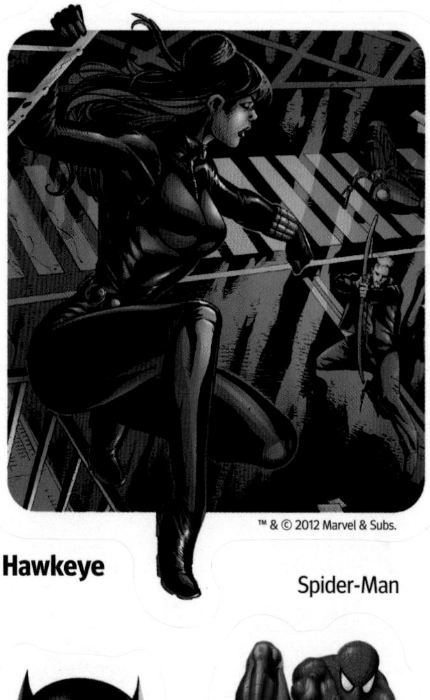
™ & © 2012 Marvel & Subs.

Web-shooters

Juggernaut

On target

Wolverine

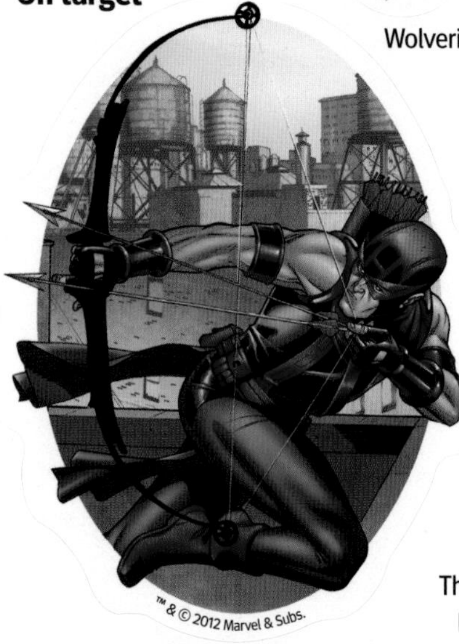
™ & © 2012 Marvel & Subs.

Hawkeye

Spider-Man

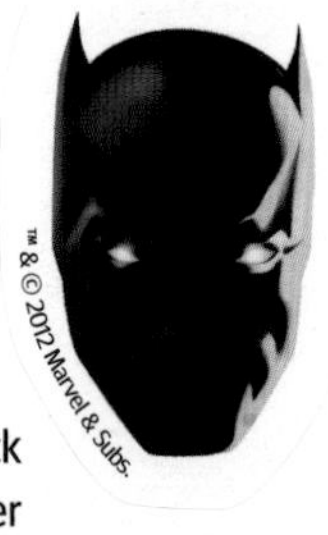
™ & © 2012 Marvel & Subs.

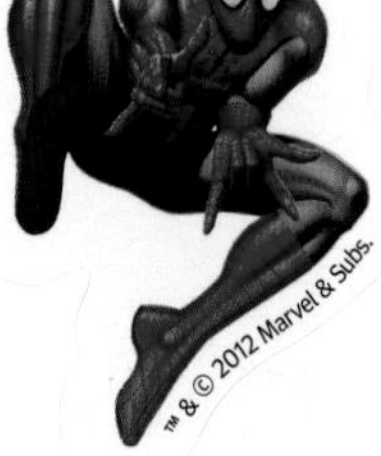
™ & © 2012 Marvel & Subs.

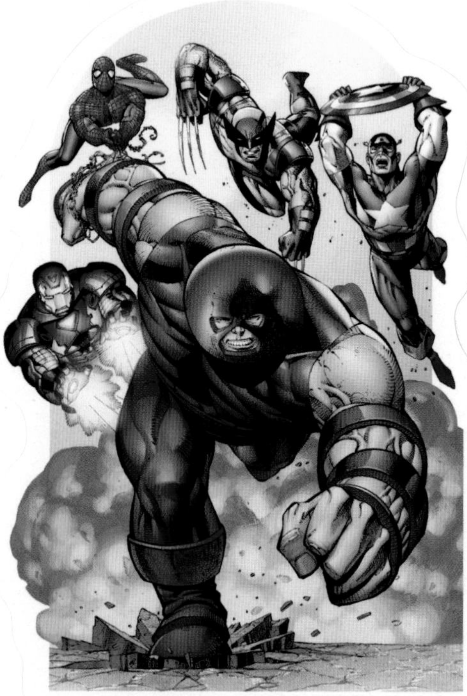
™ & © 2012 Marvel & Subs.

The Black Panther

STICKERS

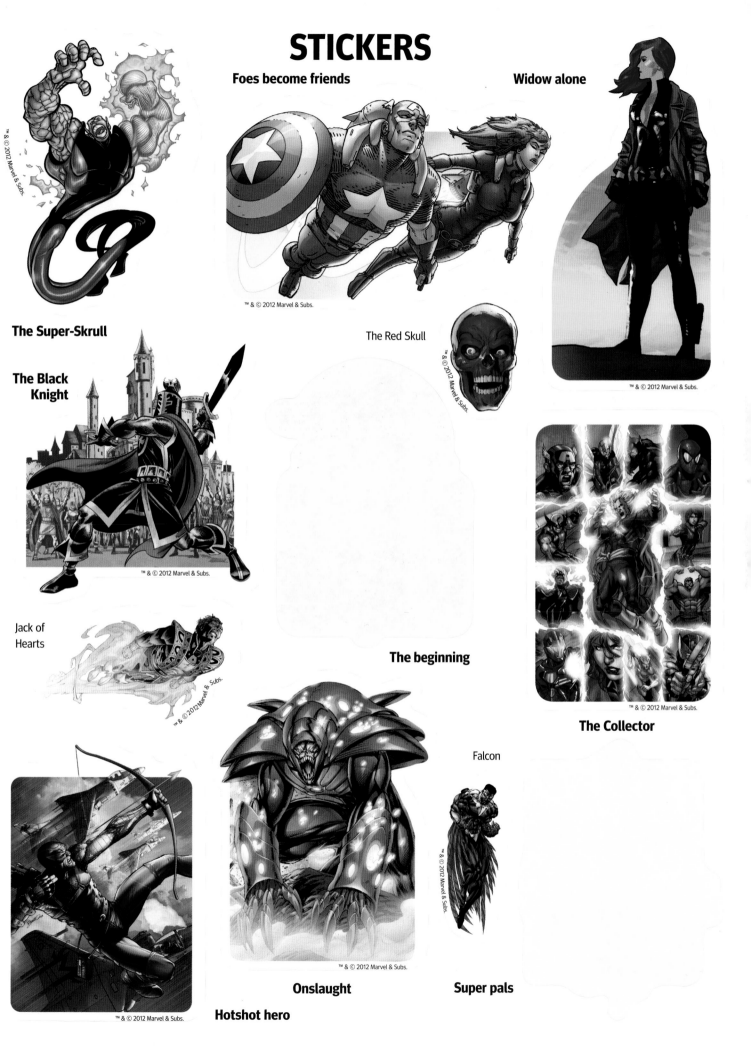

Foes become friends

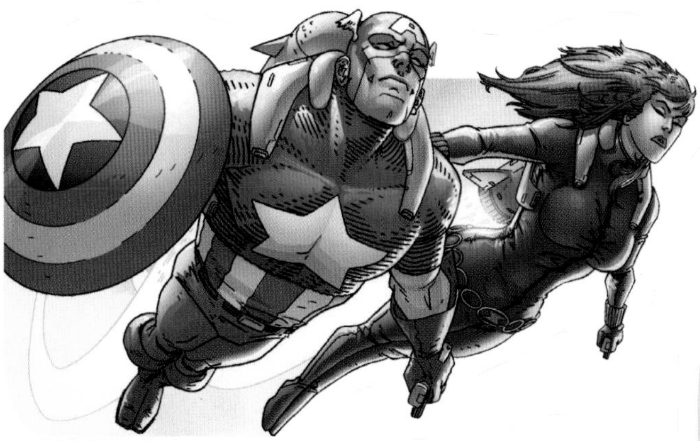

™ & © 2012 Marvel & Subs.

Widow alone

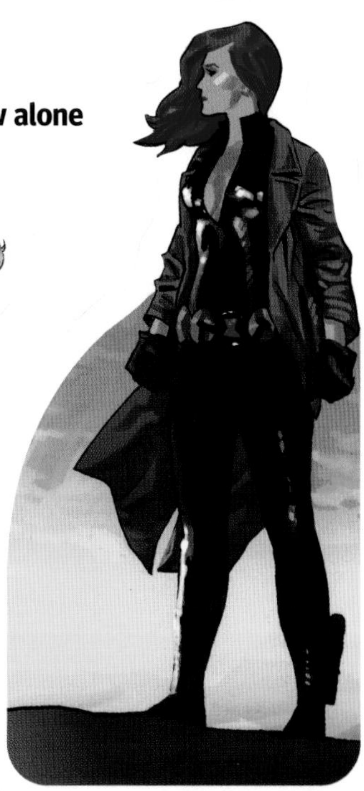

™ & © 2012 Marvel & Subs.

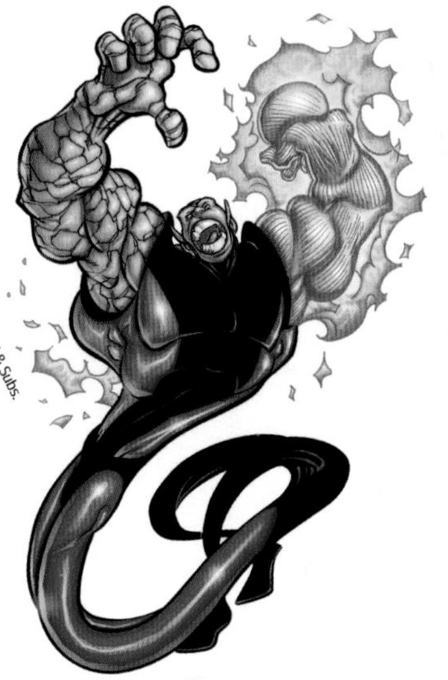

™ & © 2012 Marvel & Subs.

The Super-Skrull

The Red Skull

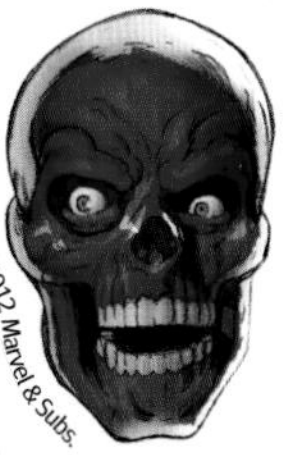

™ & © 2012 Marvel & Subs.

The Black Knight

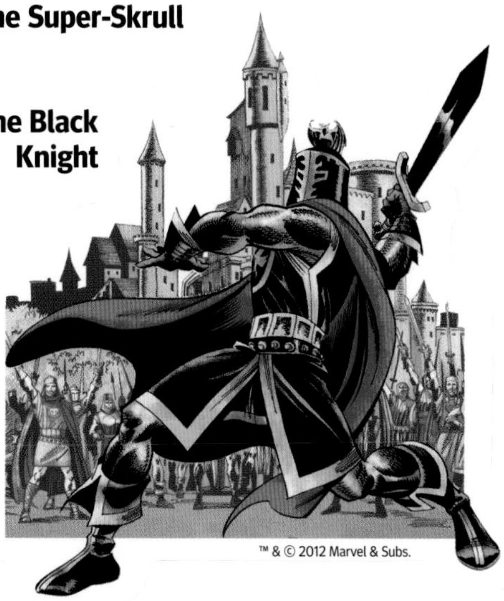

™ & © 2012 Marvel & Subs.

Jack of Hearts

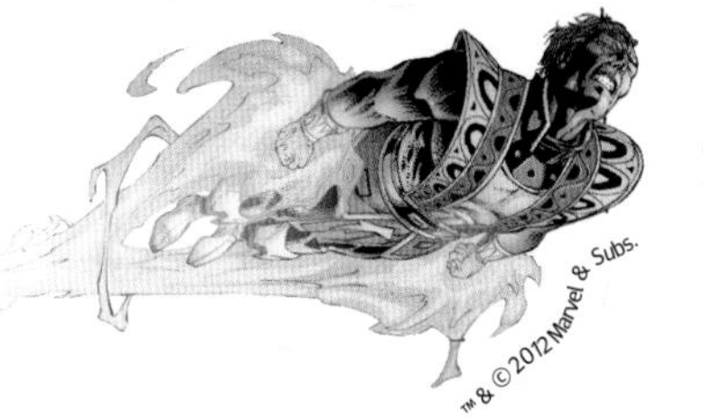

™ & © 2012 Marvel & Subs.

The beginning

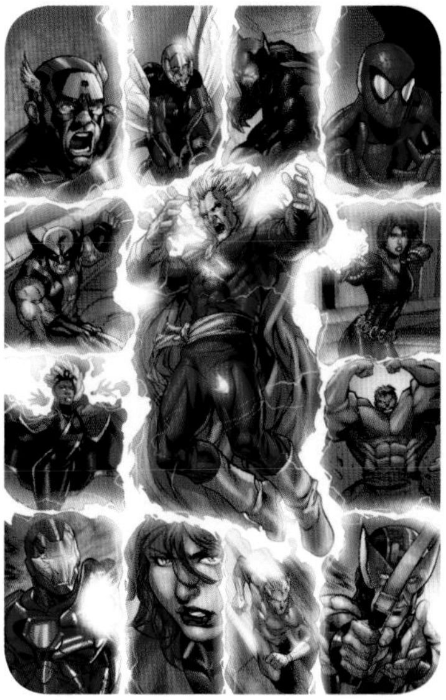

™ & © 2012 Marvel & Subs.

The Collector

Falcon

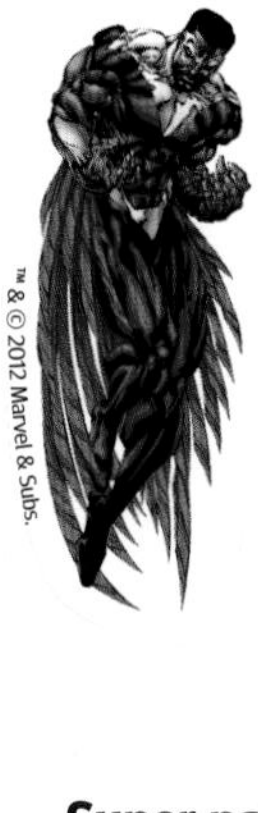

™ & © 2012 Marvel & Subs.

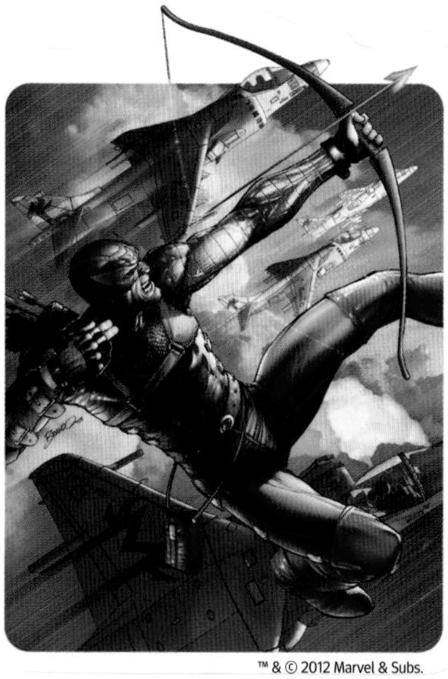

™ & © 2012 Marvel & Subs.

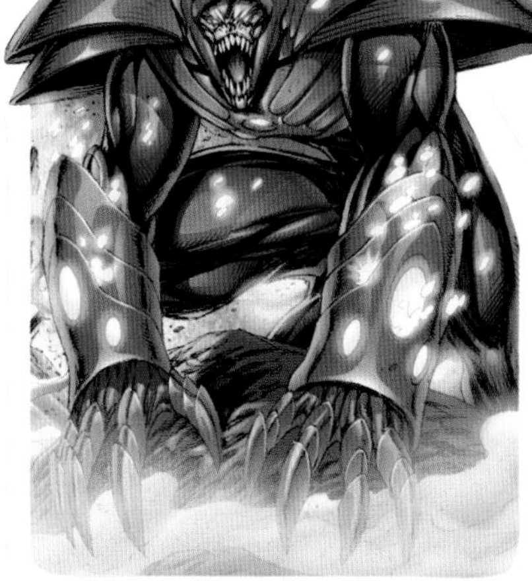

™ & © 2012 Marvel & Subs.

Onslaught

Super pals

Hotshot hero

STICKERS

Peter Parker

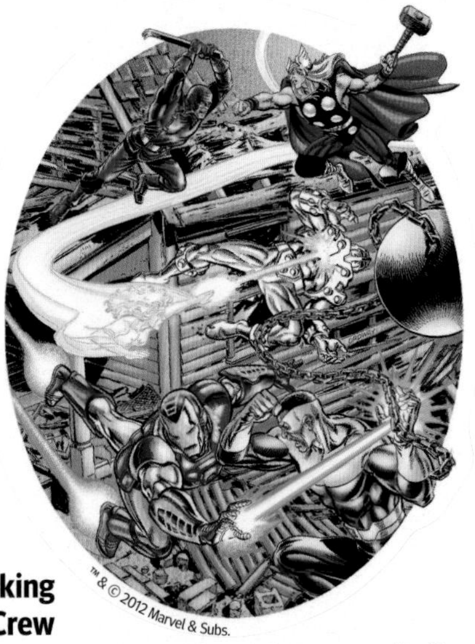

Wrecking Crew

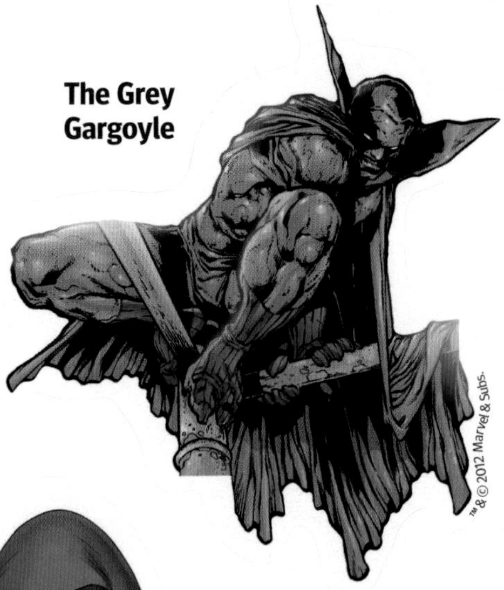

The Grey Gargoyle

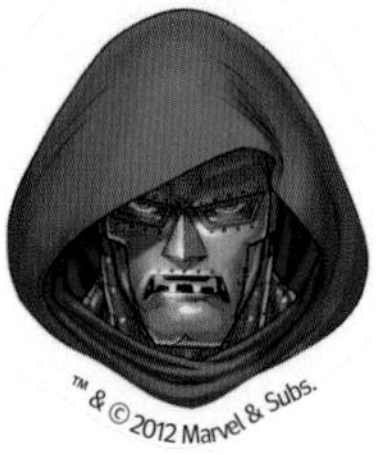

Dr. Doom

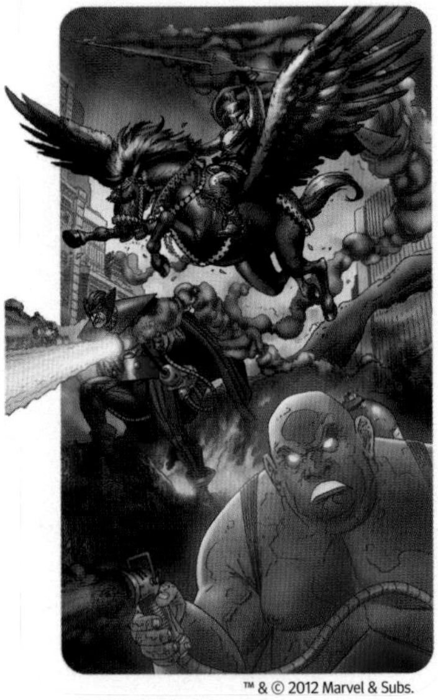

Masters of Evil

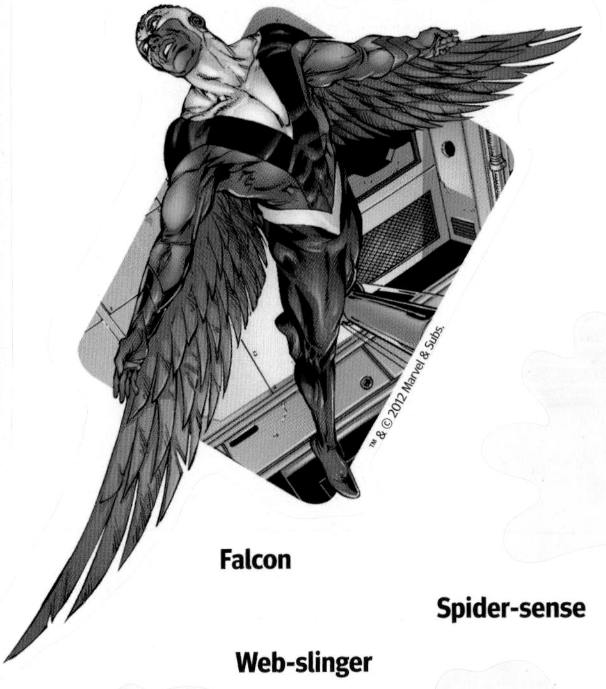

Falcon

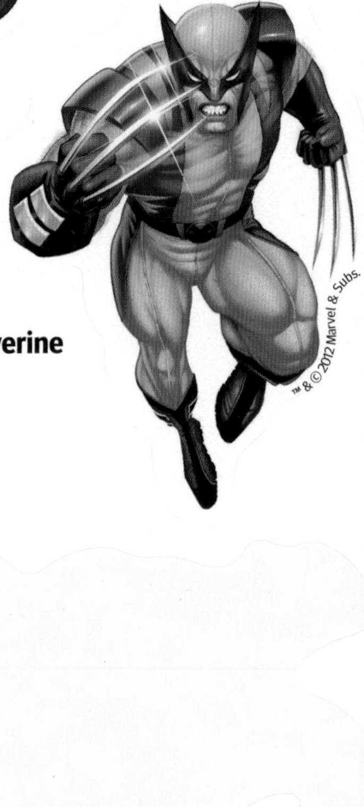

Wolverine

Spider-sense

Web-slinger

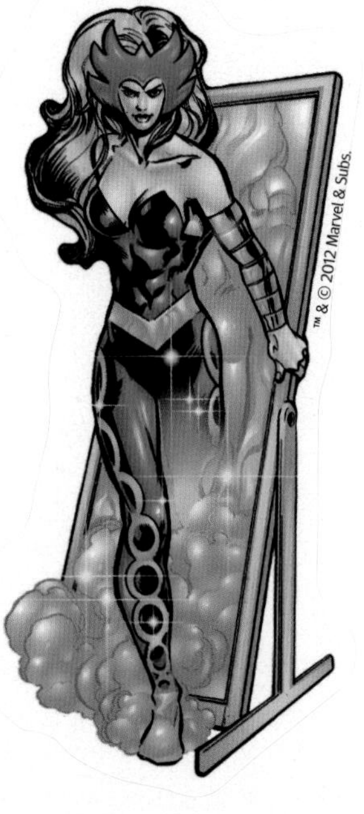

The Enchantress

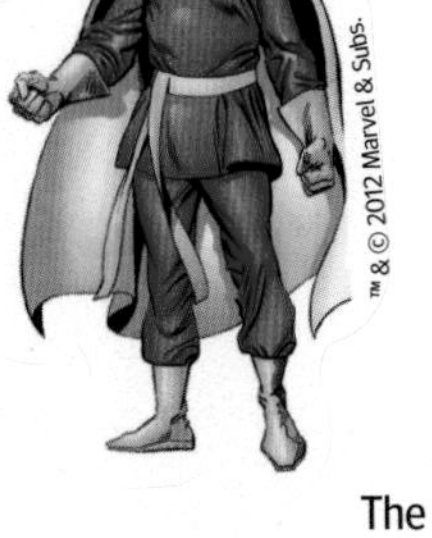

The Collector

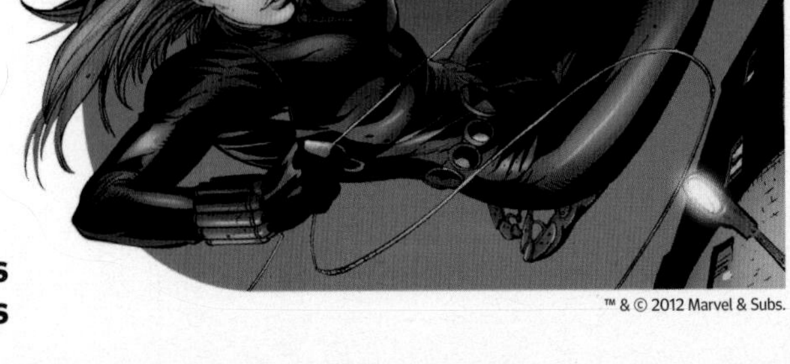

Widow's weapons

STICKERS

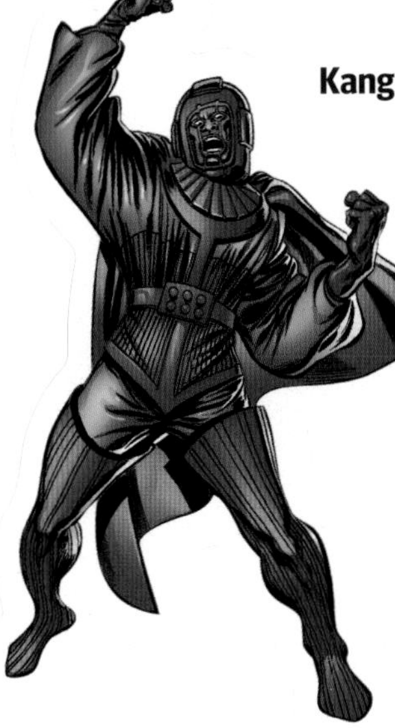

™ & © 2012 Marvel & Subs.

Kang the Conqueror

The Red Skull

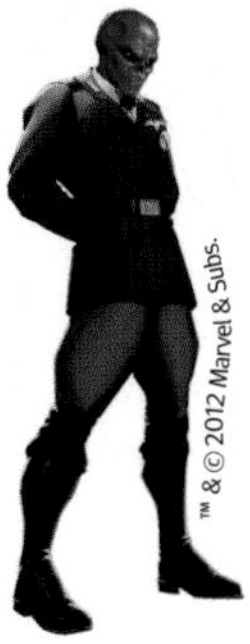

™ & © 2012 Marvel & Subs.

The Mandarin

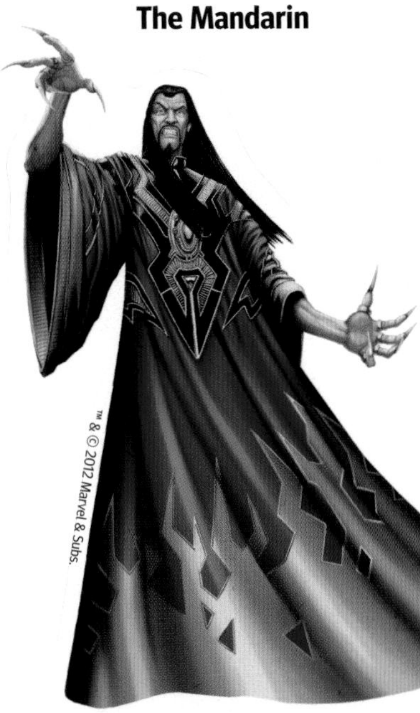

™ & © 2012 Marvel & Subs.

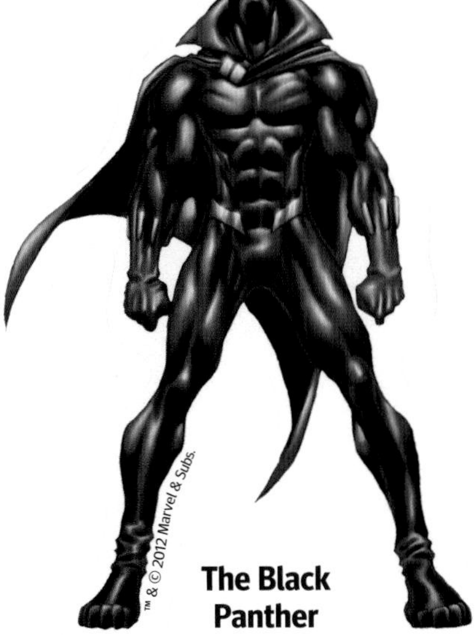

™ & © 2012 Marvel & Subs.

The Black Panther

Morgan le Fay

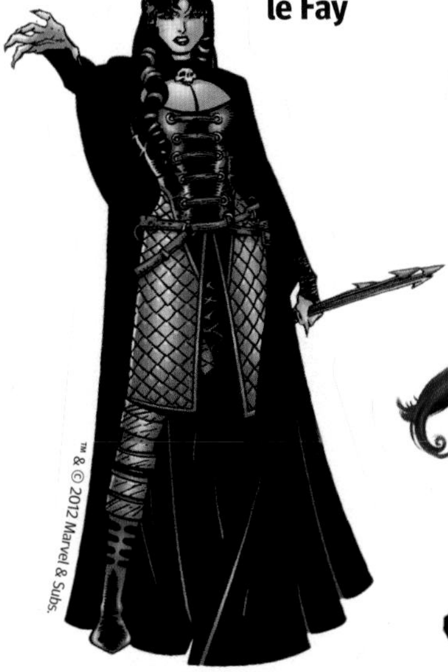

™ & © 2012 Marvel & Subs.

Serpent Society

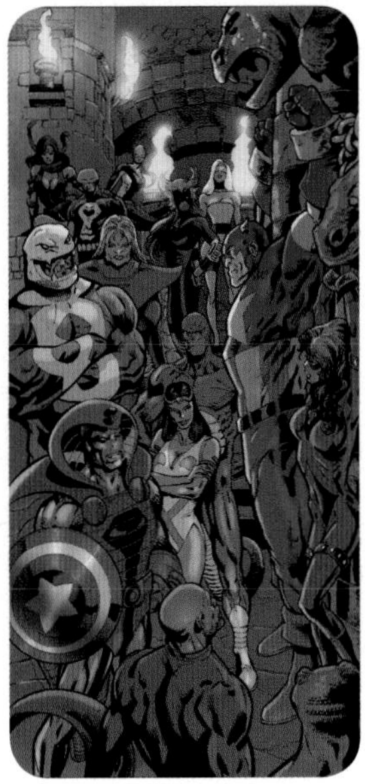

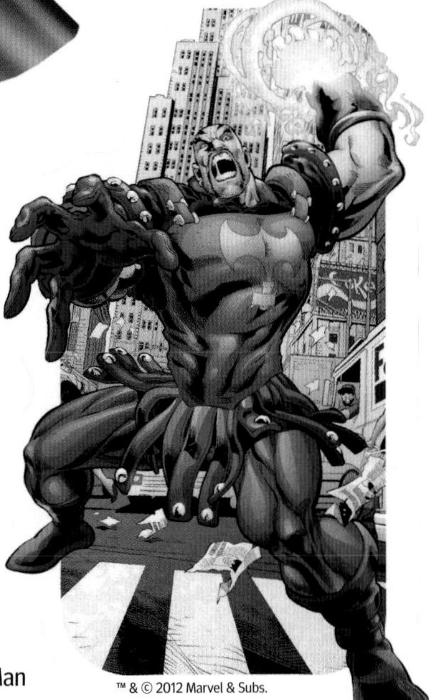

Executioner

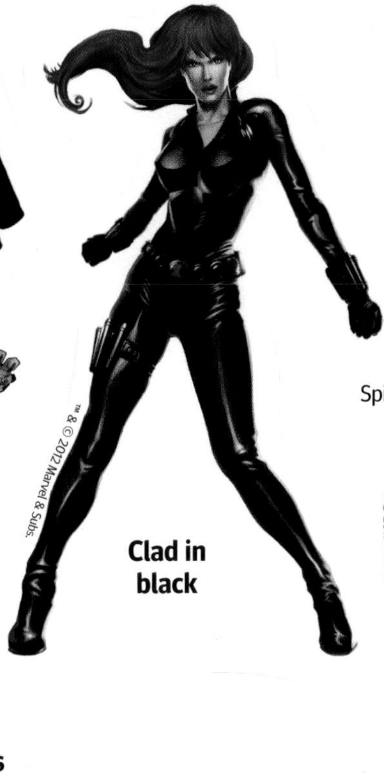

™ & © 2012 Marvel & Subs.

Clad in black

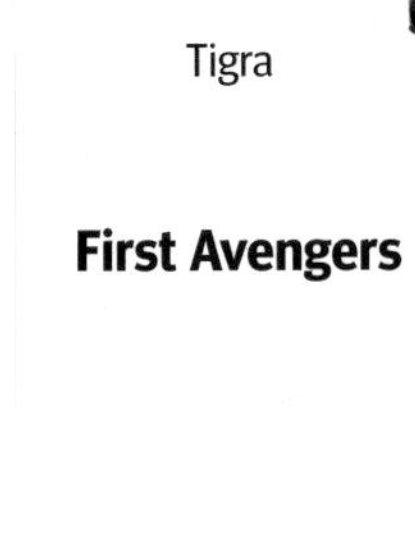

™ & © 2012 Marvel & Subs.

Tigra

Spider-Man

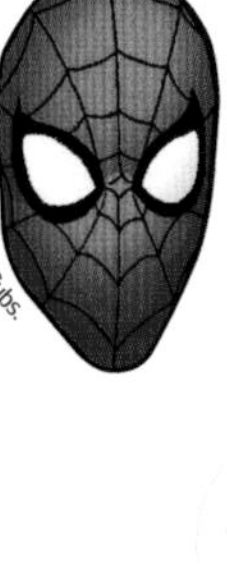

™ & © 2012 Marvel & Subs.

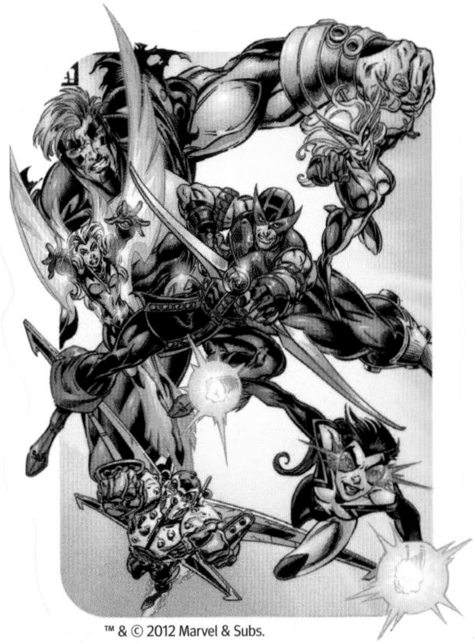

First Avengers

A dream come true

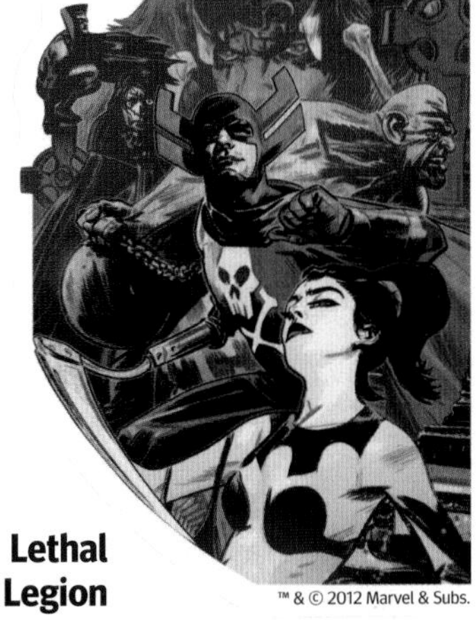

Lethal Legion

STICKERS

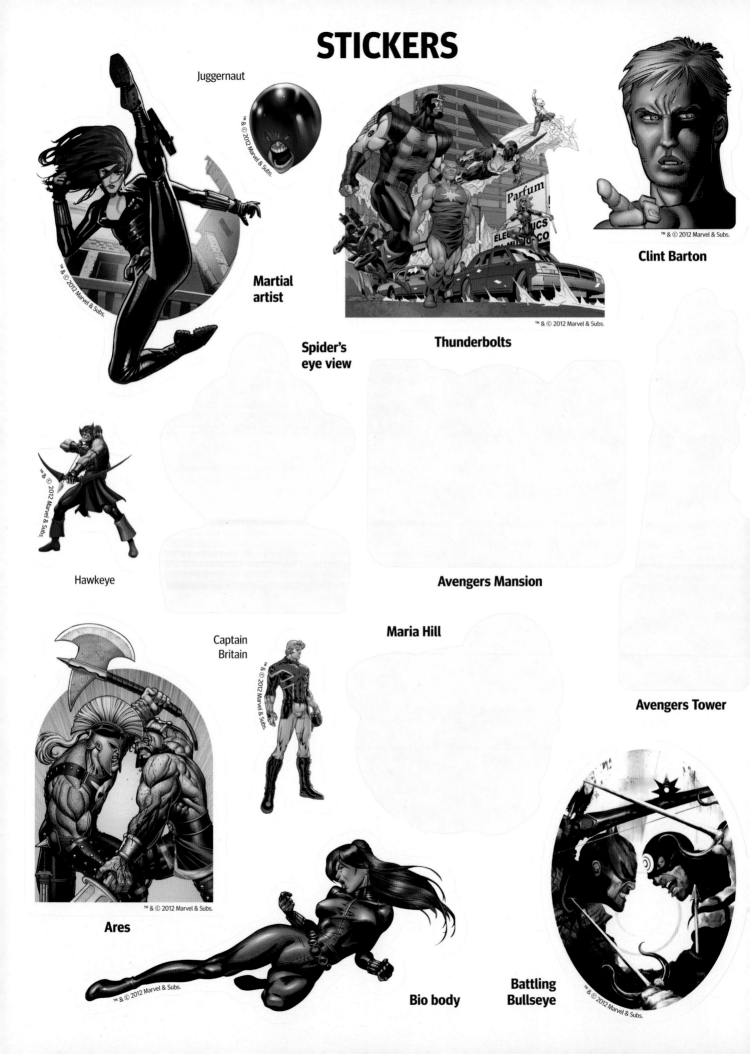

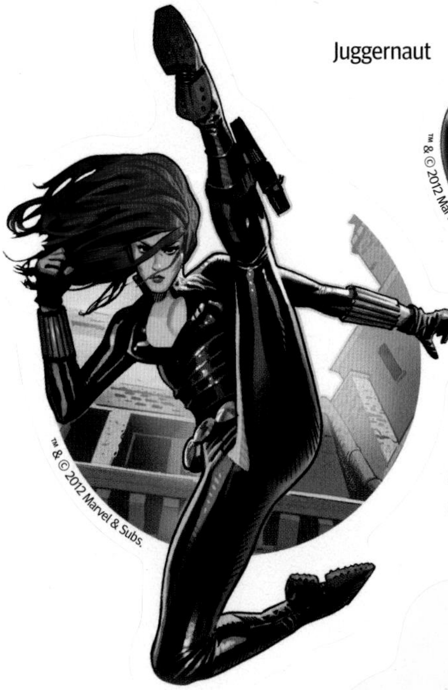
™ & © 2012 Marvel & Subs.

Martial artist

Juggernaut

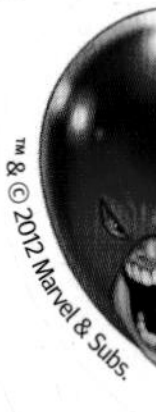
™ & © 2012 Marvel & Subs.

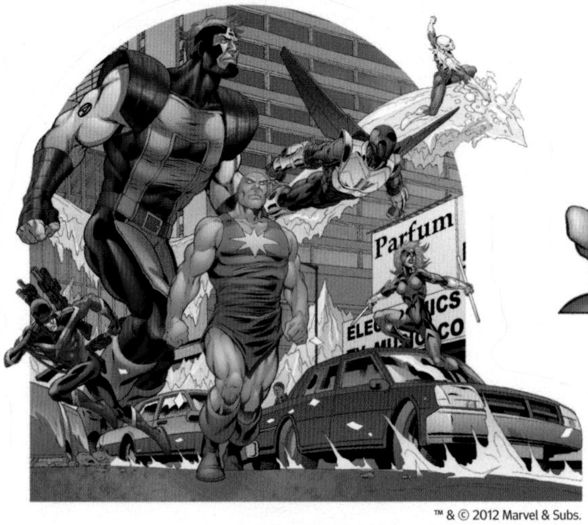
Parfum
™ & © 2012 Marvel & Subs.

Thunderbolts

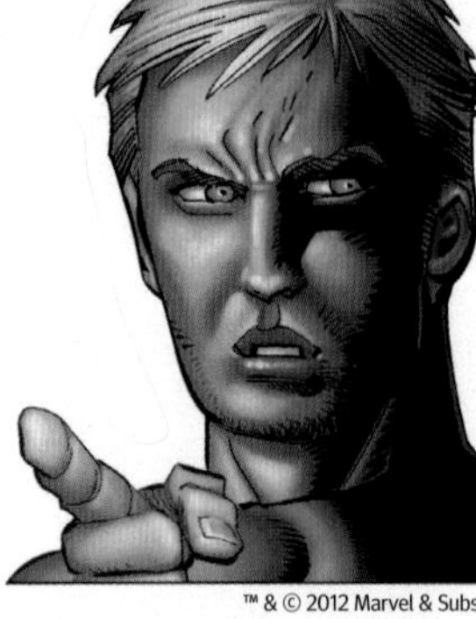
™ & © 2012 Marvel & Subs.

Clint Barton

Spider's eye view

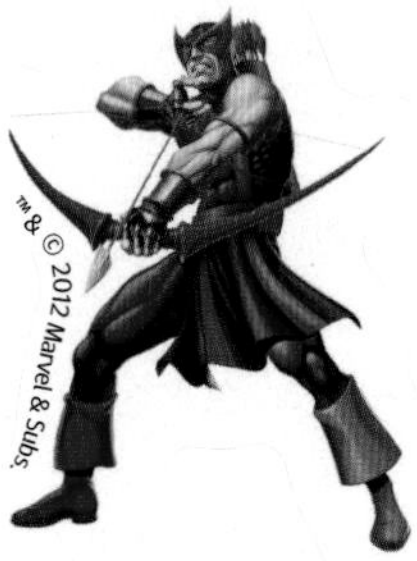
™ & © 2012 Marvel & Subs.

Hawkeye

Avengers Mansion

Maria Hill

Avengers Tower

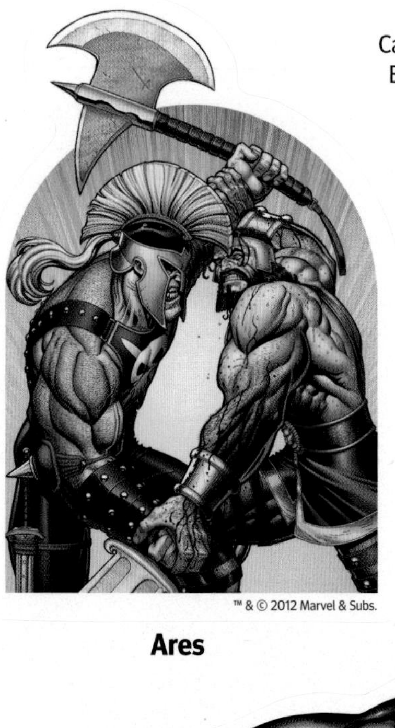
™ & © 2012 Marvel & Subs.

Ares

Captain Britain

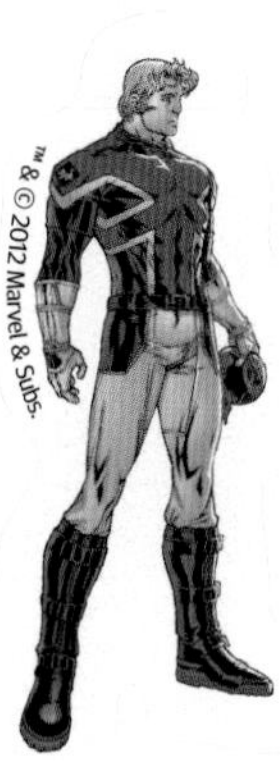
™ & © 2012 Marvel & Subs.

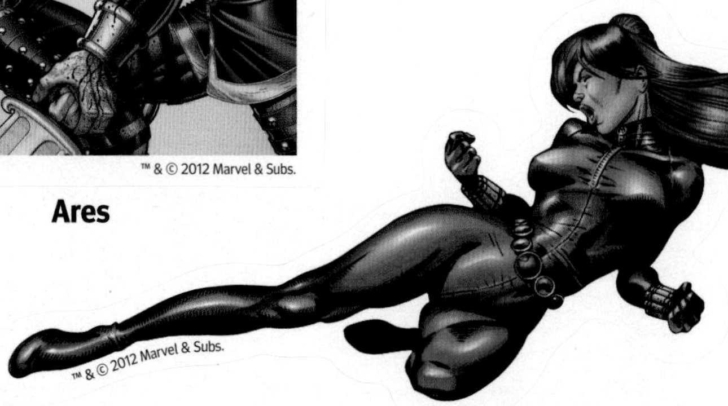
™ & © 2012 Marvel & Subs.

Bio body

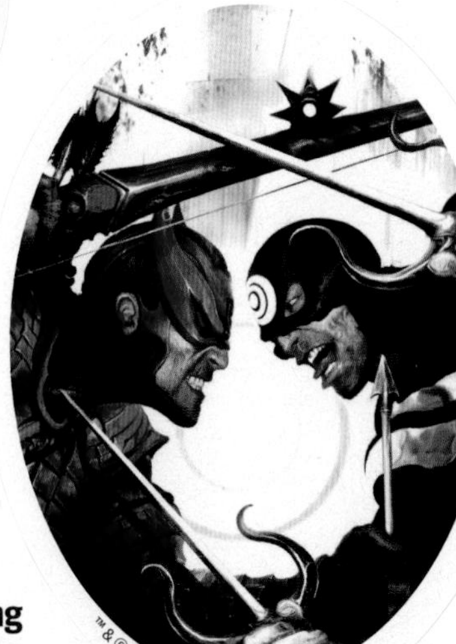
™ & © 2012 Marvel & Subs.

Battling Bullseye

STICKERS

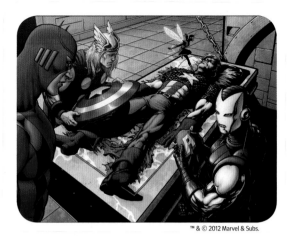

Repulsor rays

Ice Cap

Quicksilver

Deep-sea armor

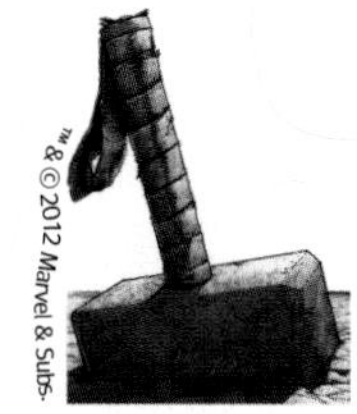

™ & © 2012 Marvel & Subs.

Mjolnir

™ & © 2012 Marvel & Subs.

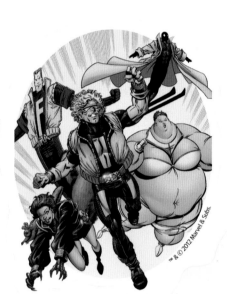

Great Lakes Avengers

Jocasta

Moondragon

™ & © 2012 Marvel & Subs.

Hulk

™ & © 2012 Marvel & Subs.

Pym particles

™ & © 2012 Marvel & Subs.

Firestar

™ & © 2012 Marvel & Subs.

Lord of lightning

The shield

™ & © 2012 Marvel & Subs.

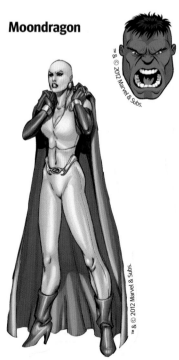

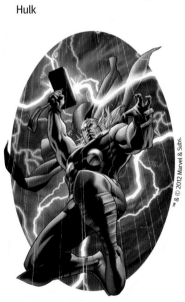

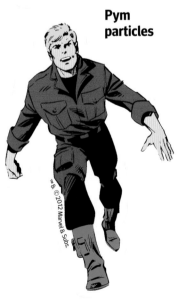

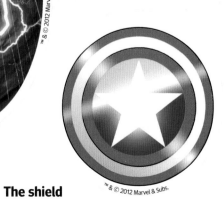

STICKERS

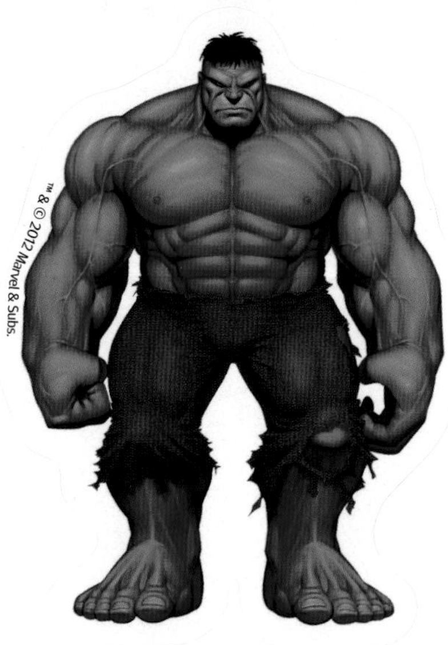
™ & © 2012 Marvel & Subs.

Mean and green

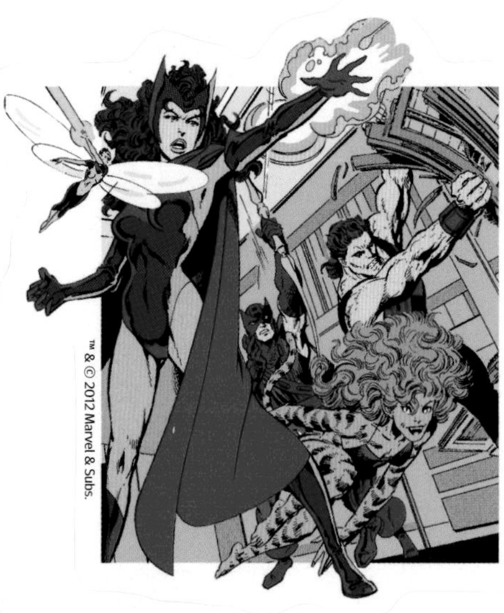
™ & © 2012 Marvel & Subs.

West Coast Avengers

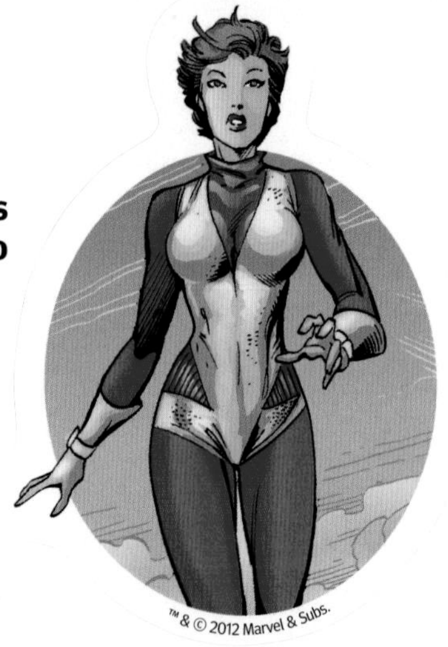
™ & © 2012 Marvel & Subs.

Heiress to hero

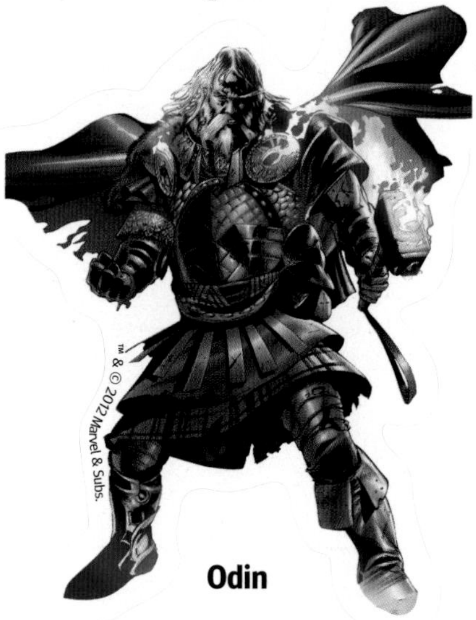
™ & © 2012 Marvel & Subs.

Odin

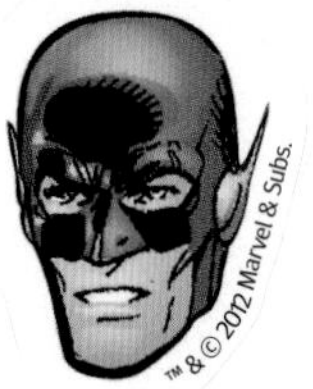
™ & © 2012 Marvel & Subs.

Ant-Man

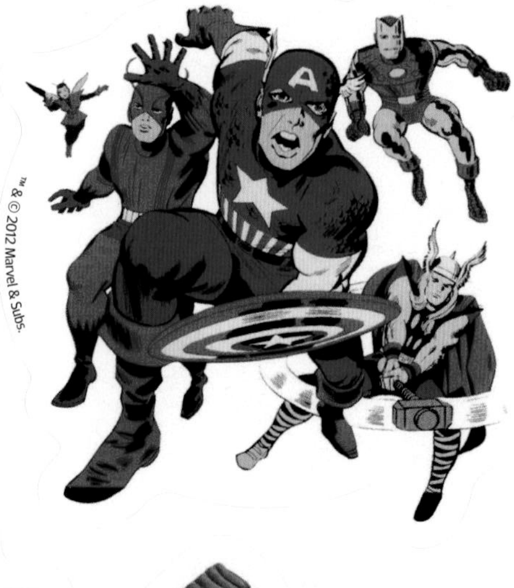
™ & © 2012 Marvel & Subs.

The Avengers' leader

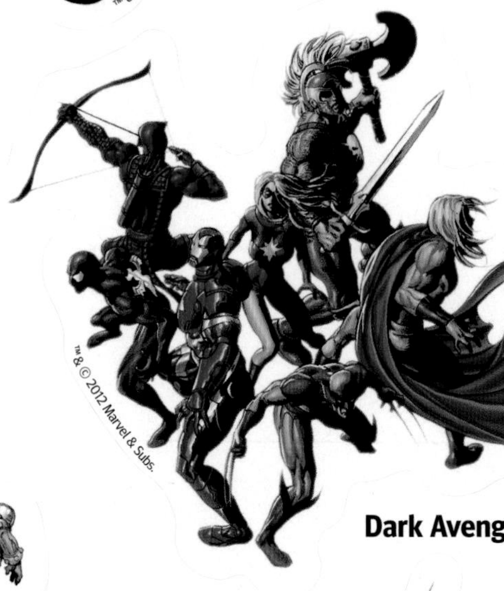
™ & © 2012 Marvel & Subs.

Dark Avengers

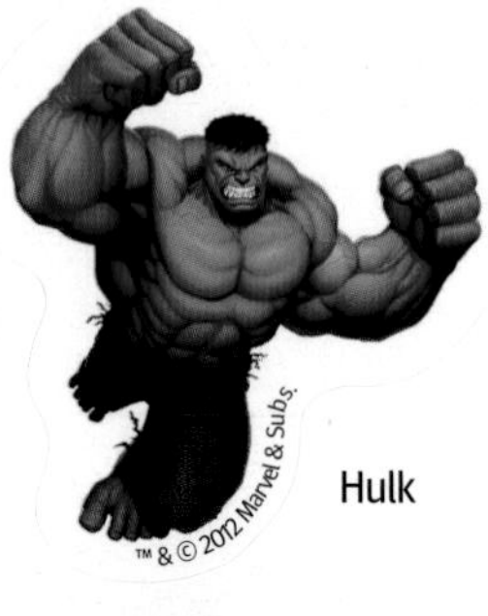
™ & © 2012 Marvel & Subs.

Hulk

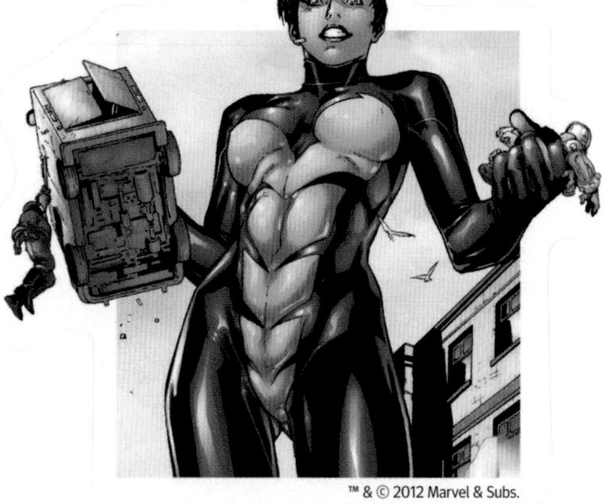
™ & © 2012 Marvel & Subs.

Giant Wasp

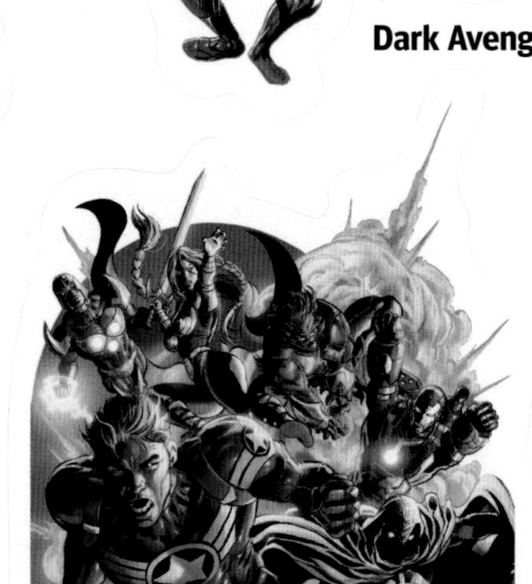
™ & © 2012 Marvel & Subs.

Secret Avengers

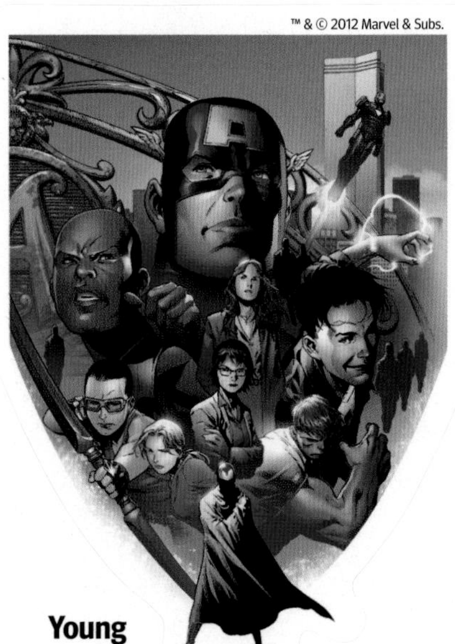
™ & © 2012 Marvel & Subs.

Young Avengers

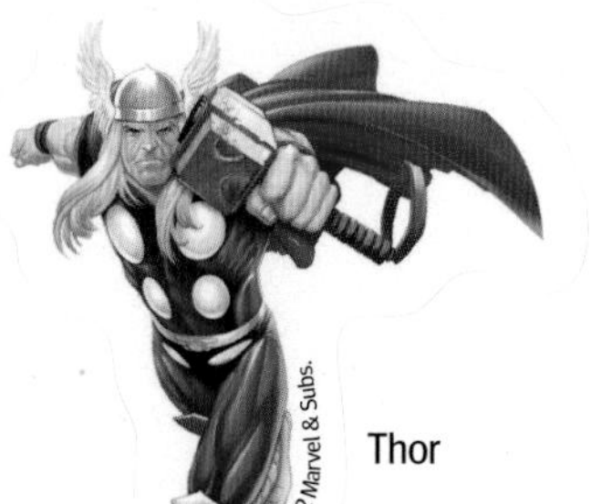
™ & © 2012 Marvel & Subs.

Thor

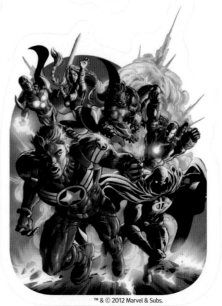

STICKERS

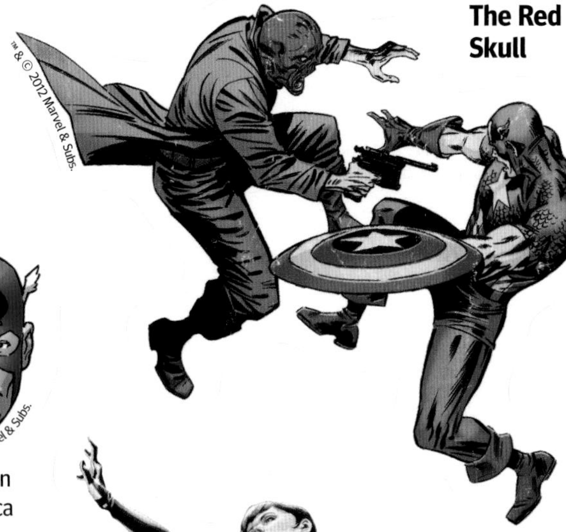
™ & © 2012 Marvel & Subs.

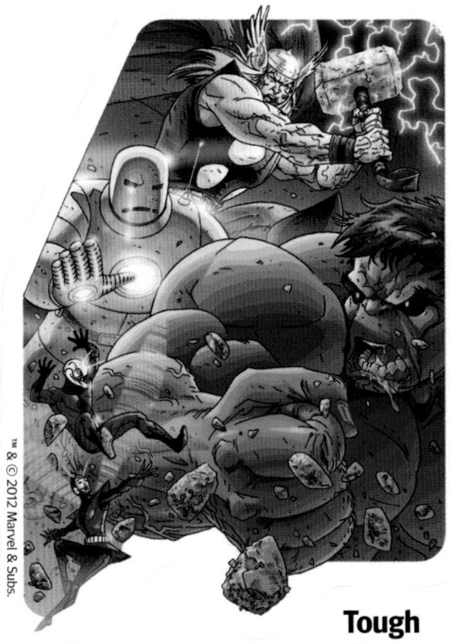
™ & © 2012 Marvel & Subs.

The Red Skull

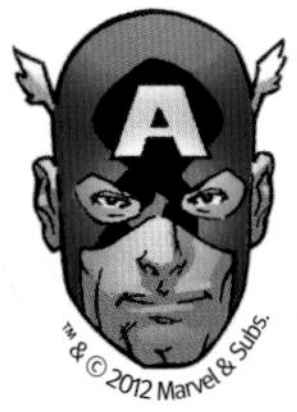
™ & © 2012 Marvel & Subs.

Man of metal

Captain America

Tough love

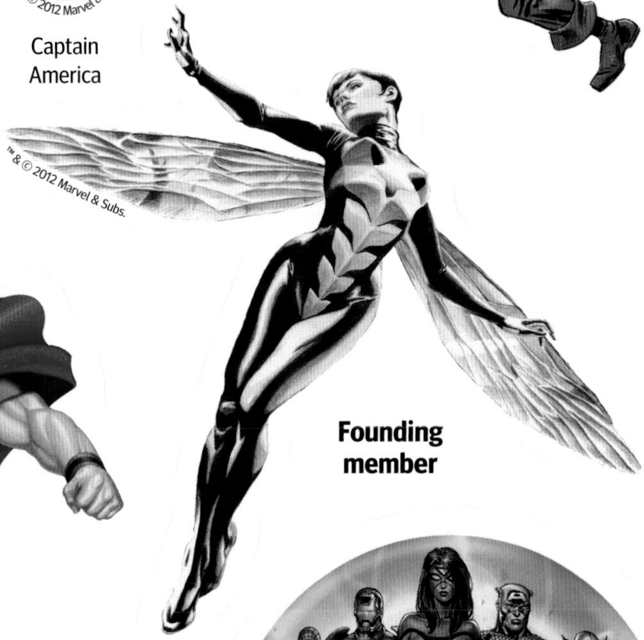
™ & © 2012 Marvel & Subs.

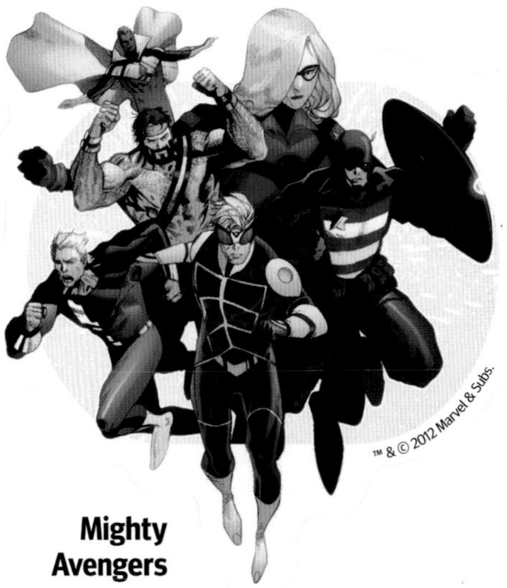
™ & © 2012 Marvel & Subs.

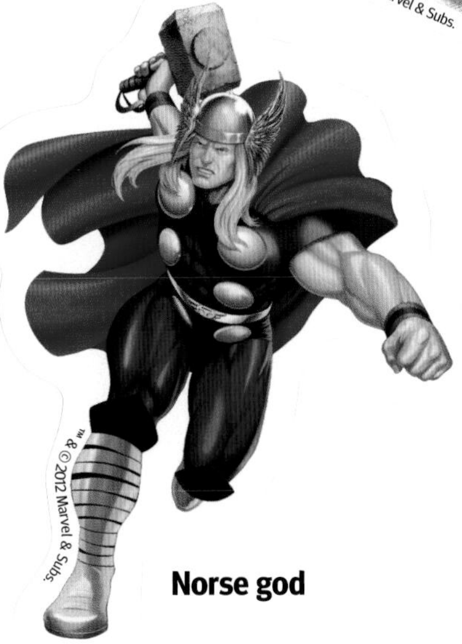
™ & © 2012 Marvel & Subs.

Founding member

Mighty Avengers

Norse god

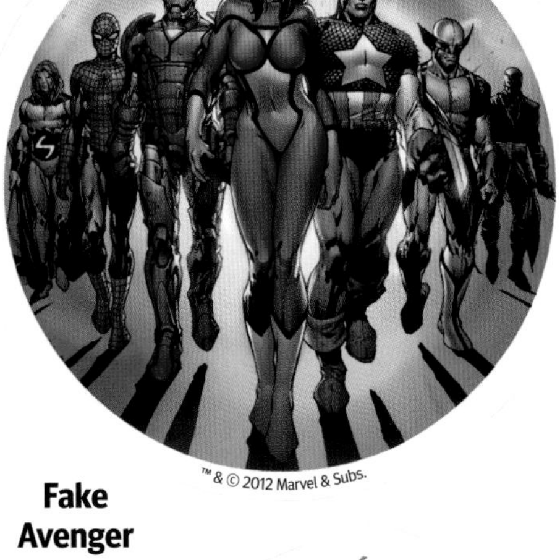
™ & © 2012 Marvel & Subs.

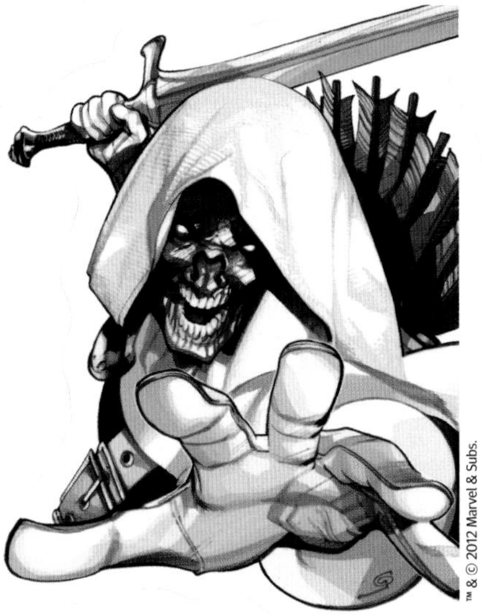
™ & © 2012 Marvel & Subs.

Fake Avenger

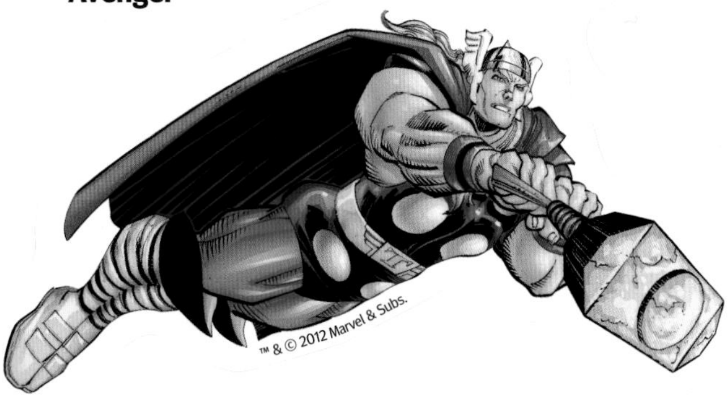
™ & © 2012 Marvel & Subs.

The Scarlet Witch

Taskmaster

Mjolnir

STICKERS

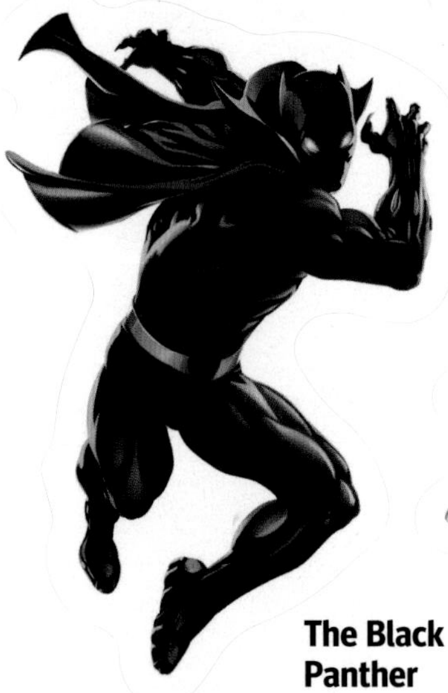

The Black Panther

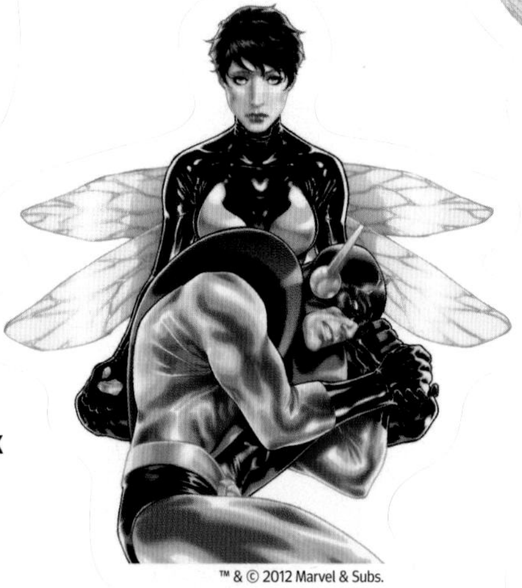
™ & © 2012 Marvel & Subs.

Ant fan

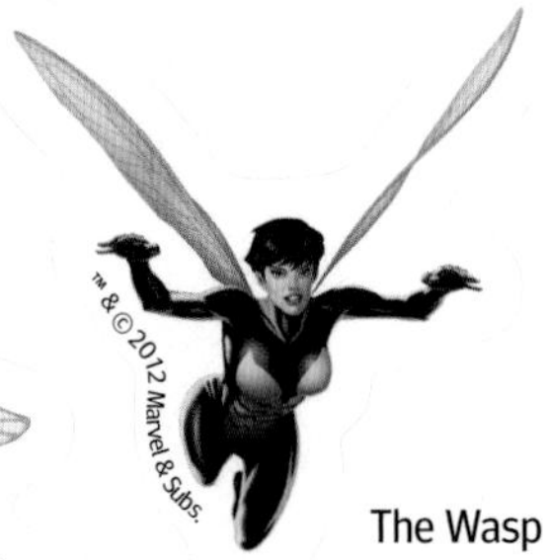
™ & © 2012 Marvel & Subs.

The Wasp

Yellowjacket

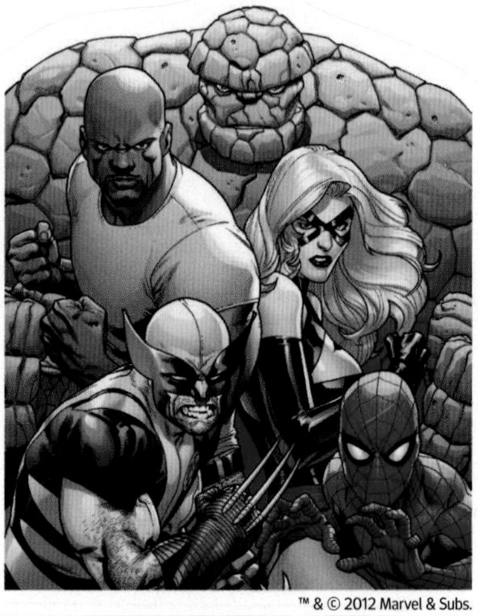
™ & © 2012 Marvel & Subs.

New Avengers

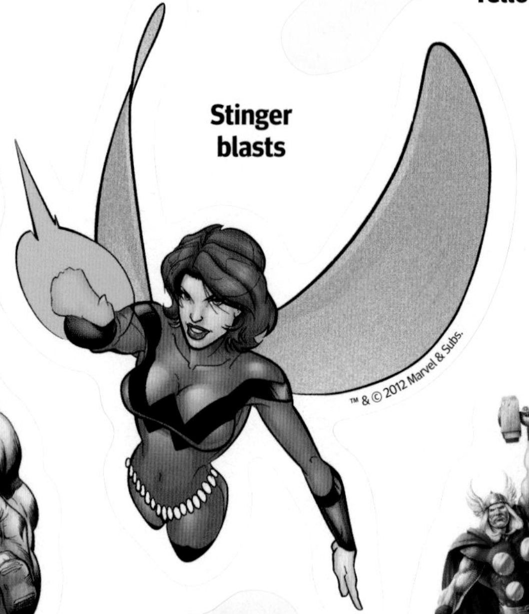
™ & © 2012 Marvel & Subs.

Stinger blasts

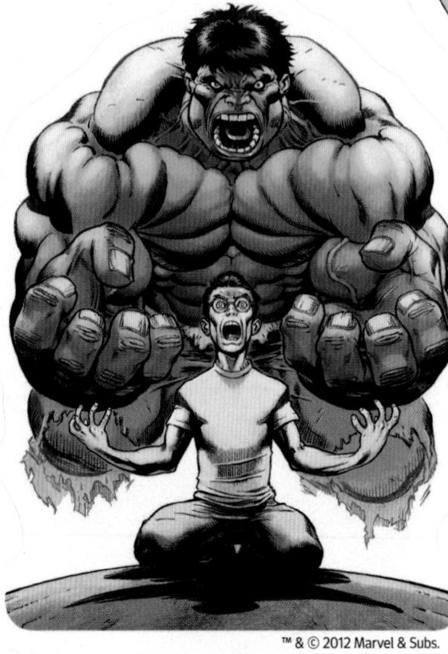
™ & © 2012 Marvel & Subs.

Transformation

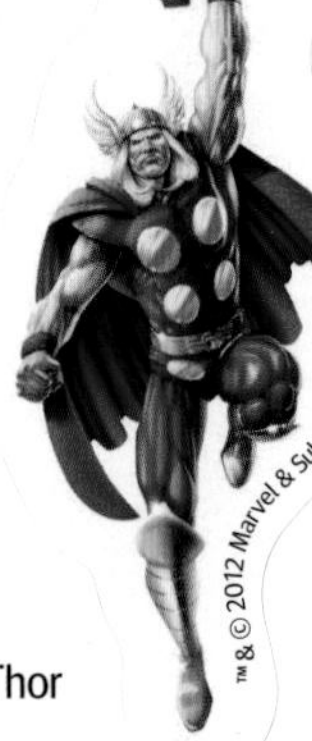
™ & © 2012 Marvel & Subs.

Thor

Iron Man

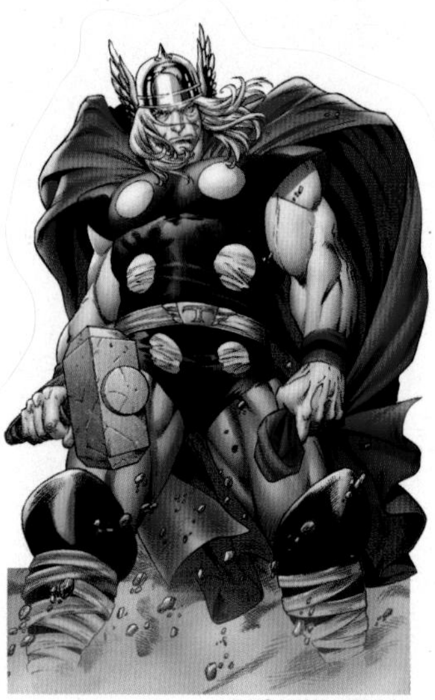
™ & © 2012 Marvel & Subs.

Such power

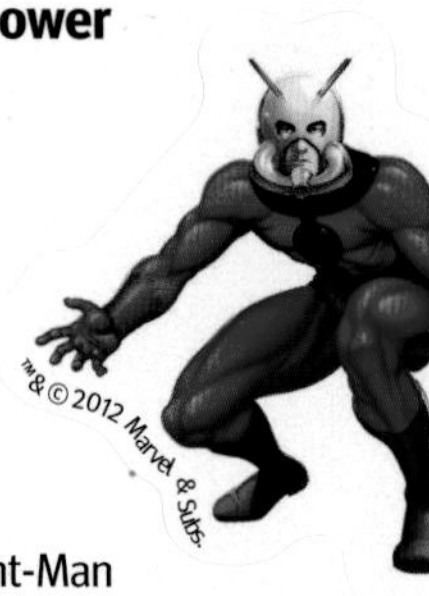
™ & © 2012 Marvel & Subs.

Ant-Man

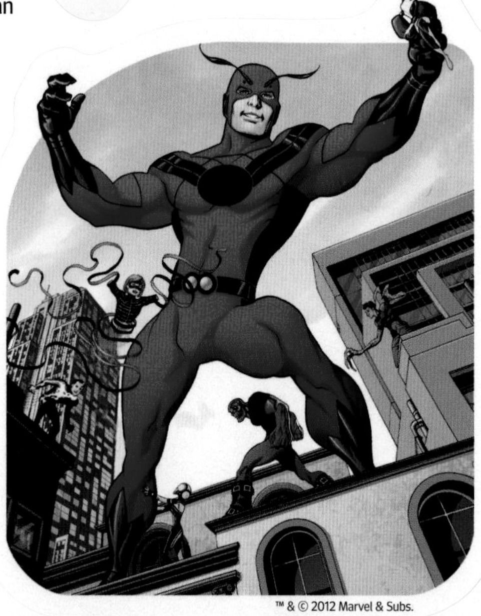
™ & © 2012 Marvel & Subs.

Giant-Man

Beast

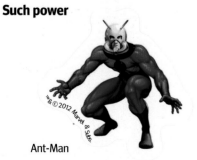

STICKERS

Tony Stark

Lady Sif

Firestar

Ant-Man

Armor

The Leader

Zero to hero

Captain America

Wonderful wings

Ant army

Team player

Donald Blake

Hercules

Jet boots

STICKERS

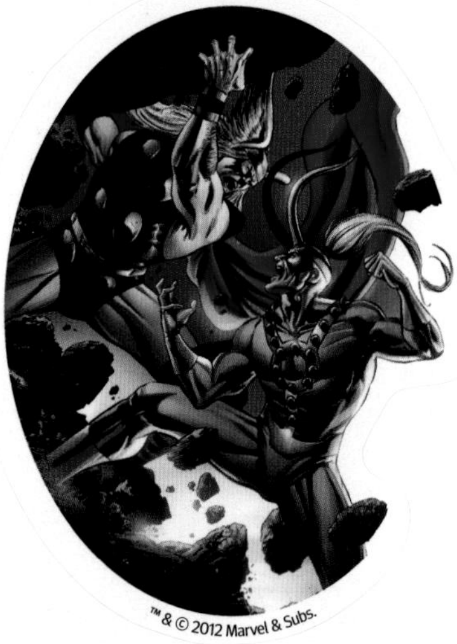
™ & © 2012 Marvel & Subs.

Battling brothers

The Mandarin

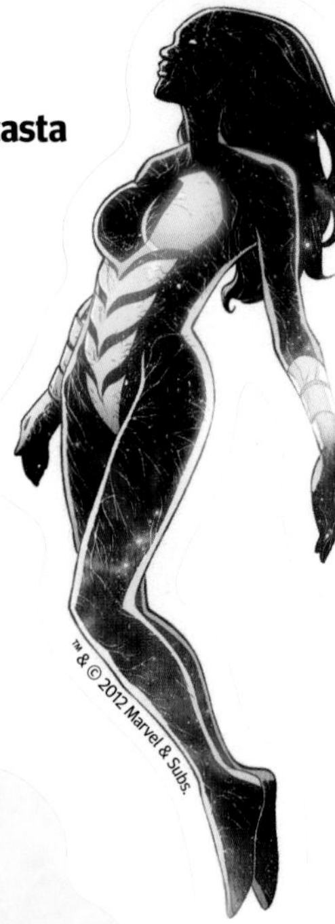
™ & © 2012 Marvel & Subs.

Jocasta

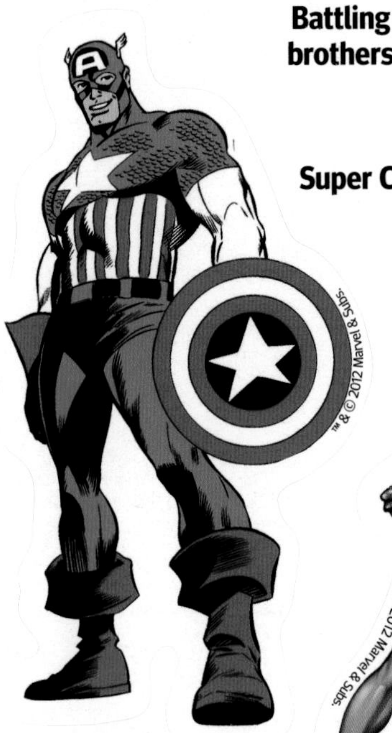
™ & © 2012 Marvel & Subs.

Super Cap

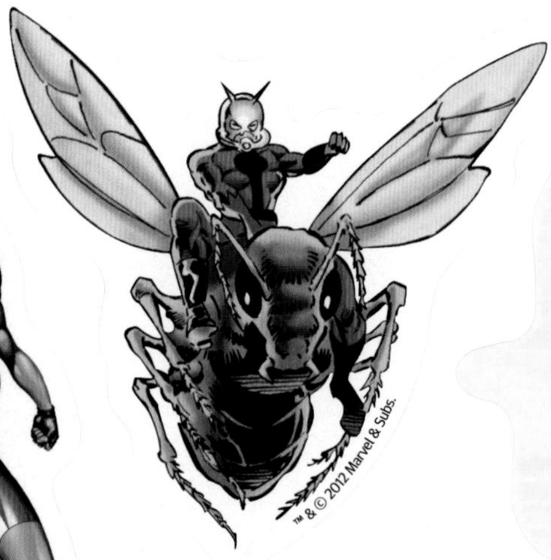
™ & © 2012 Marvel & Subs.

Ant rider

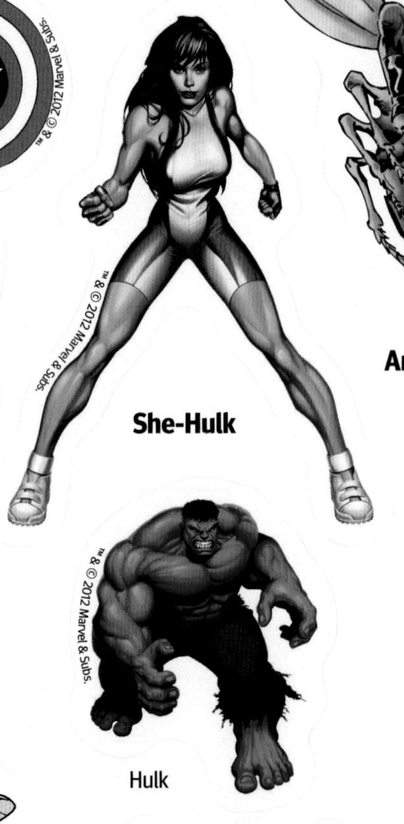
™ & © 2012 Marvel & Subs.

She-Hulk

Sentry

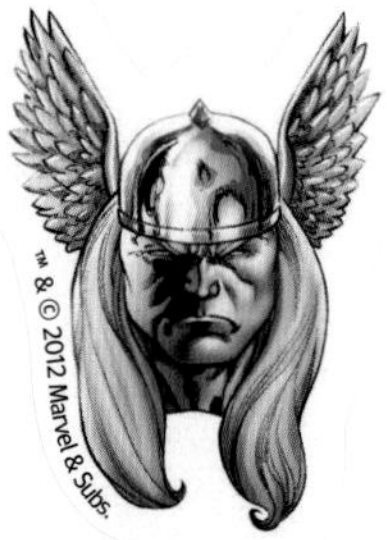
™ & © 2012 Marvel & Subs.

Thor

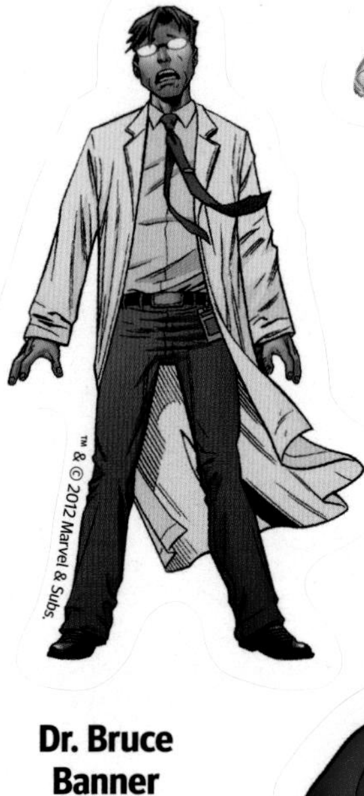
™ & © 2012 Marvel & Subs.

Dr. Bruce Banner

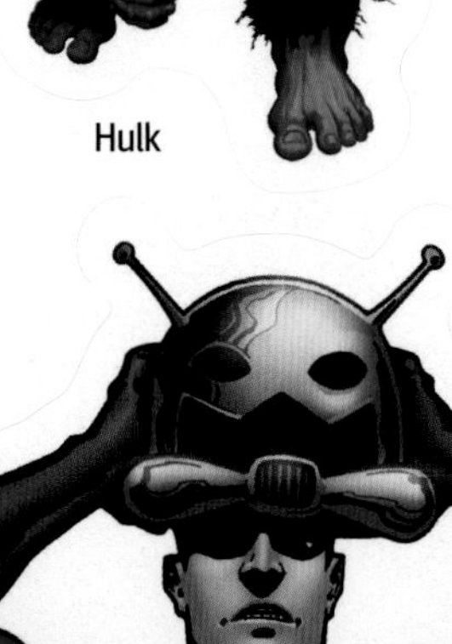
™ & © 2012 Marvel & Subs.

Hulk

Captain Marvel

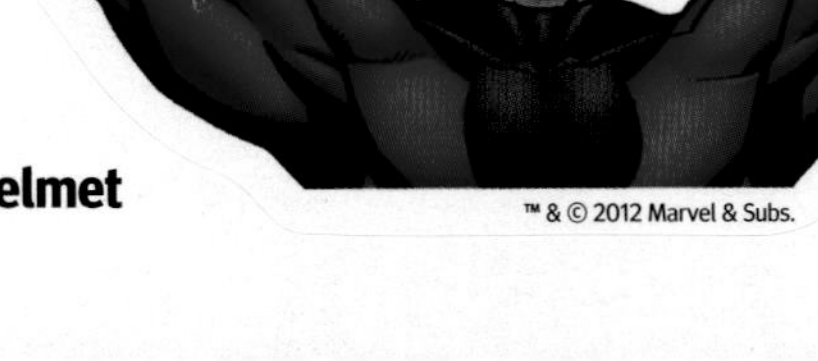
™ & © 2012 Marvel & Subs.

Hard helmet

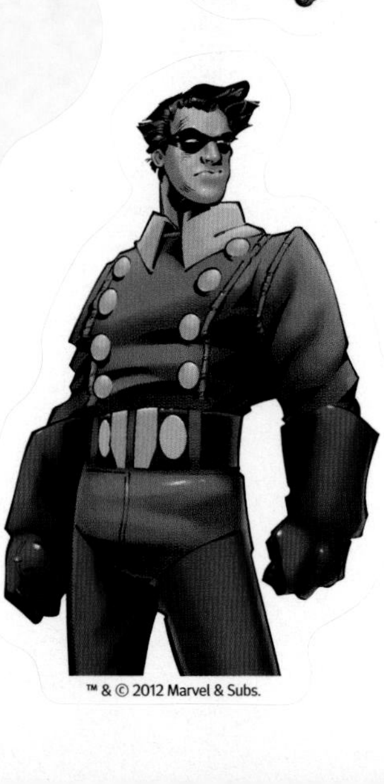
™ & © 2012 Marvel & Subs.

Bucky Barnes

STICKERS

Girl power

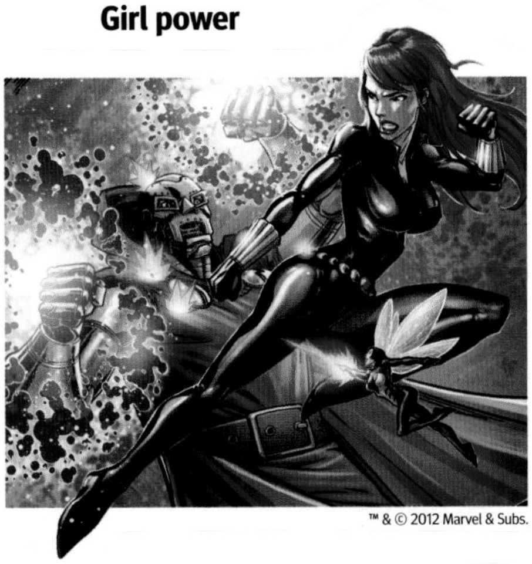
™ & © 2012 Marvel & Subs.

Ice breaker

Iron Man

Power Man

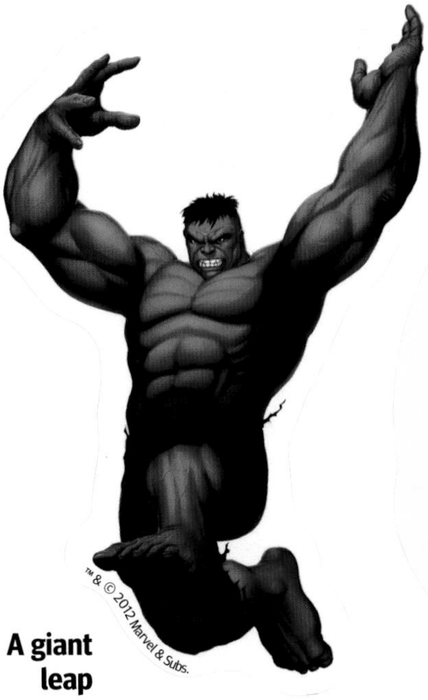
™ & © 2012 Marvel & Subs.

A giant leap

Dr. Doom

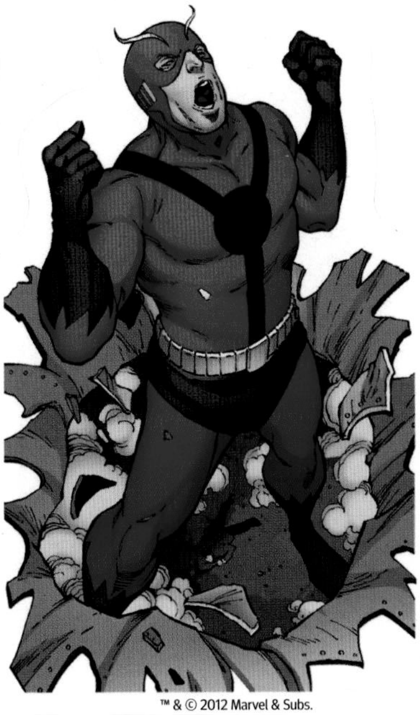
™ & © 2012 Marvel & Subs.

Sizing up

Ant Avenger

The Wasp

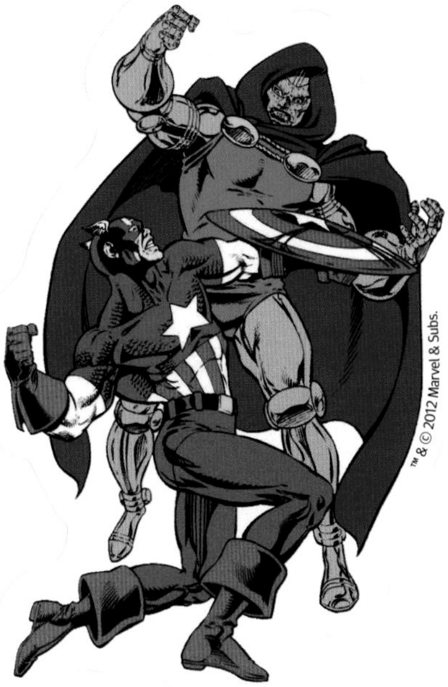
™ & © 2012 Marvel & Subs.

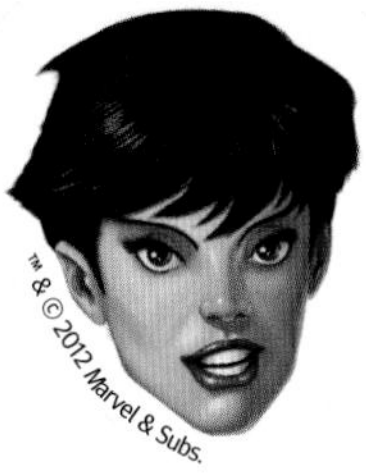
™ & © 2012 Marvel & Subs.

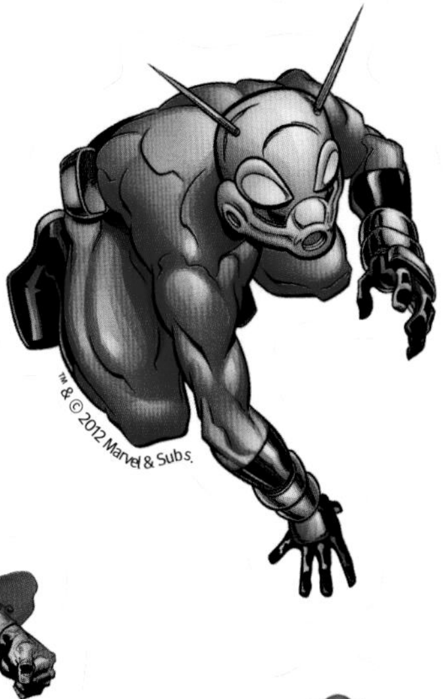
™ & © 2012 Marvel & Subs.

Cap v. Doom

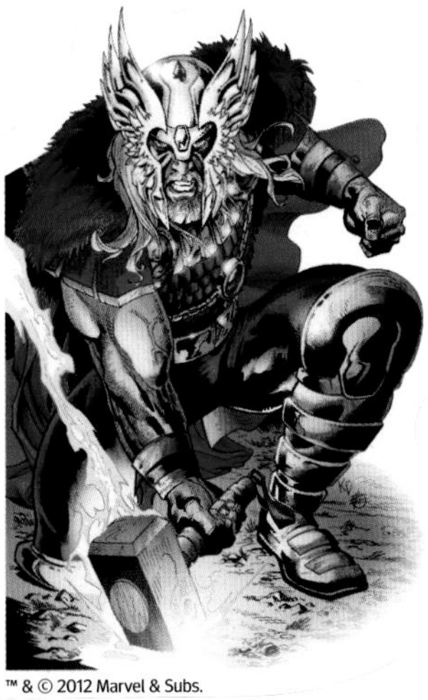
™ & © 2012 Marvel & Subs.

Quick temper

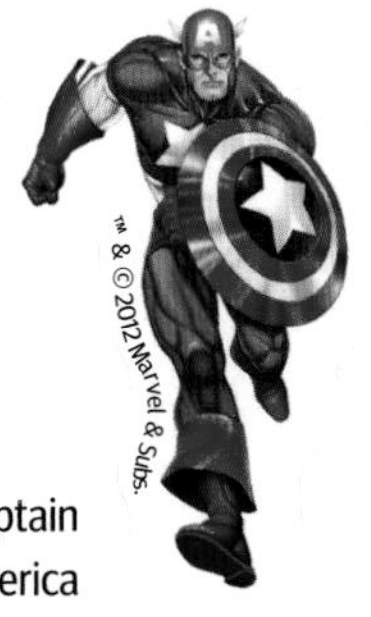
™ & © 2012 Marvel & Subs.

Captain America

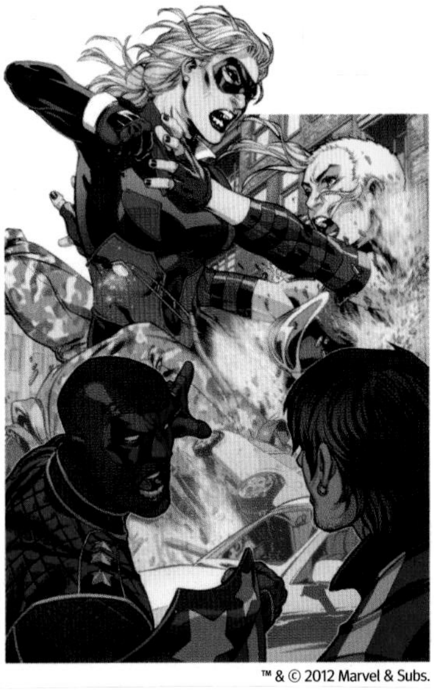
™ & © 2012 Marvel & Subs.

Young Avengers v. Dark Avengers

STICKERS

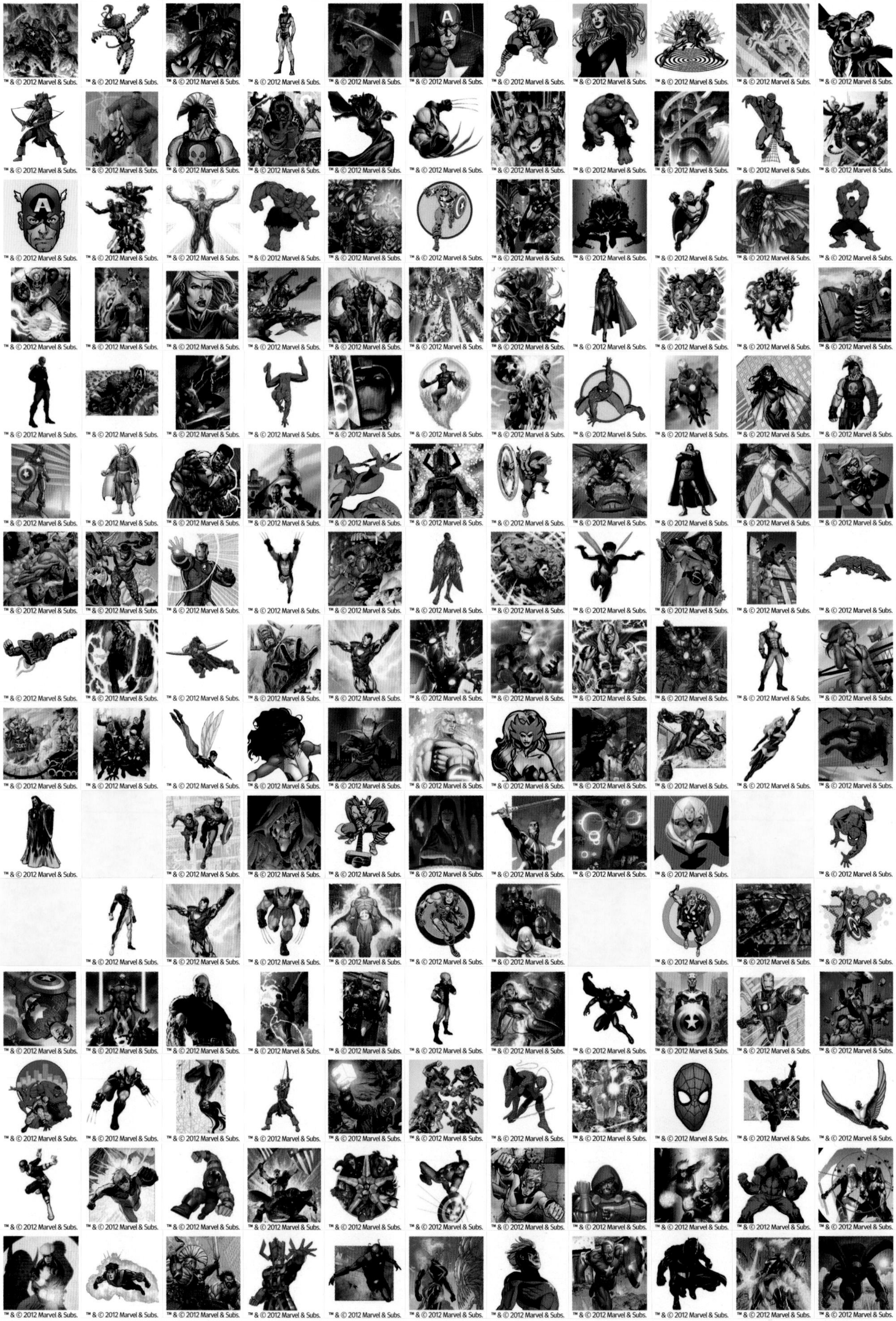
™ & © 2012 Marvel & Subs.

STICKERS

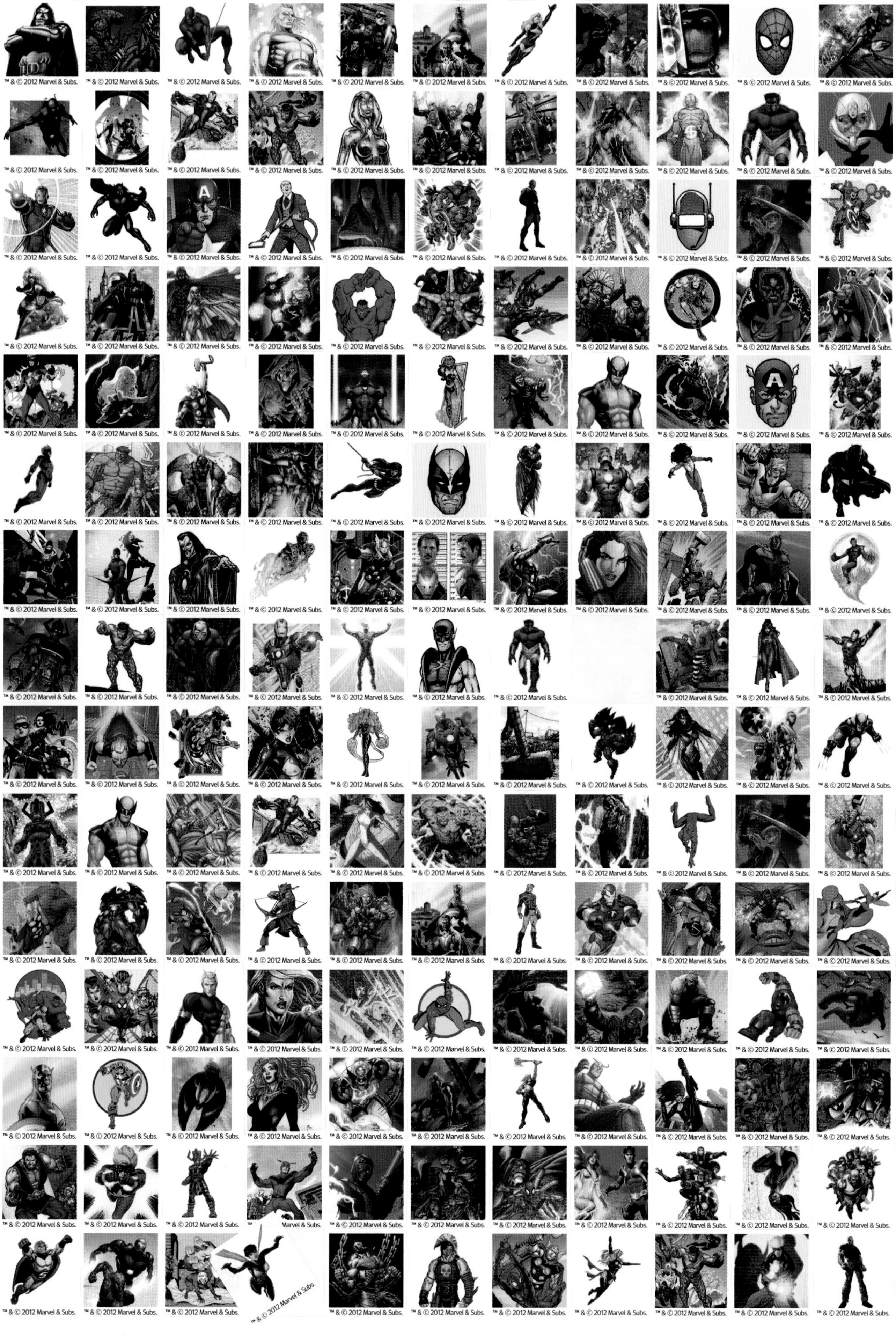
™ & © 2012 Marvel & Subs.

EXTRA STICKERS

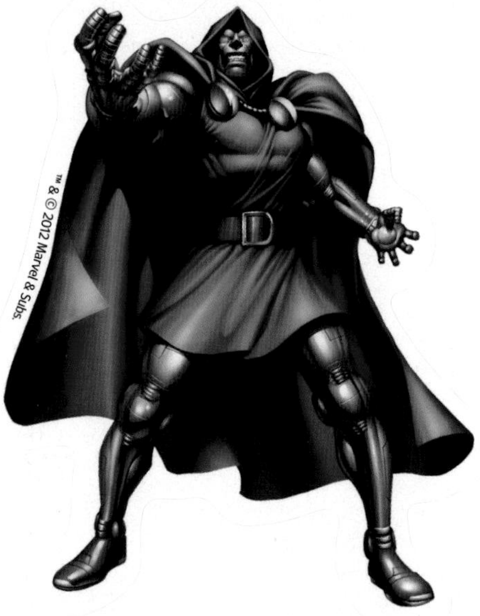

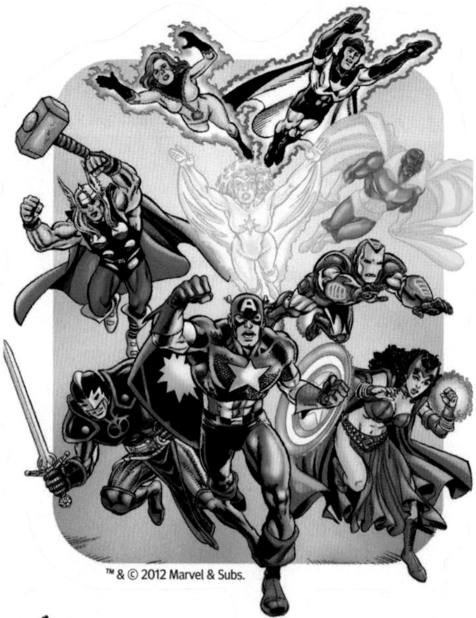

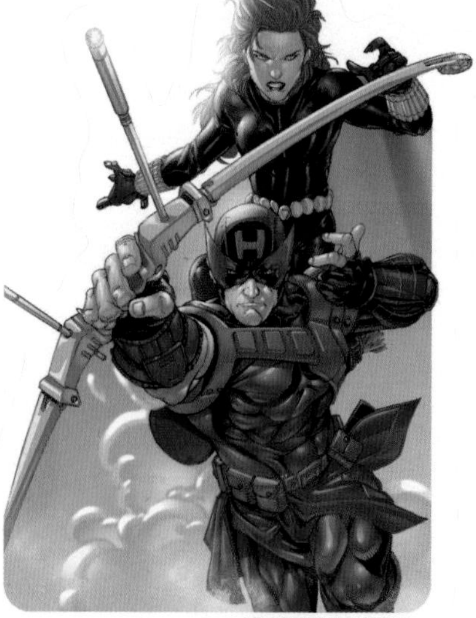

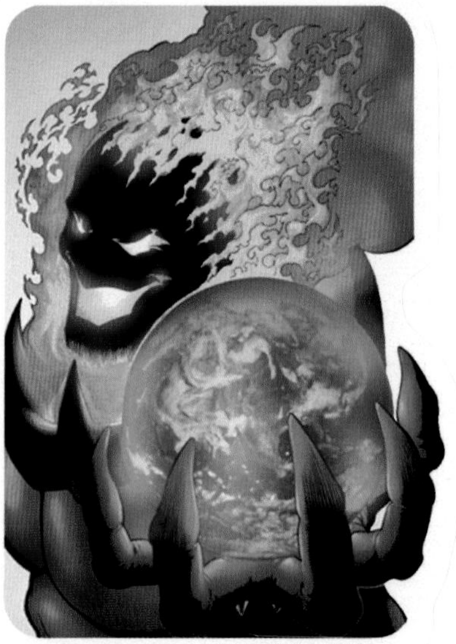

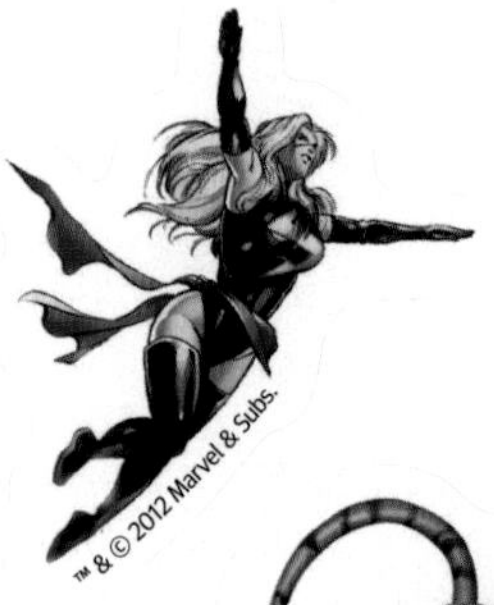

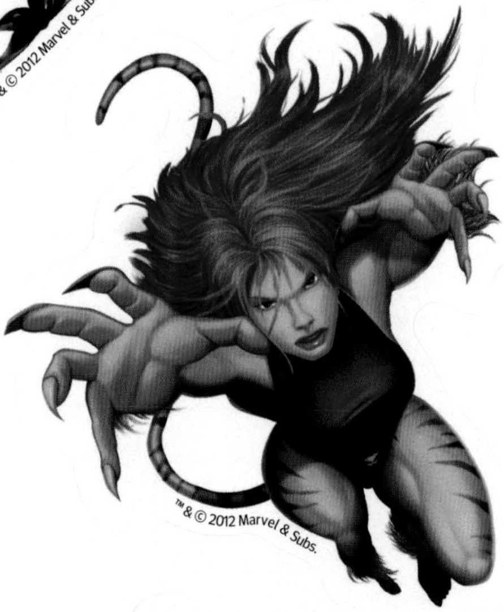

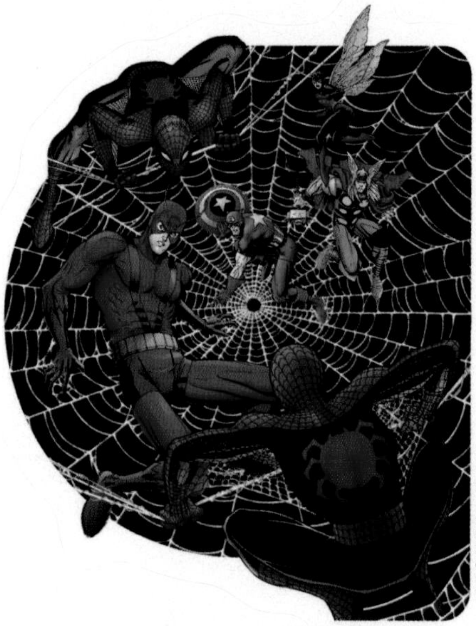

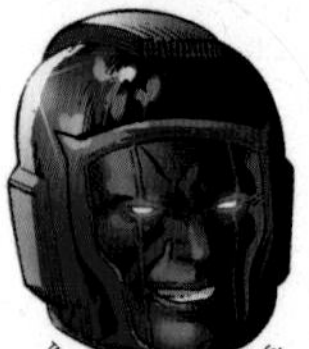

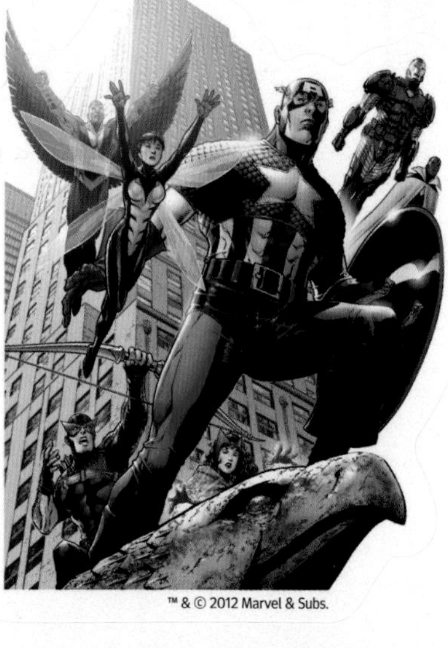

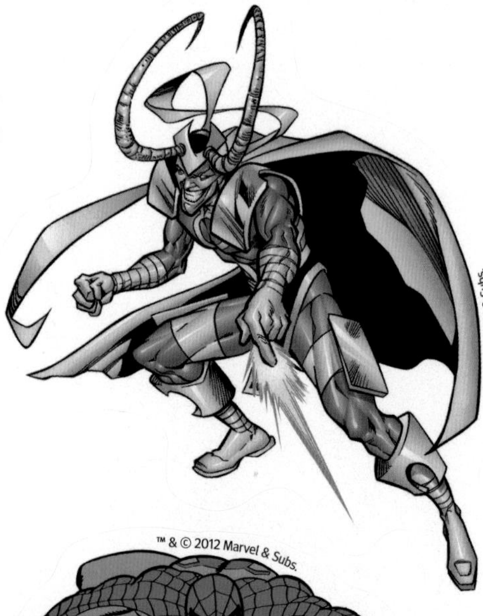

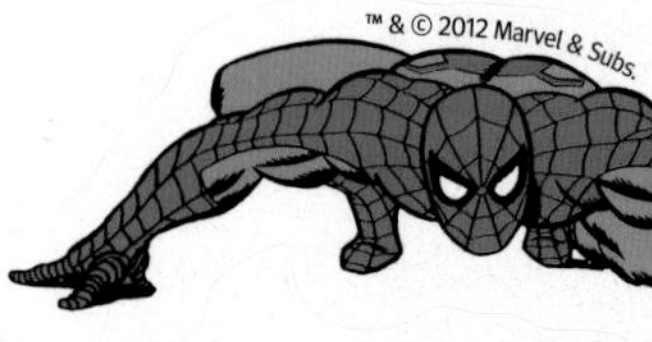

EXTRA STICKERS

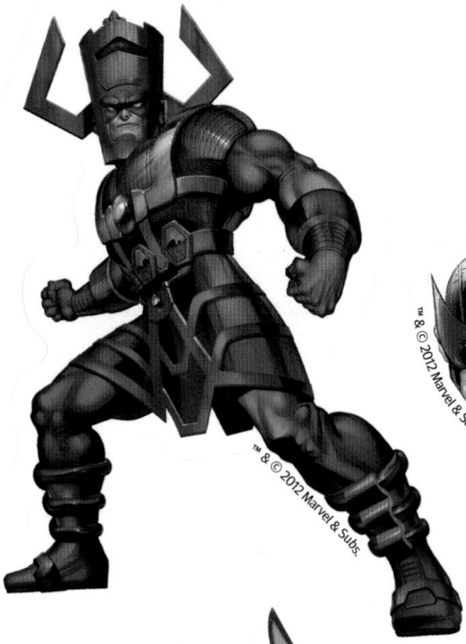

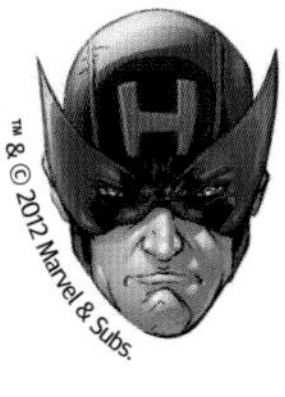

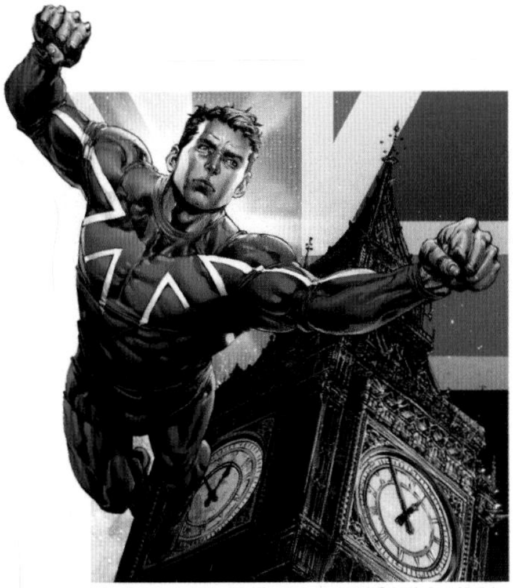

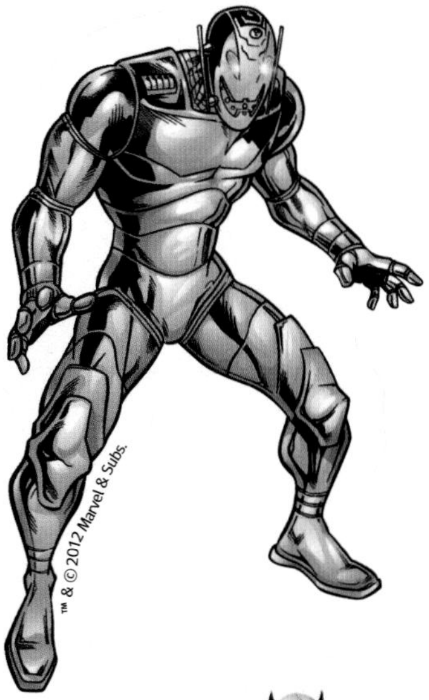

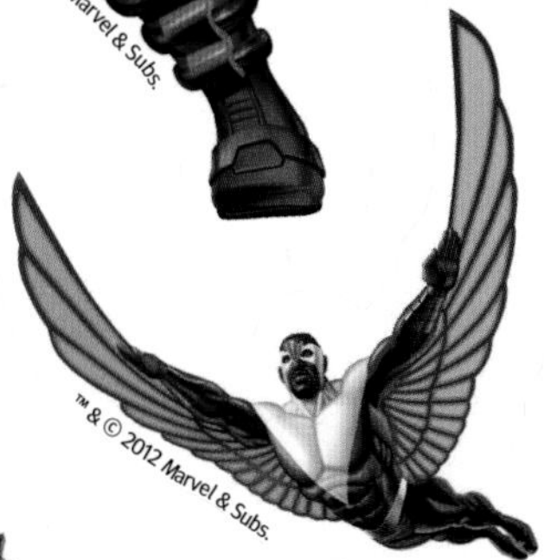

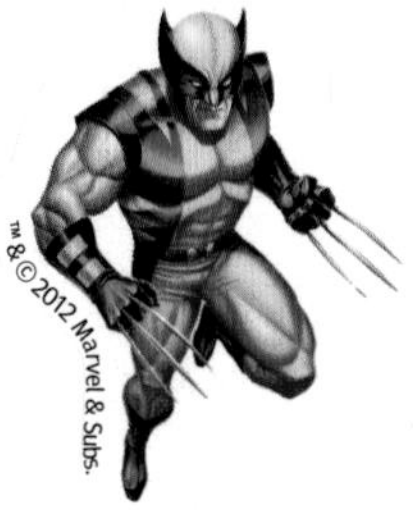

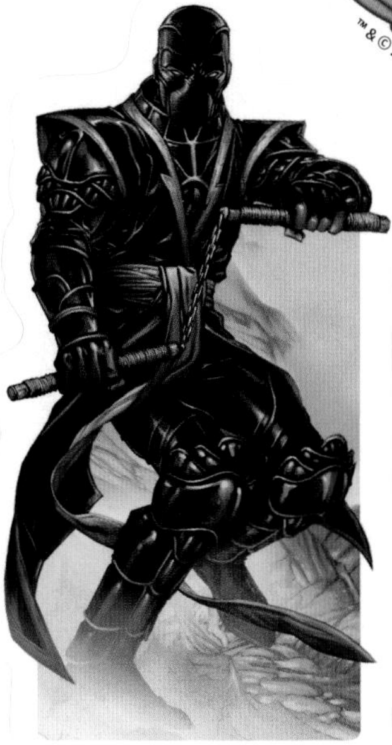

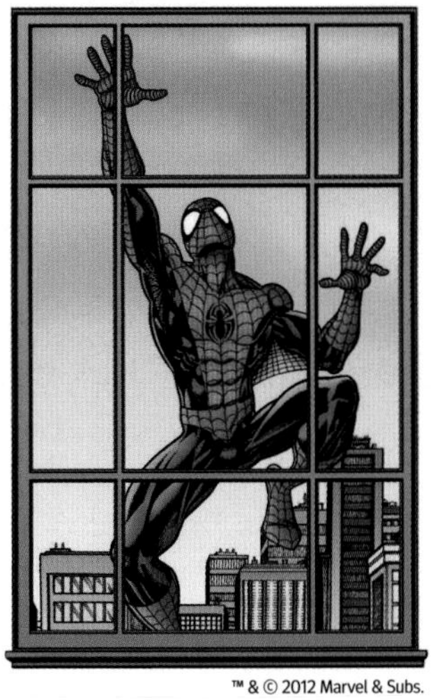

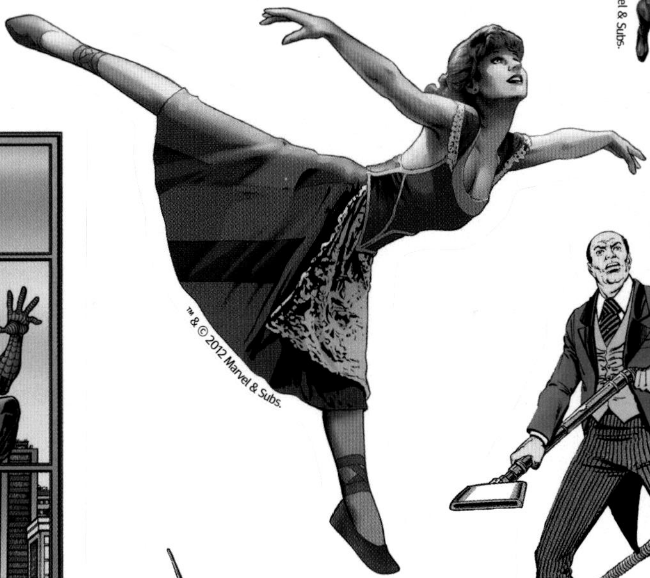

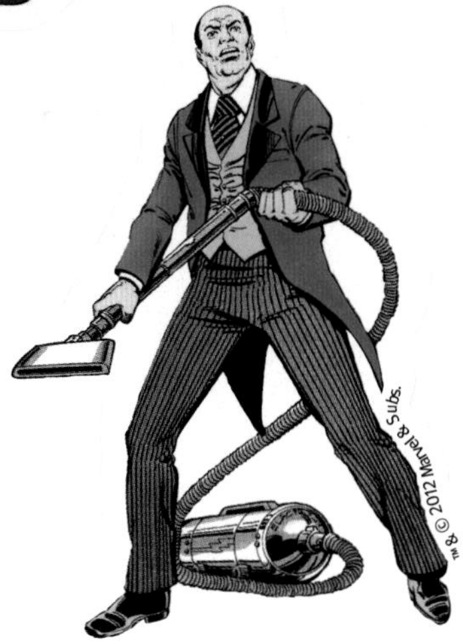

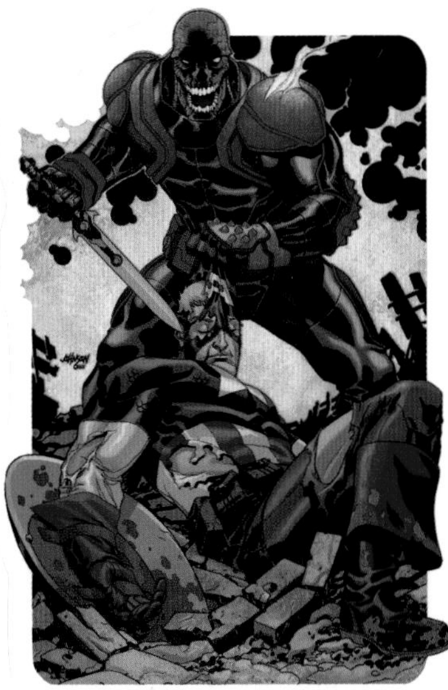

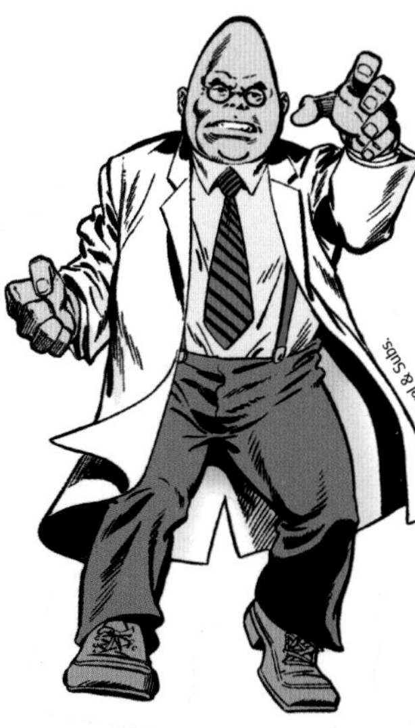

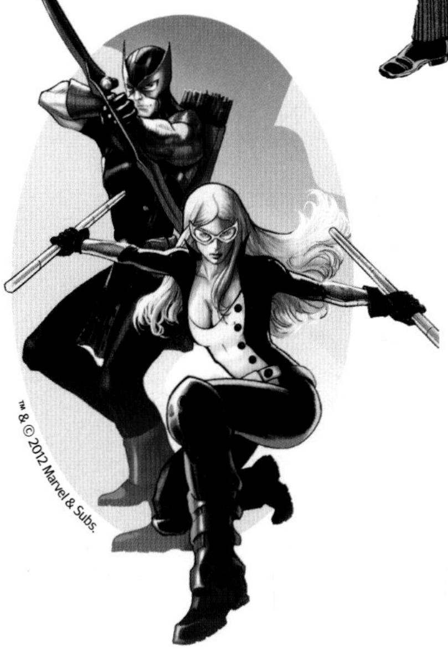

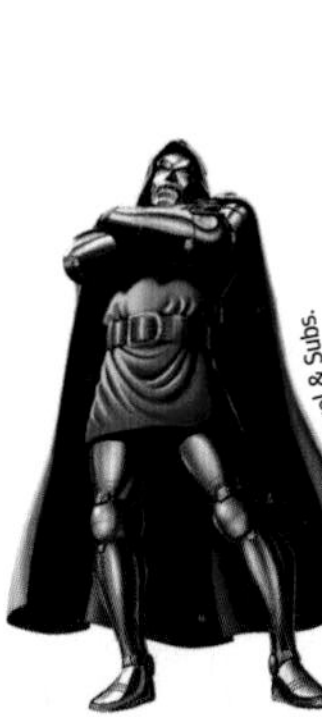

EXTRA STICKERS

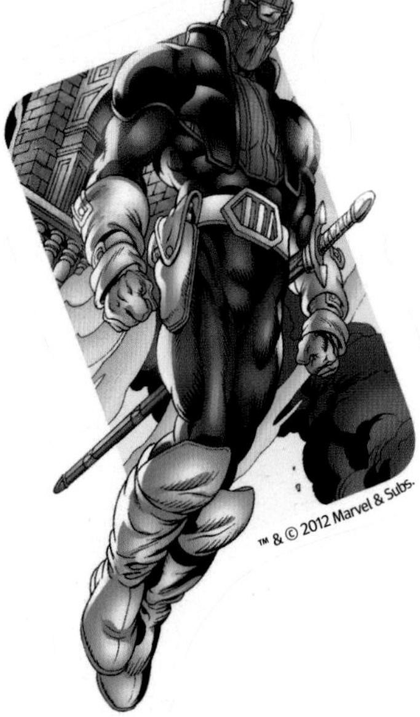

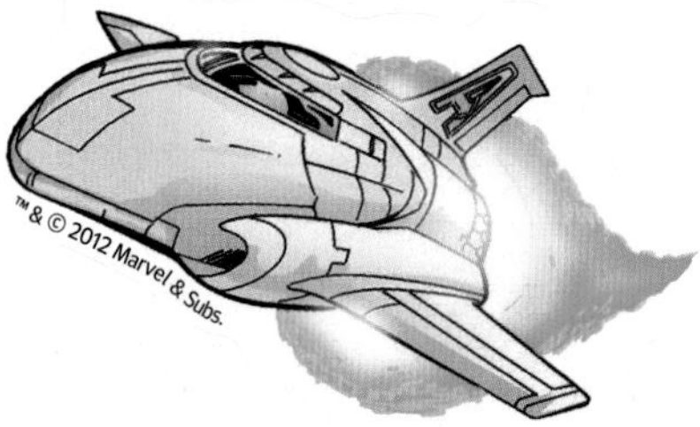

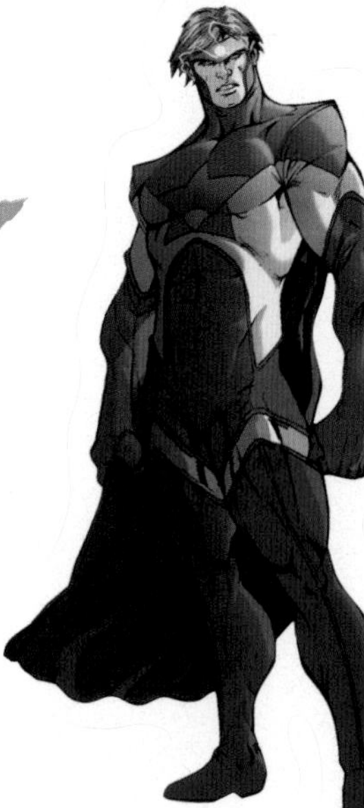

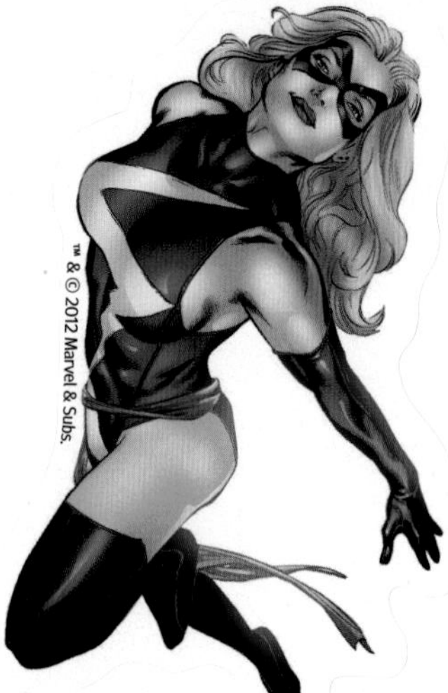

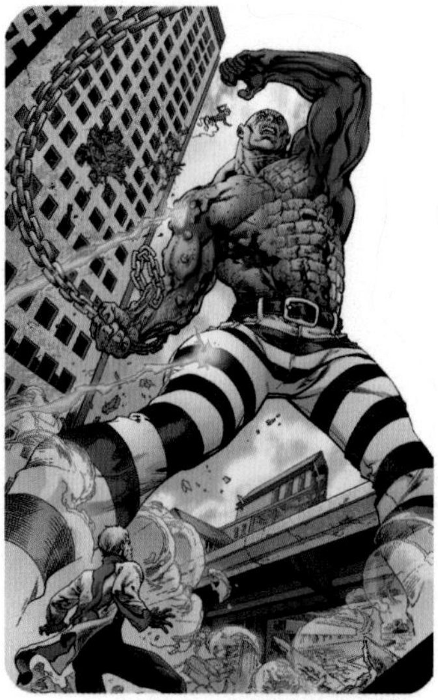

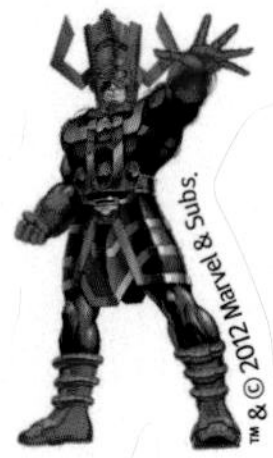

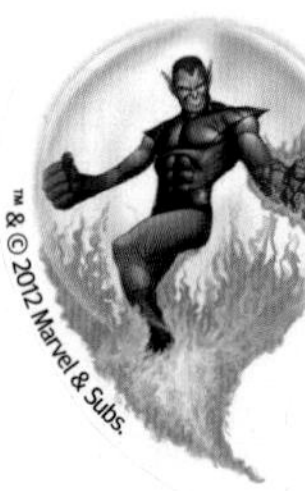

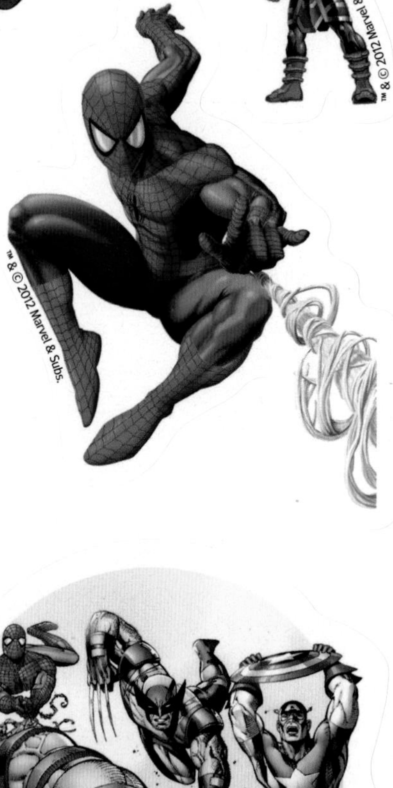

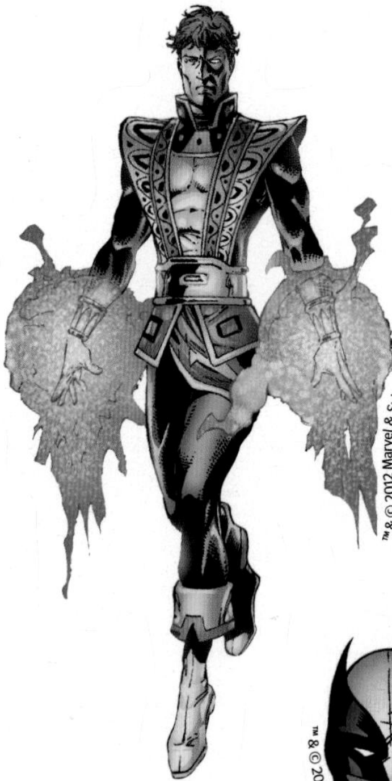

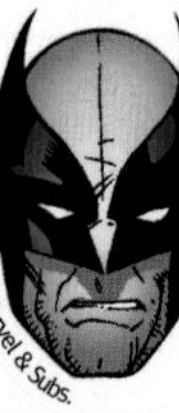

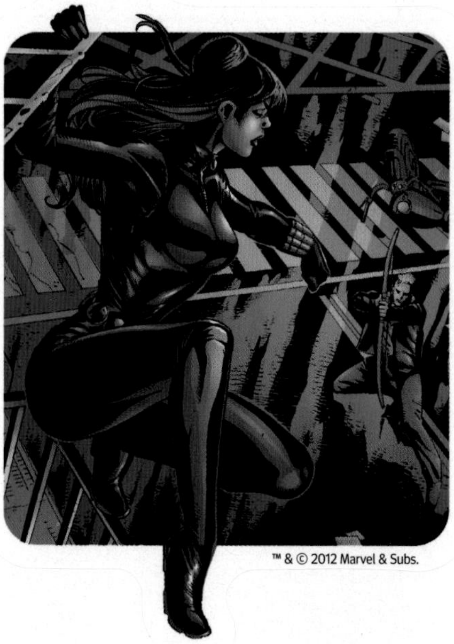

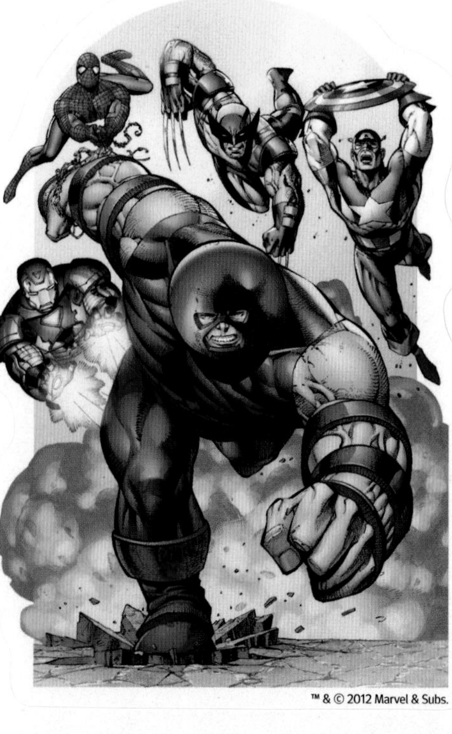

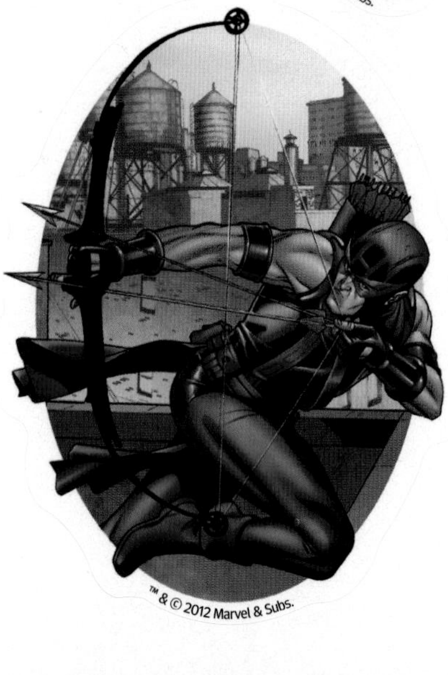

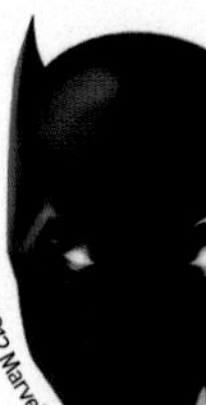

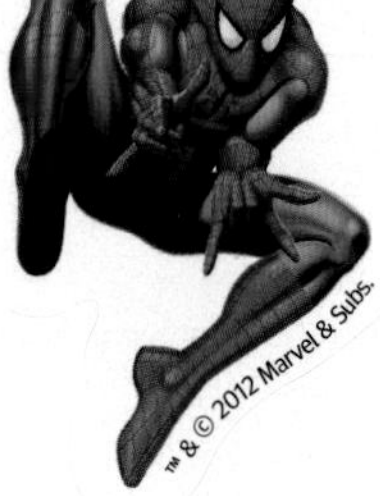

EXTRA STICKERS

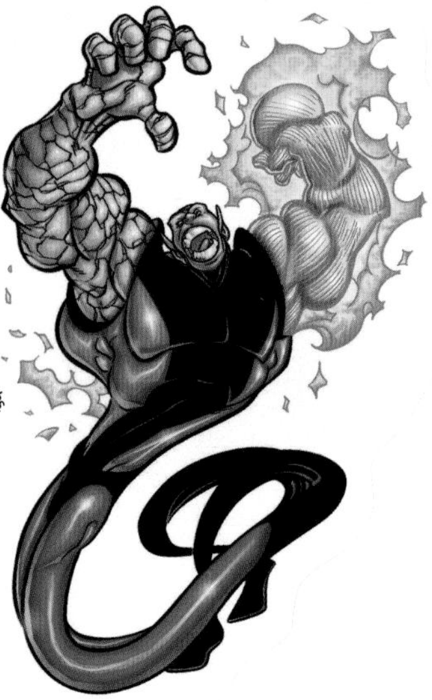

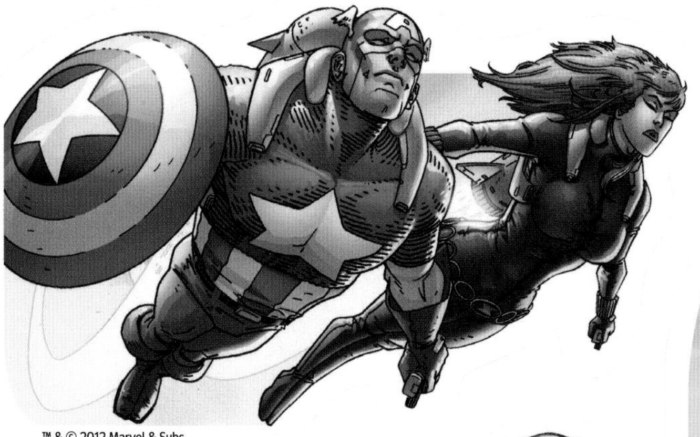

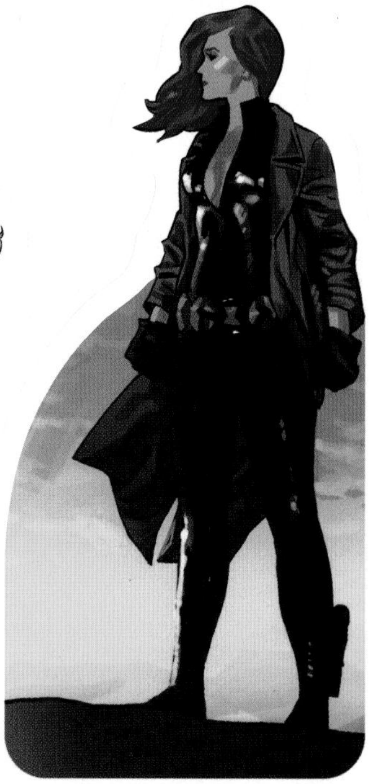

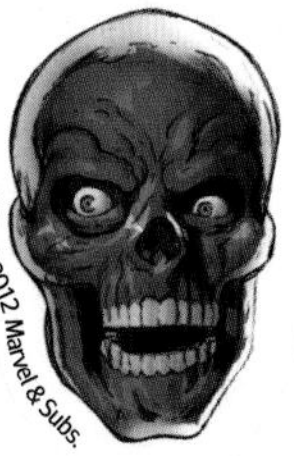

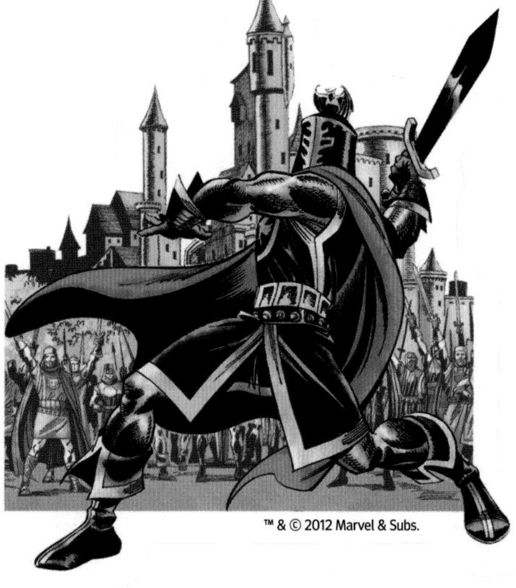

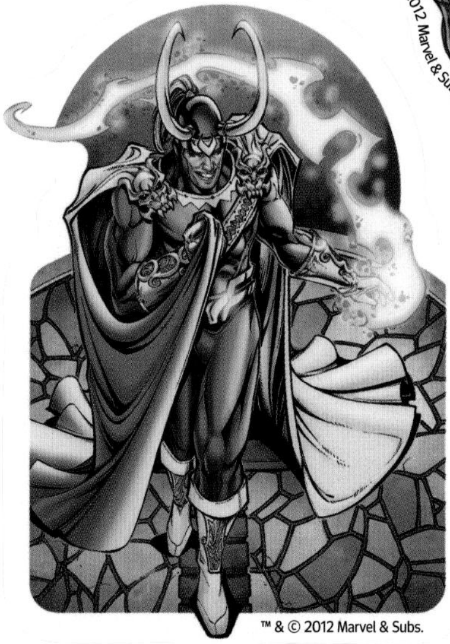

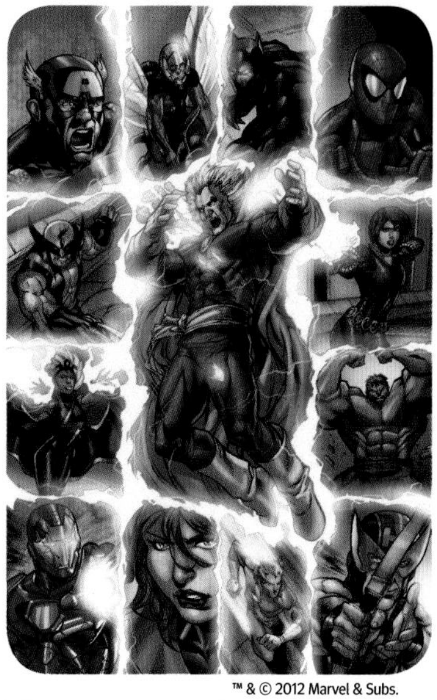

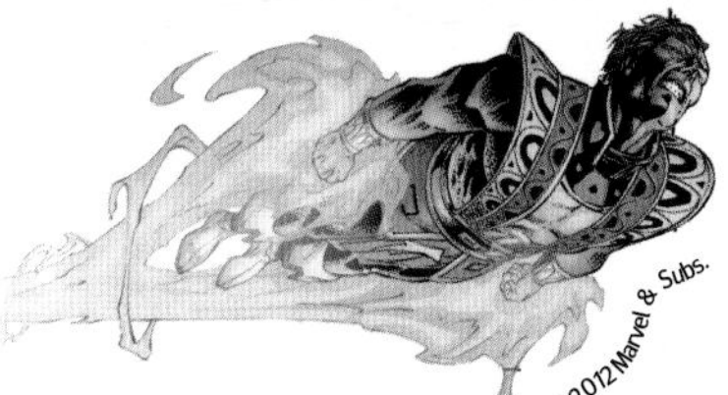

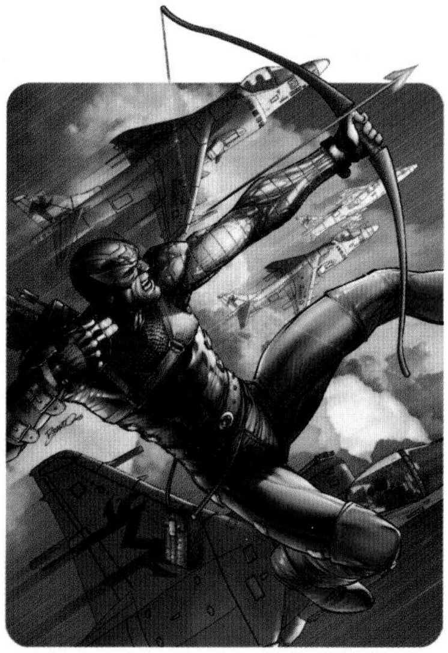

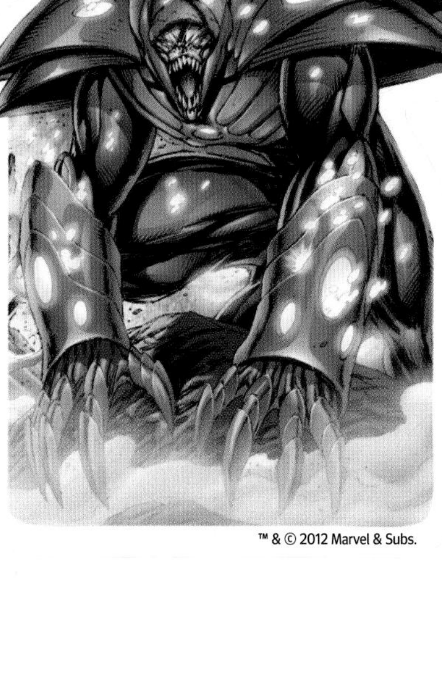

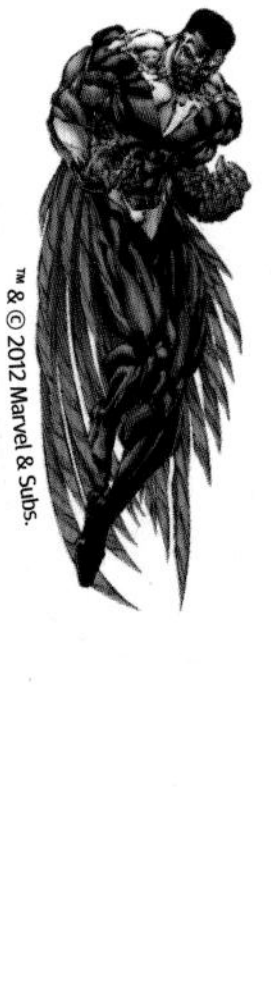

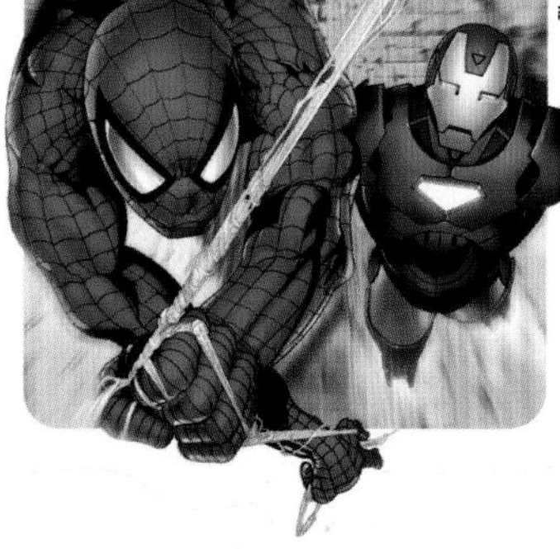

EXTRA STICKERS

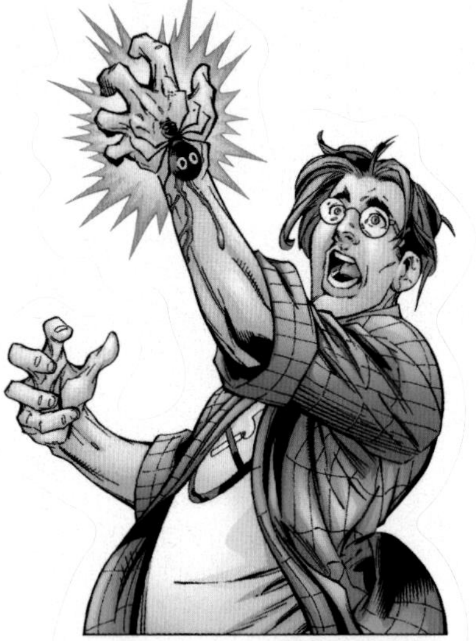

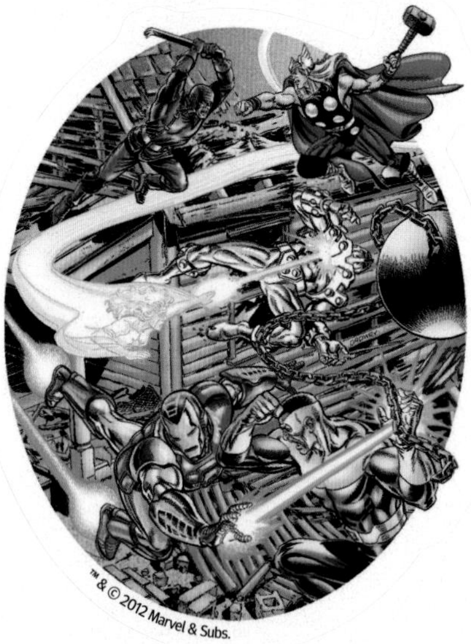

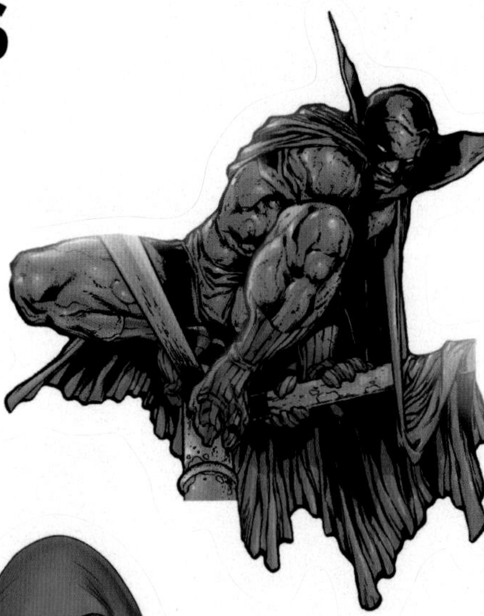

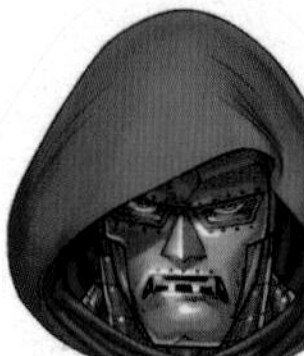

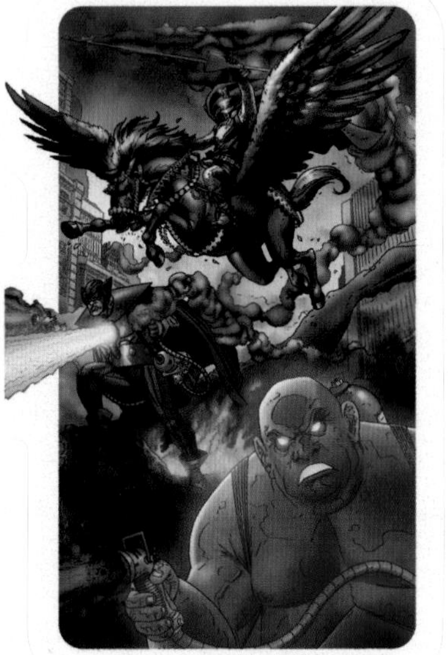

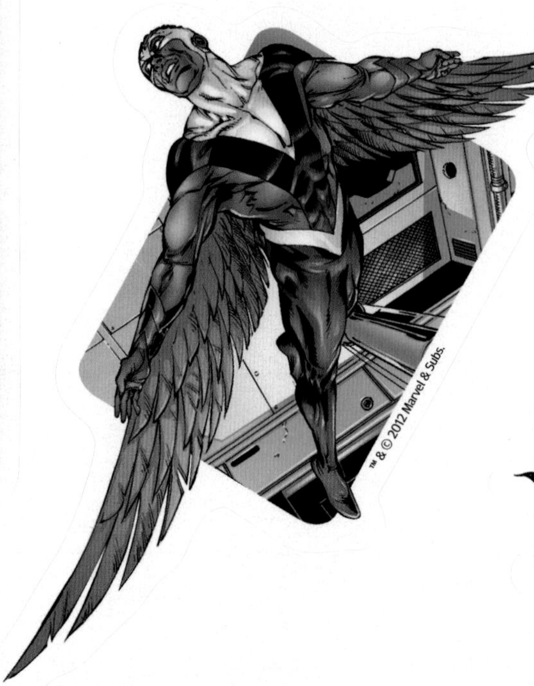

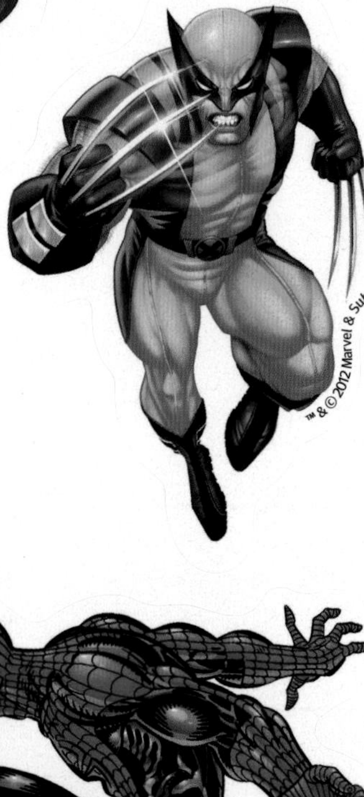

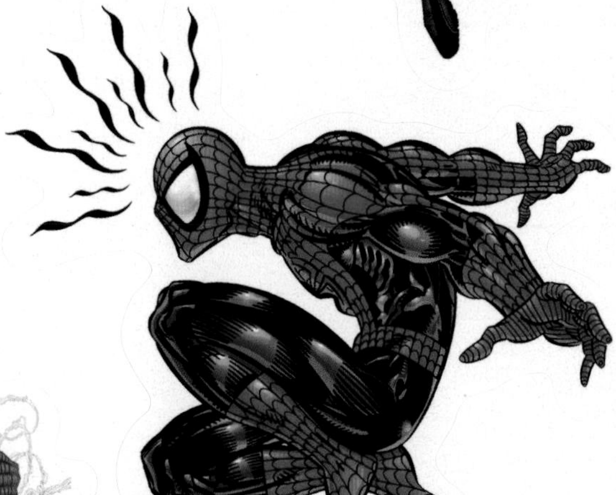

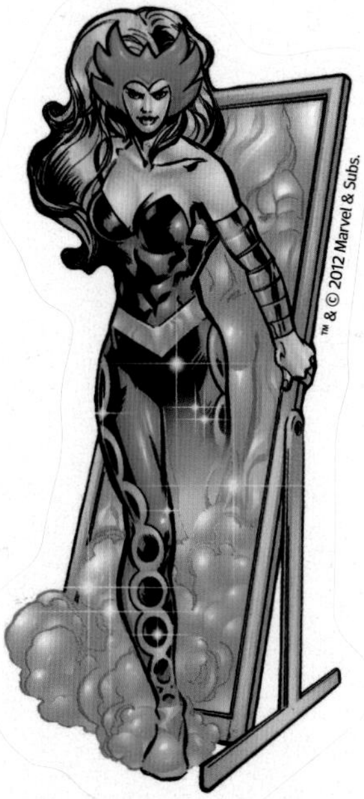

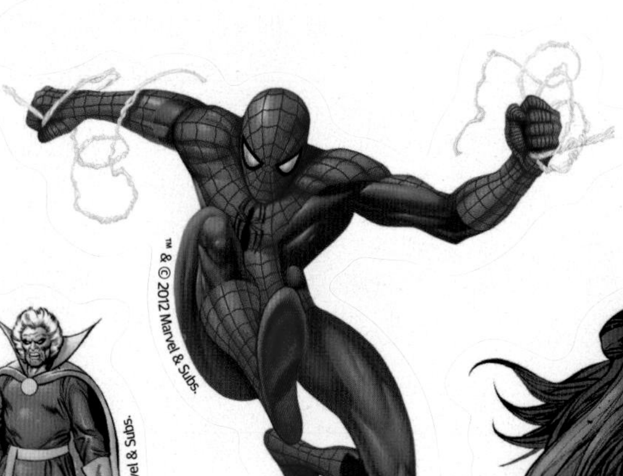

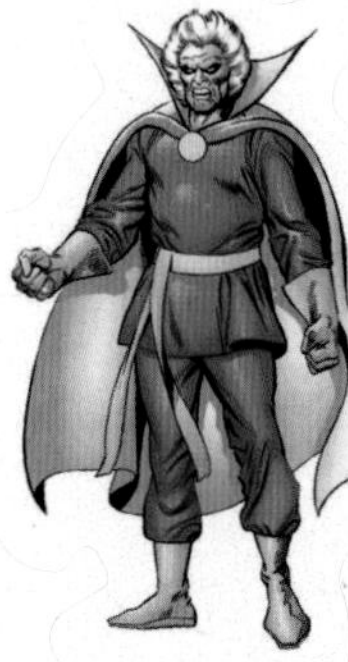

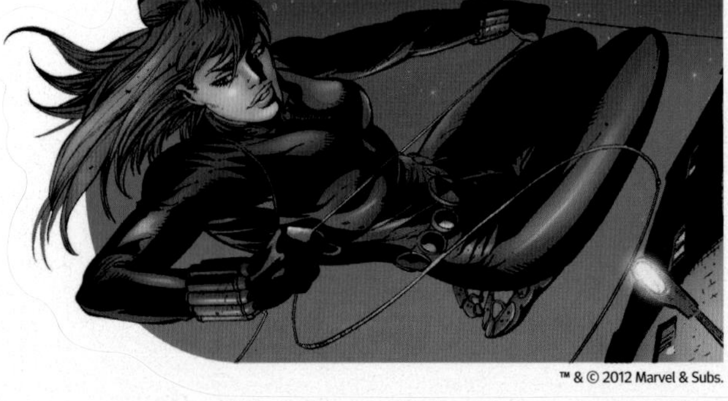

EXTRA STICKERS

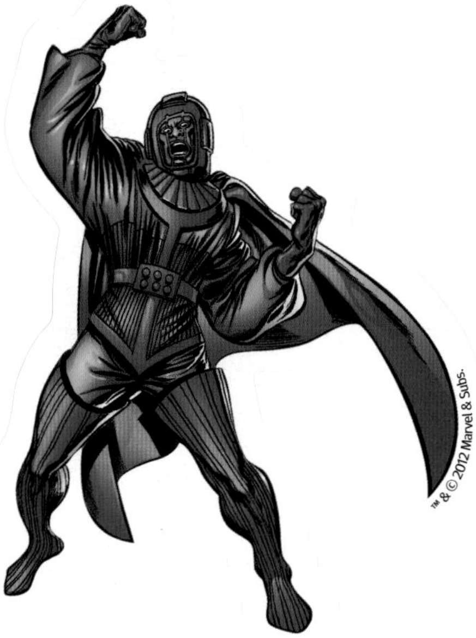

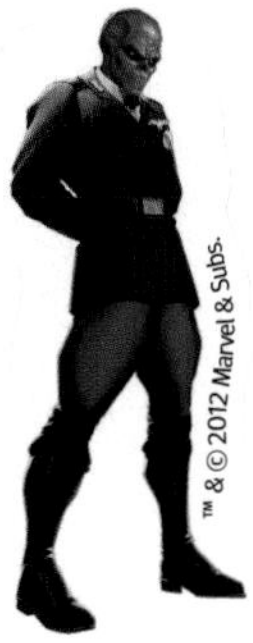

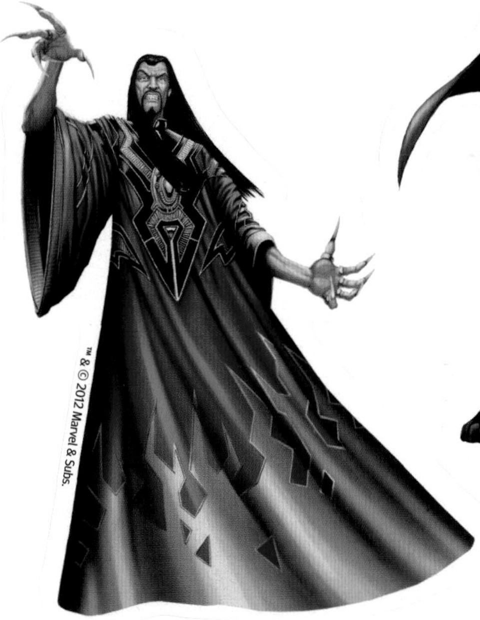

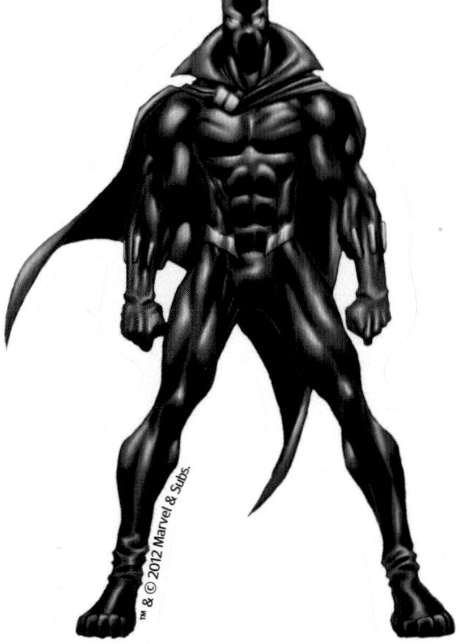

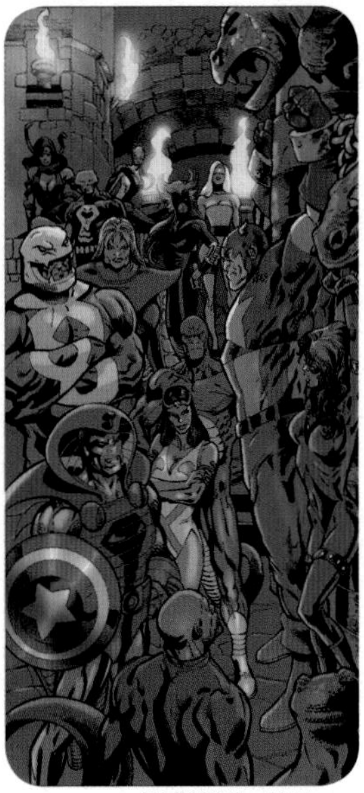

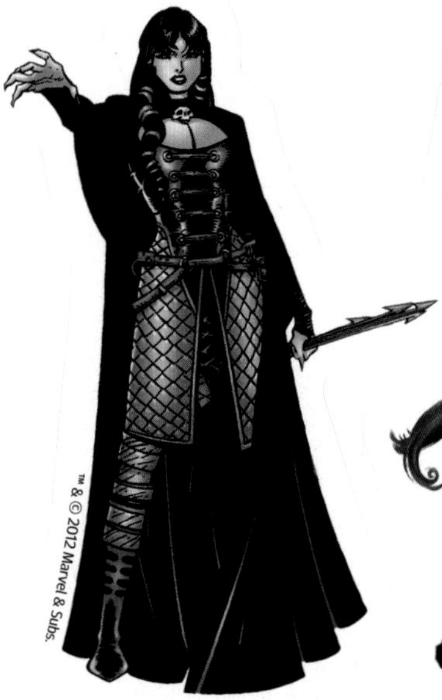

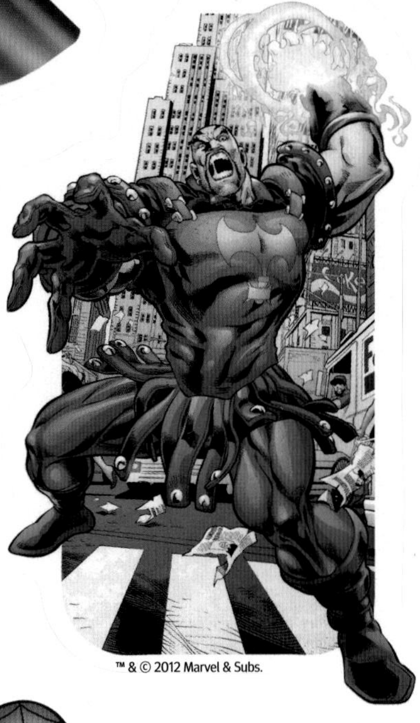

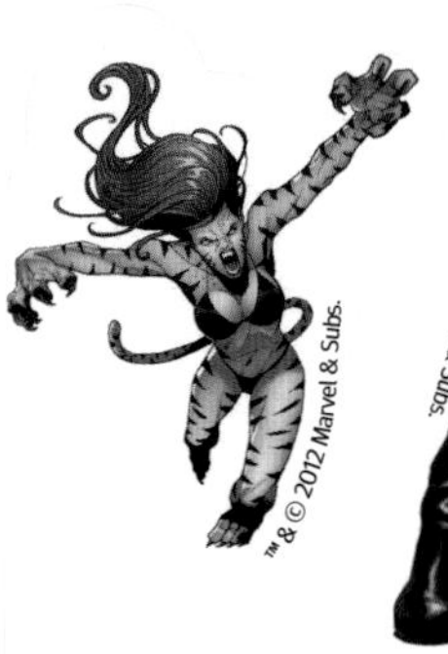

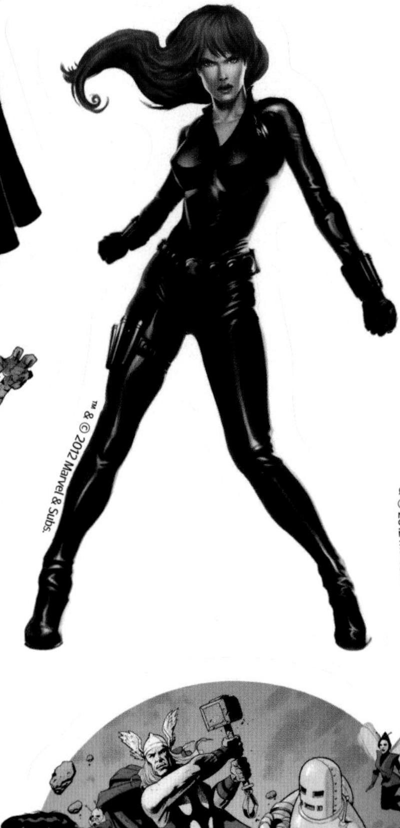

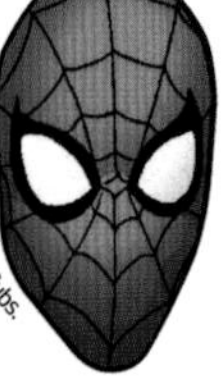

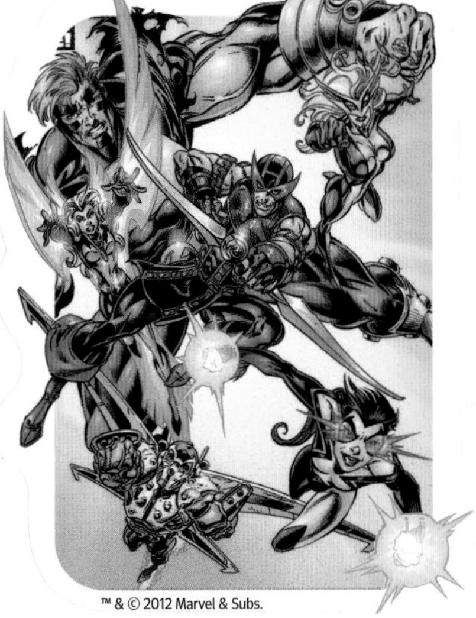

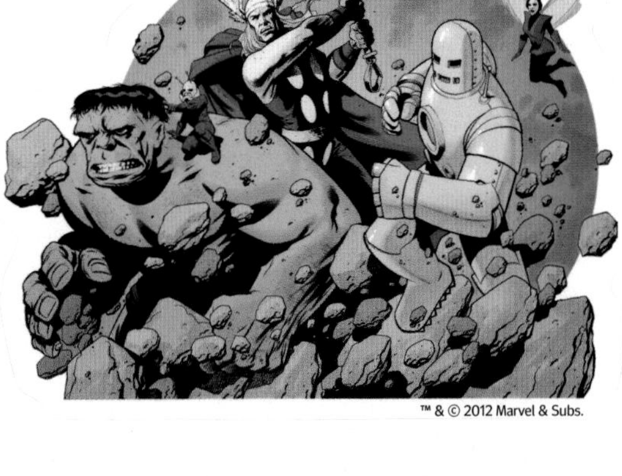

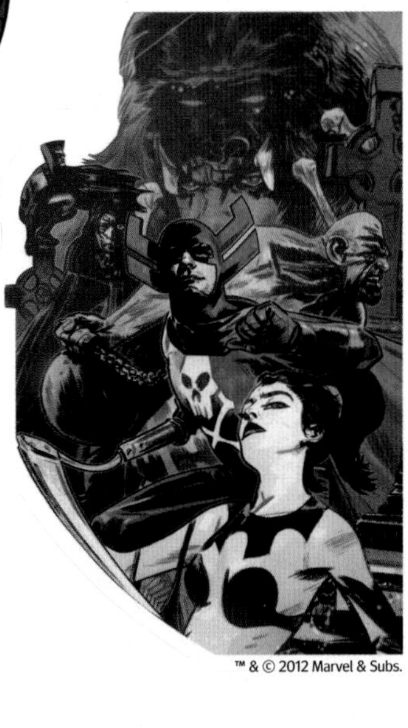

EXTRA STICKERS

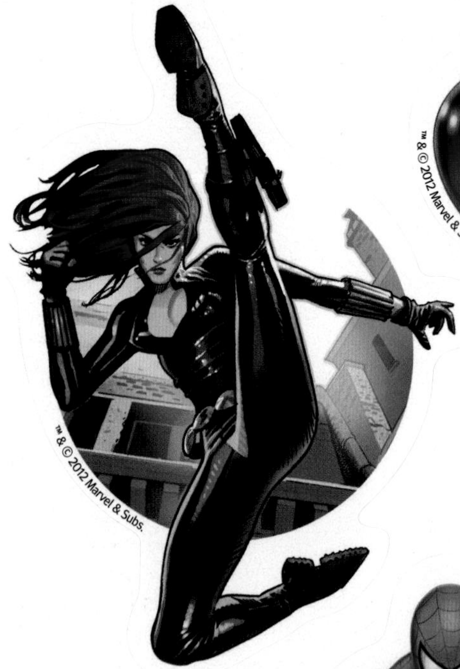

™ & © 2012 Marvel & Subs.

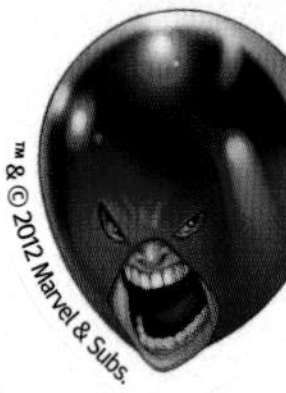

™ & © 2012 Marvel & Subs.

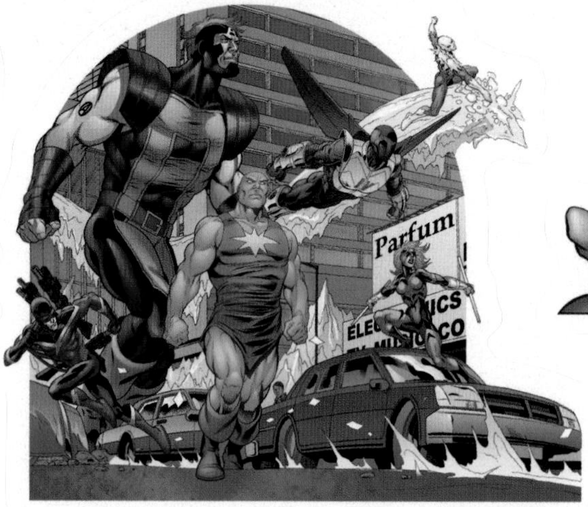

Parfum

™ & © 2012 Marvel & Subs.

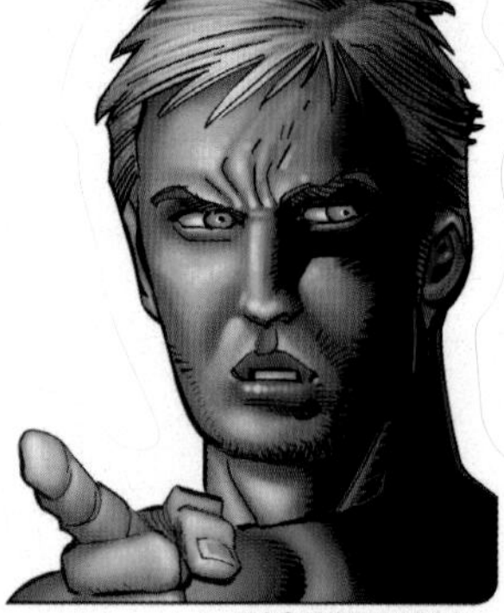

™ & © 2012 Marvel & Subs.

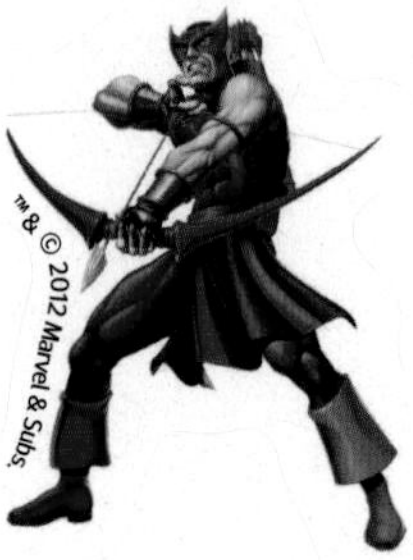

™ & © 2012 Marvel & Subs.

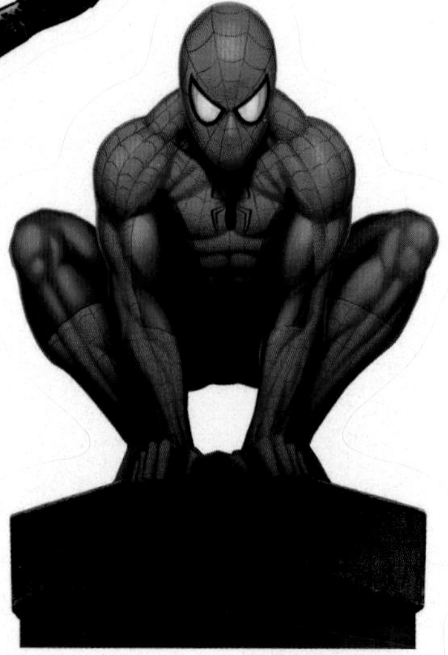

™ & © 2012 Marvel & Subs.

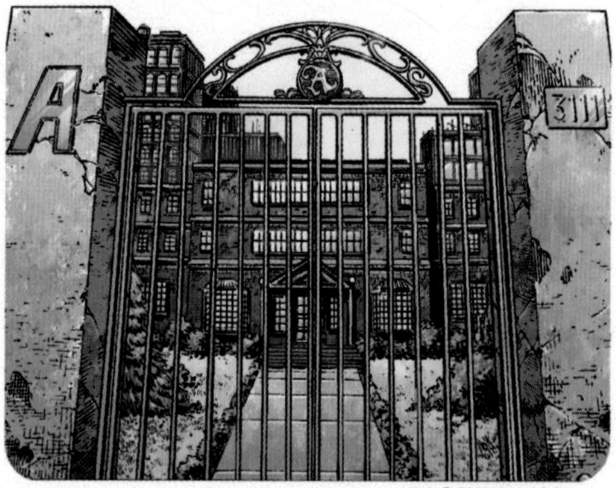

™ & © 2012 Marvel & Subs.

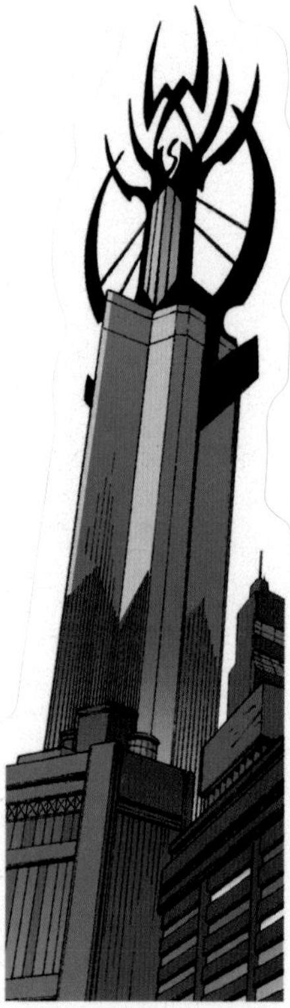

™ & © 2012 Marvel & Subs.

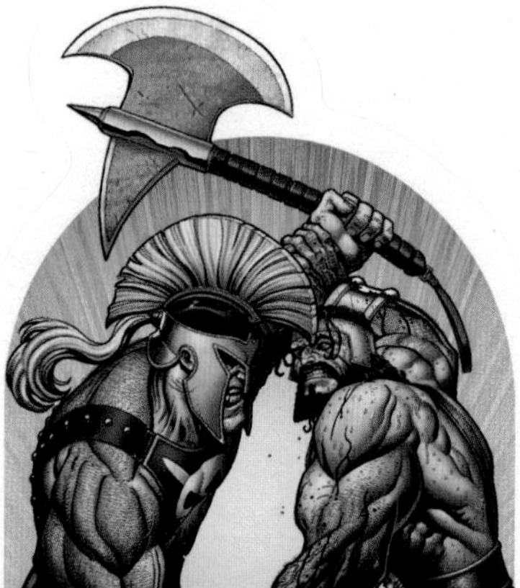

™ & © 2012 Marvel & Subs.

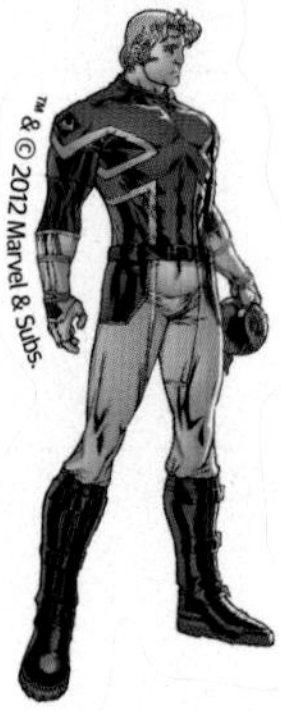

™ & © 2012 Marvel & Subs.

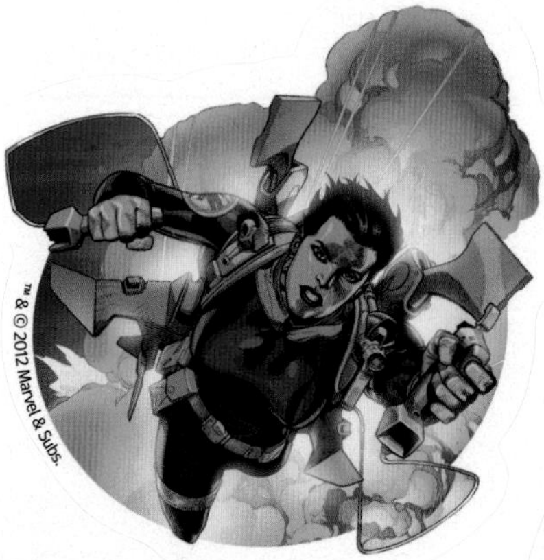

™ & © 2012 Marvel & Subs.

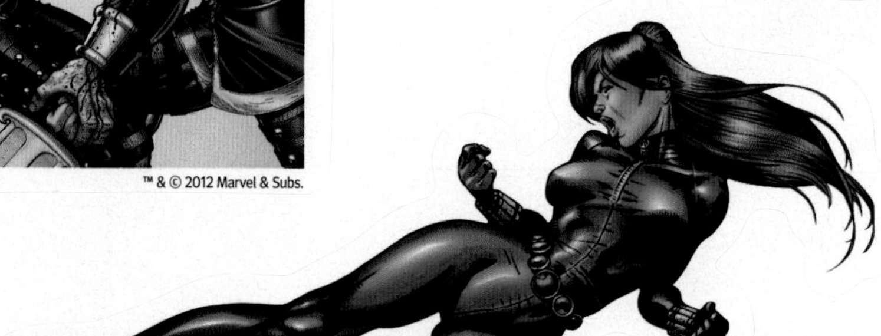

™ & © 2012 Marvel & Subs.

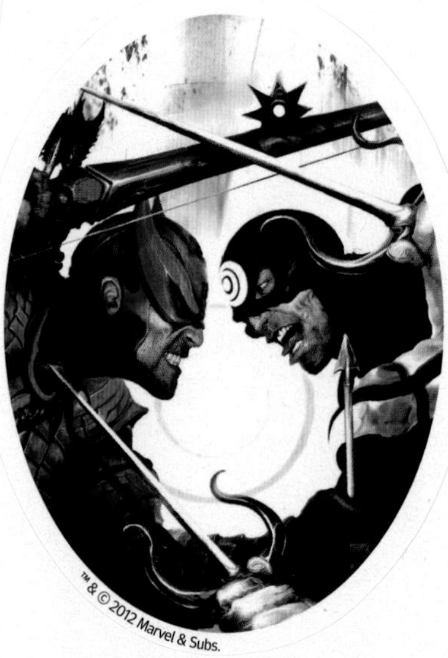

™ & © 2012 Marvel & Subs.

EXTRA STICKERS

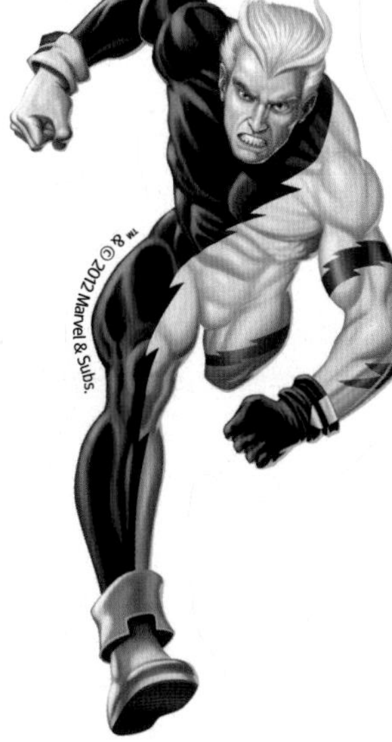

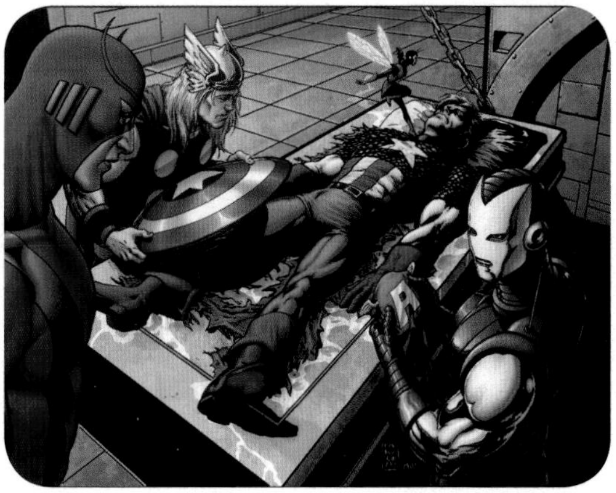

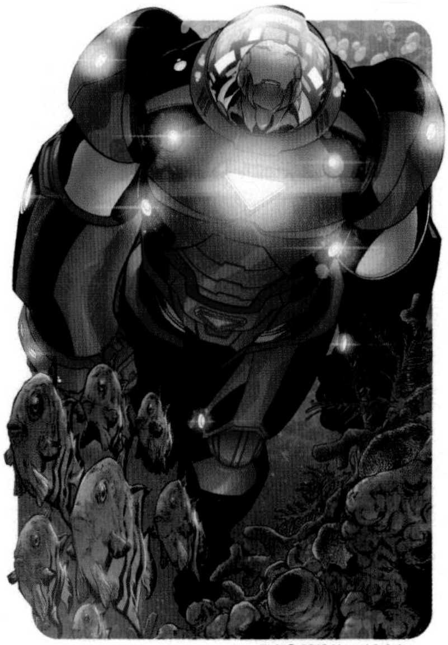

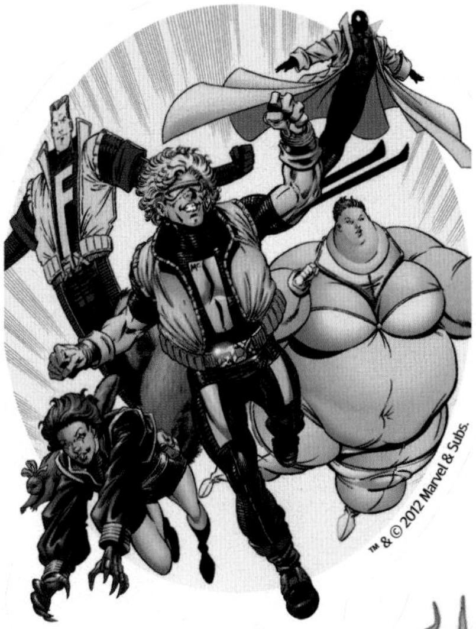

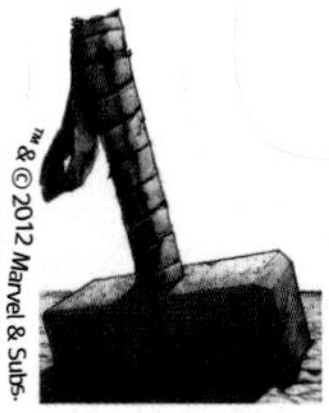

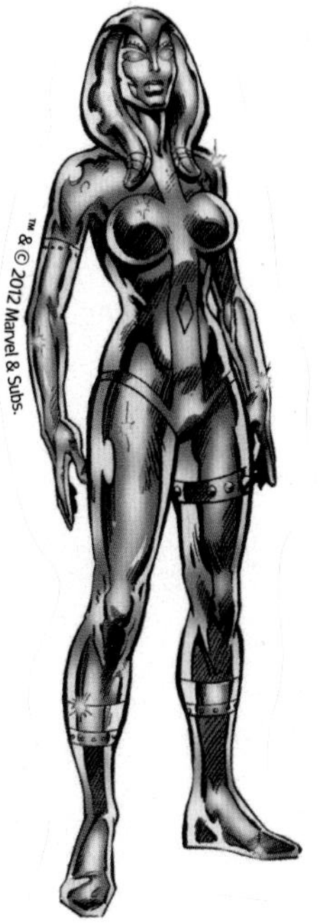

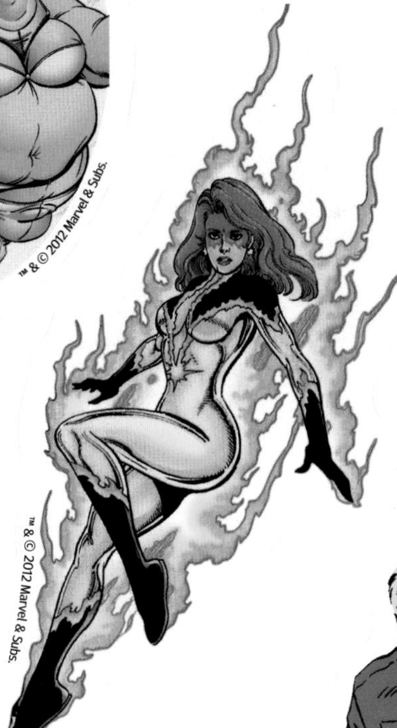

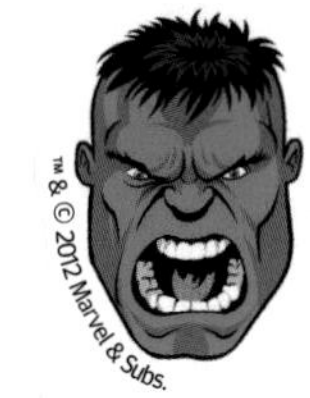

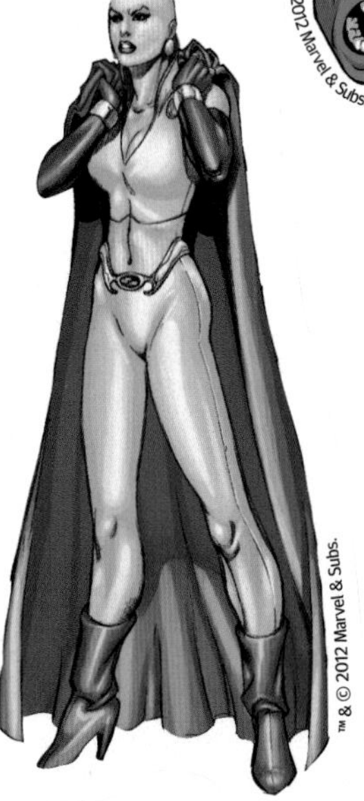

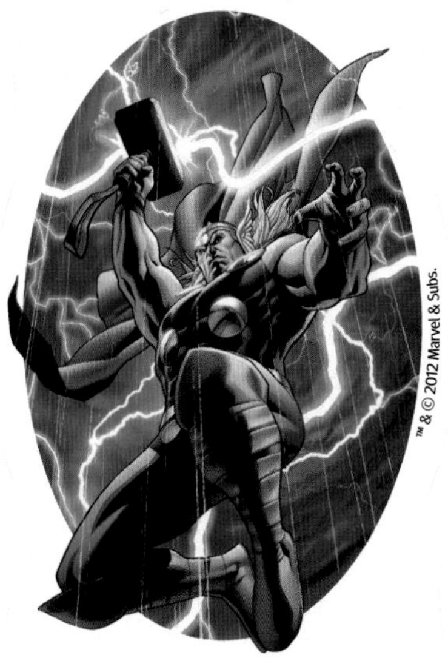

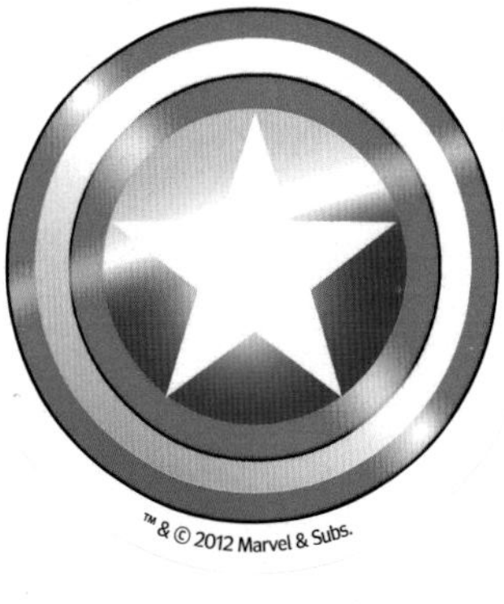

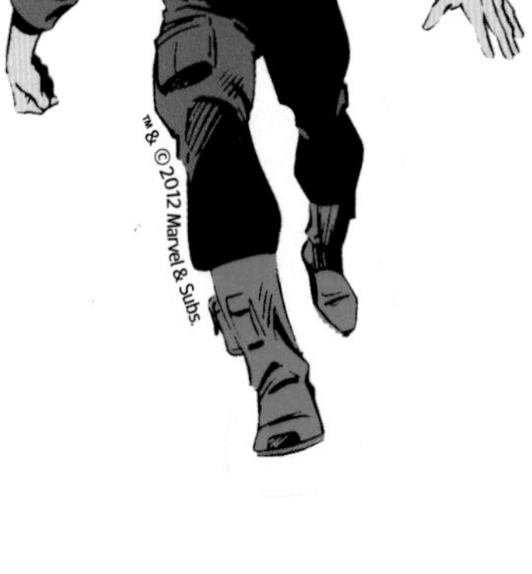

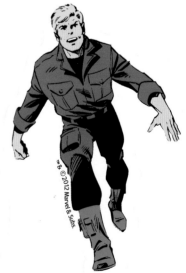

EXTRA STICKERS

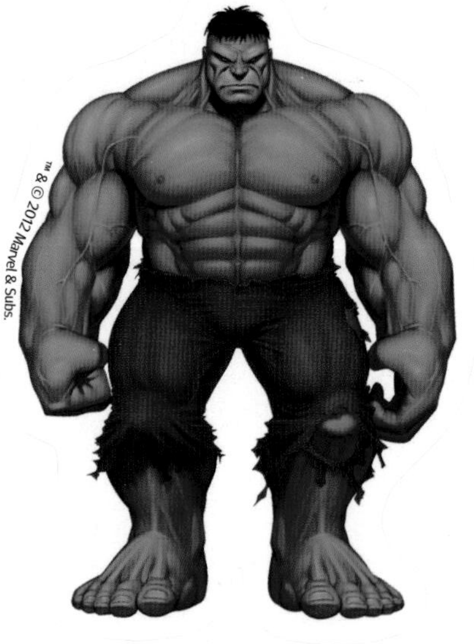

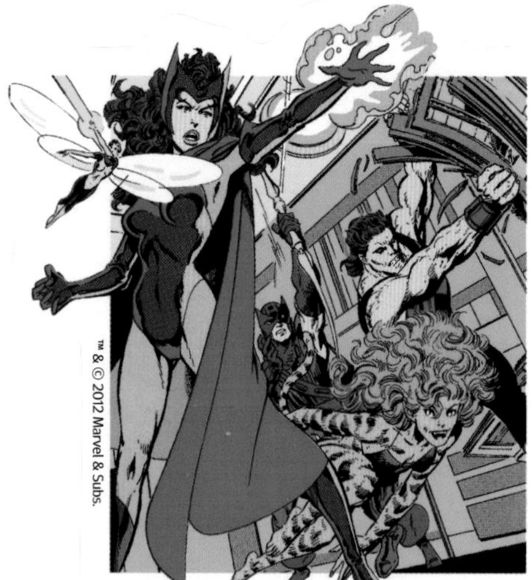

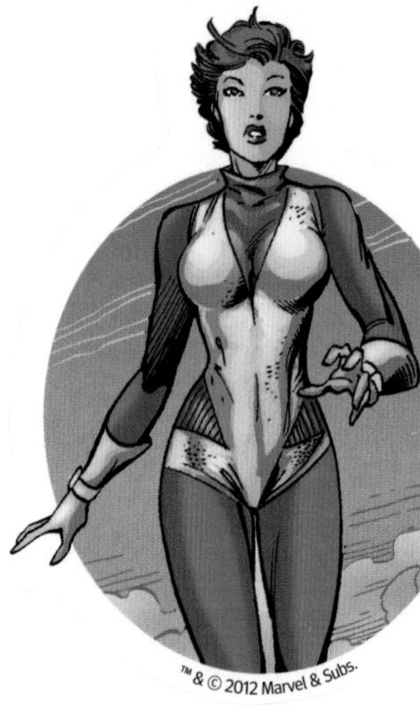

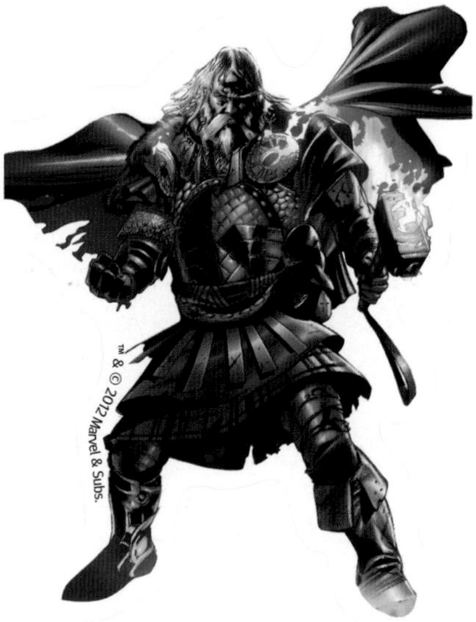

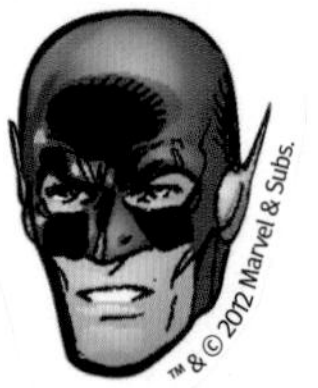

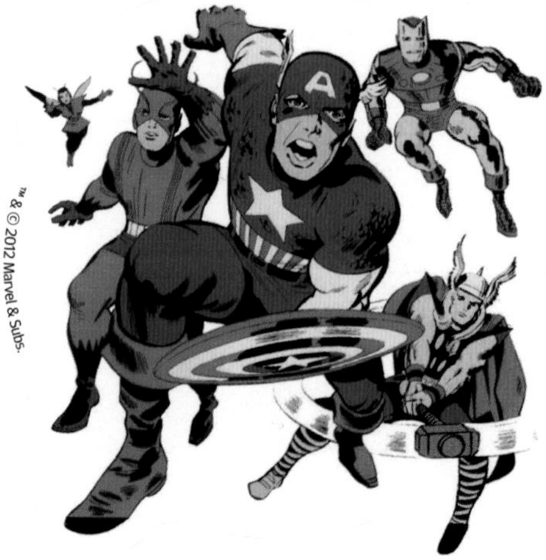

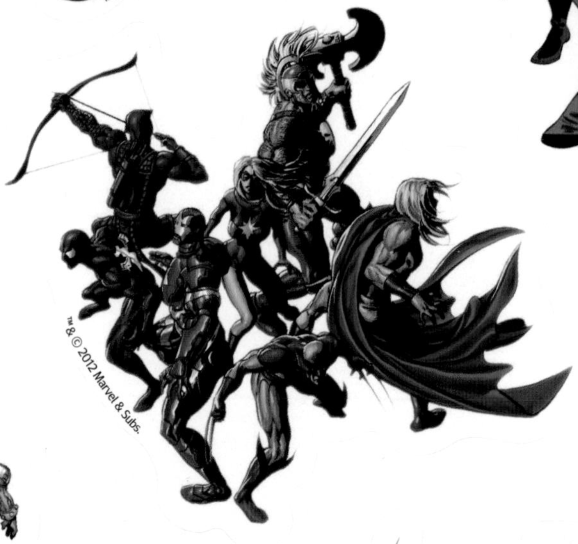

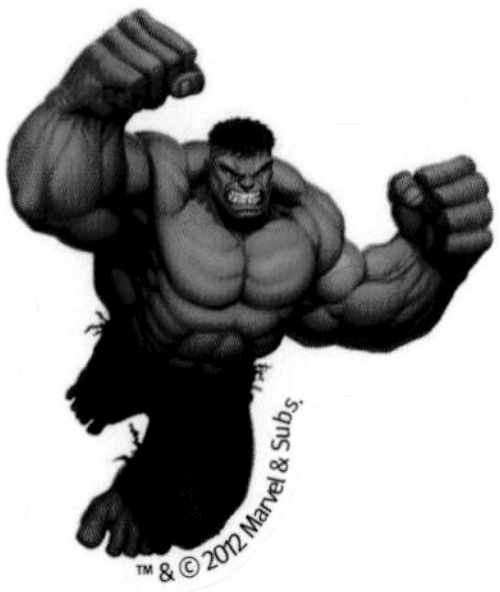

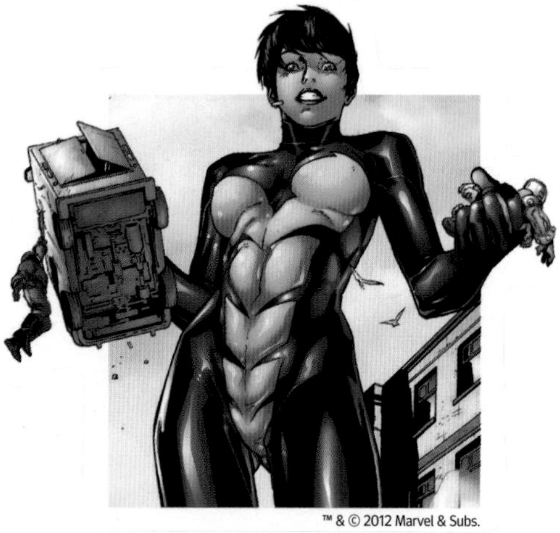

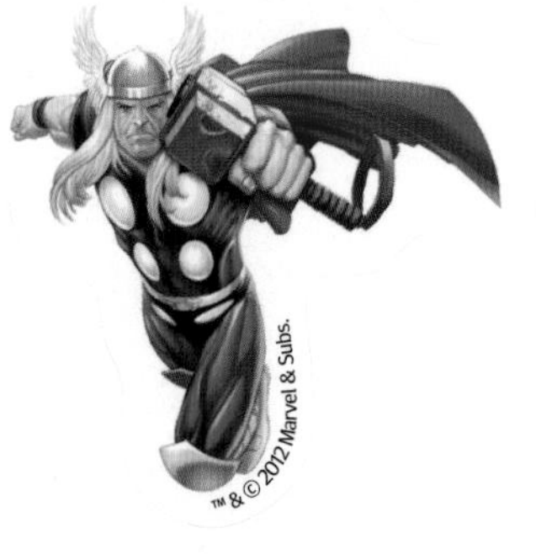

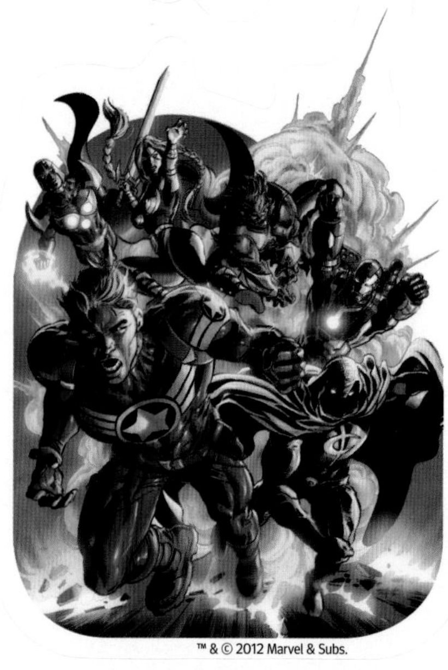

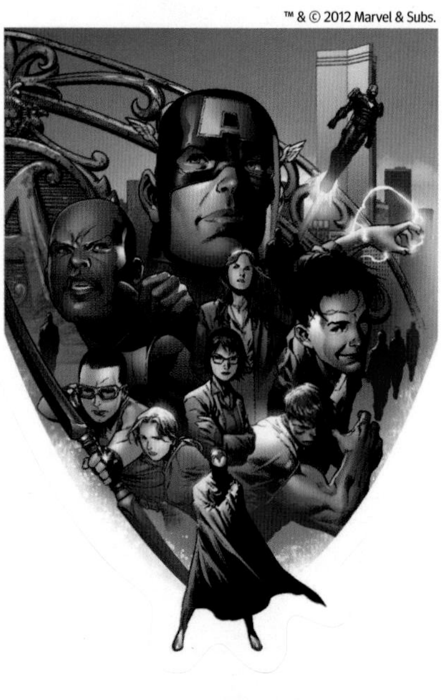

EXTRA STICKERS

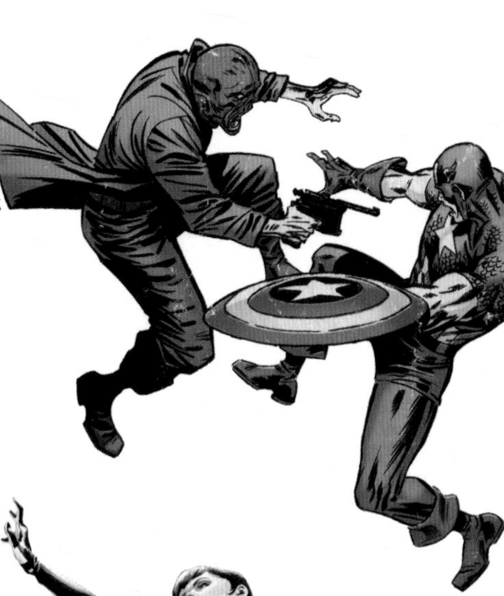

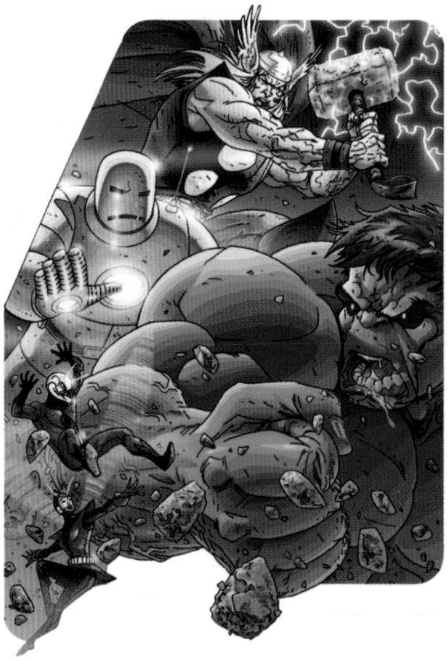

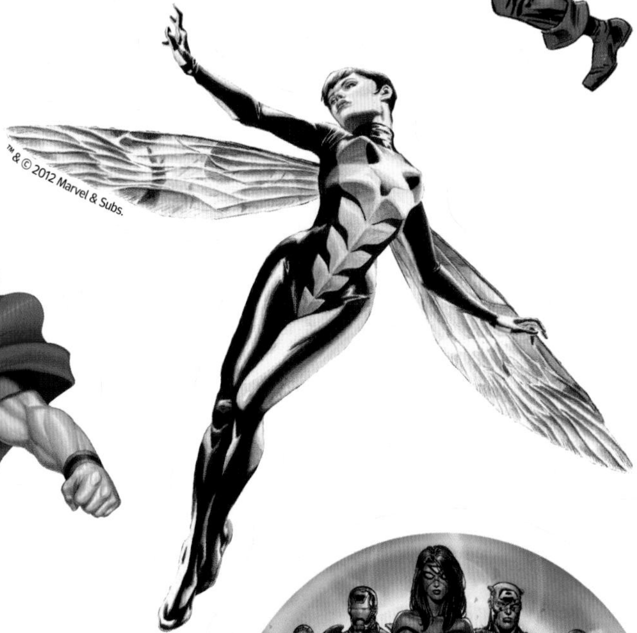

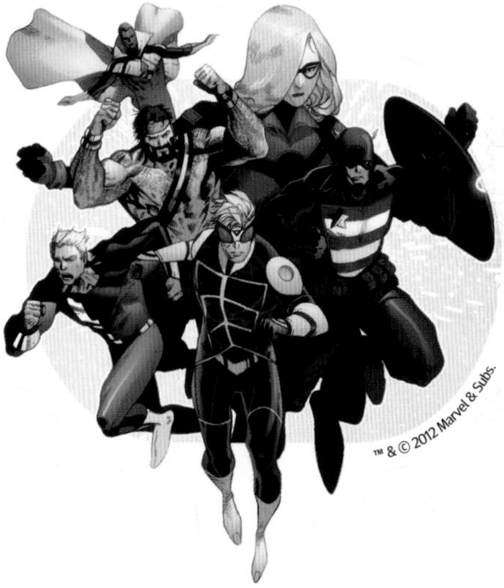

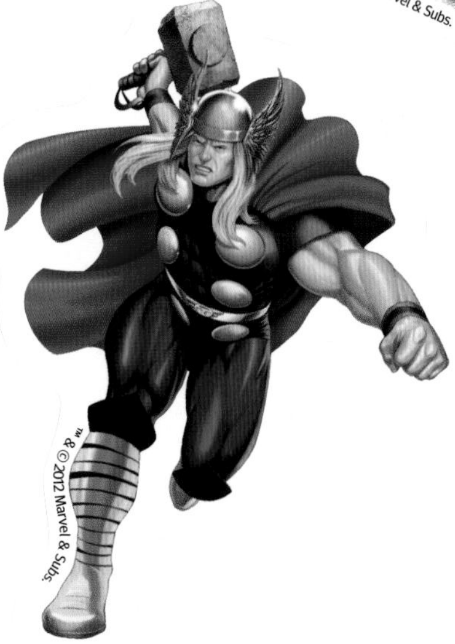

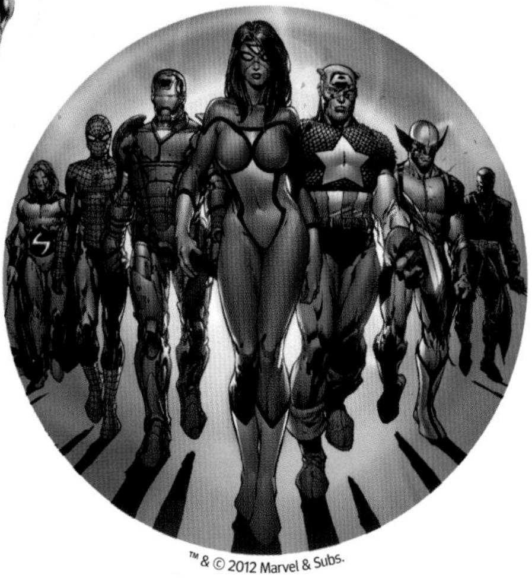

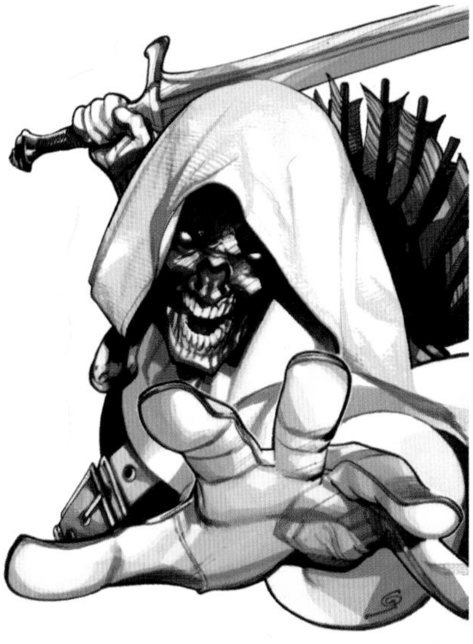

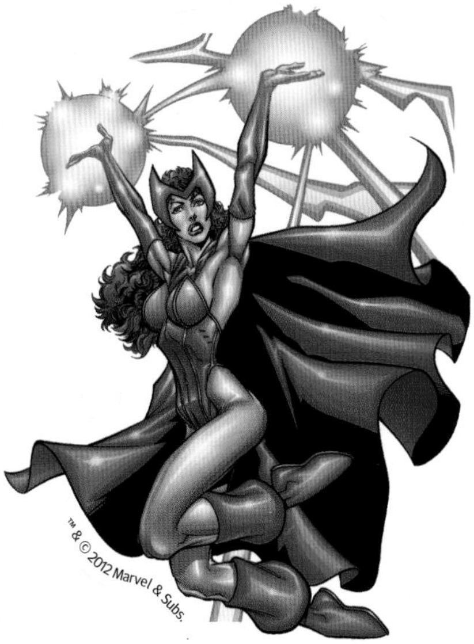

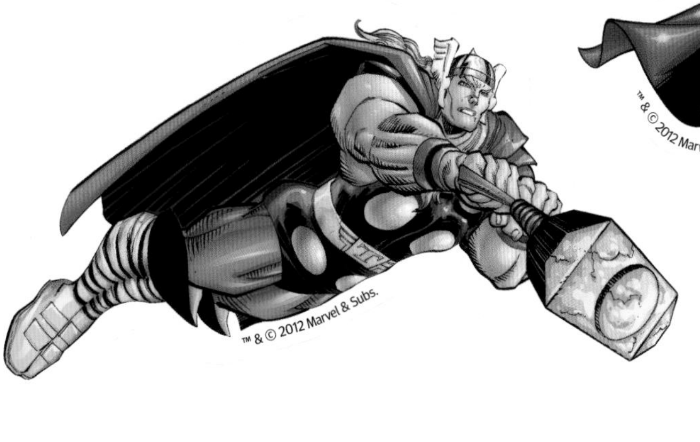

EXTRA STICKERS

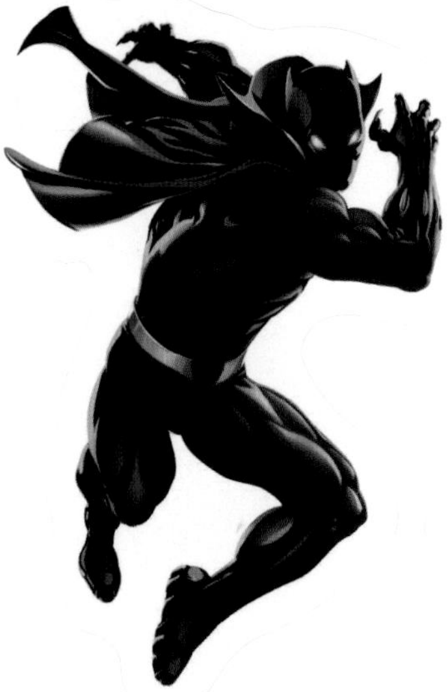

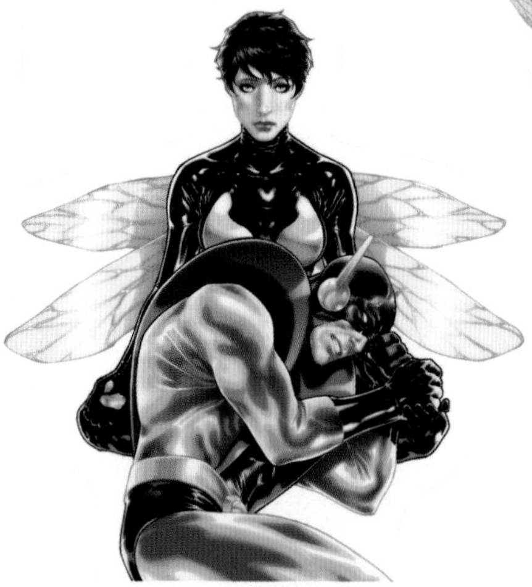

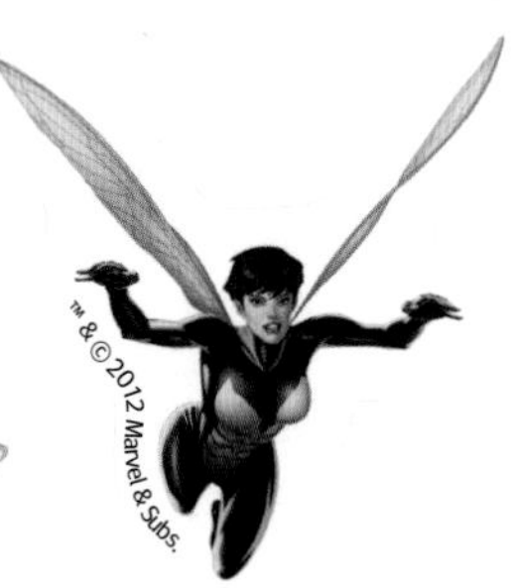

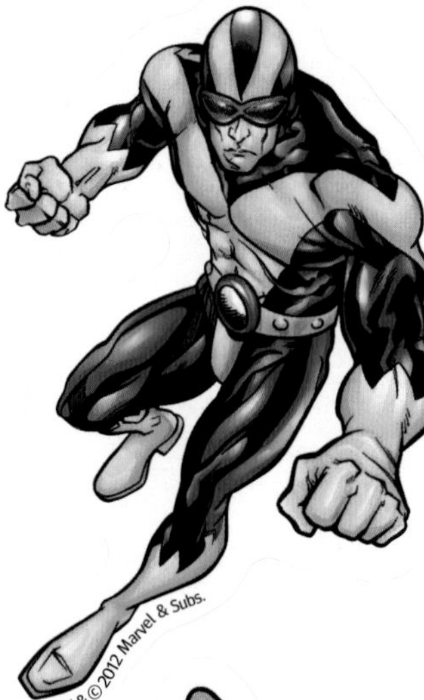

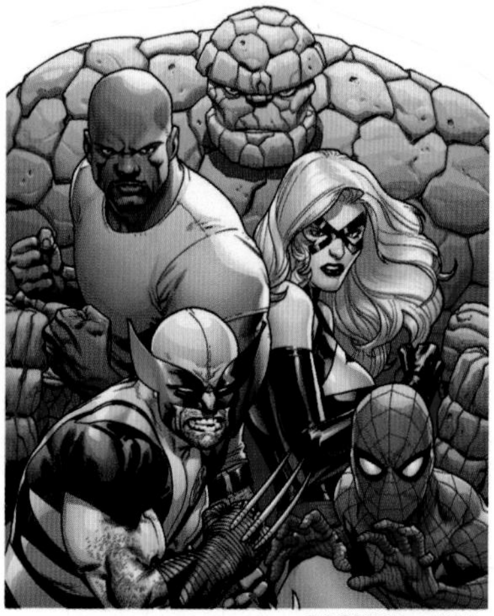

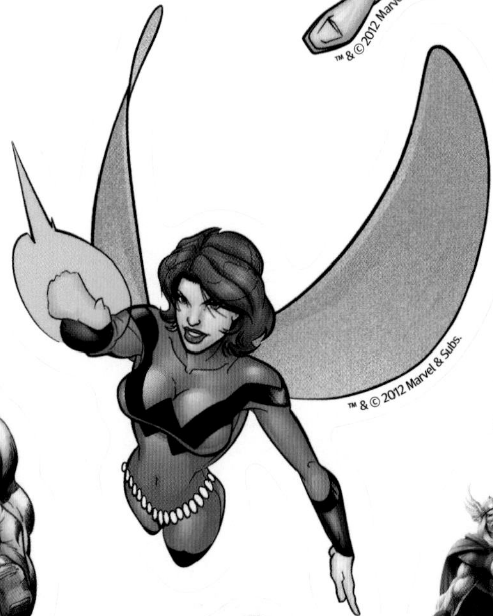

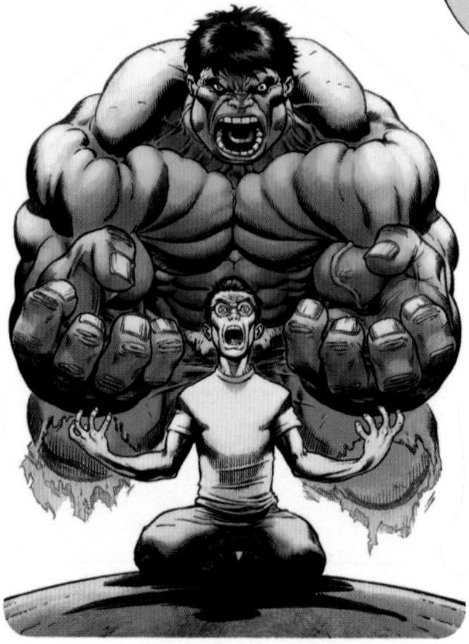

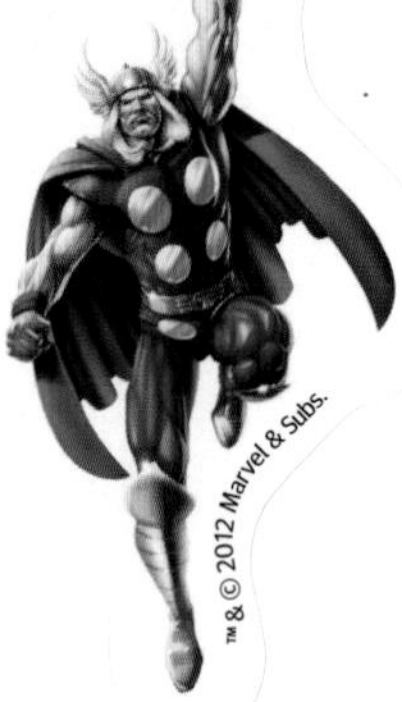

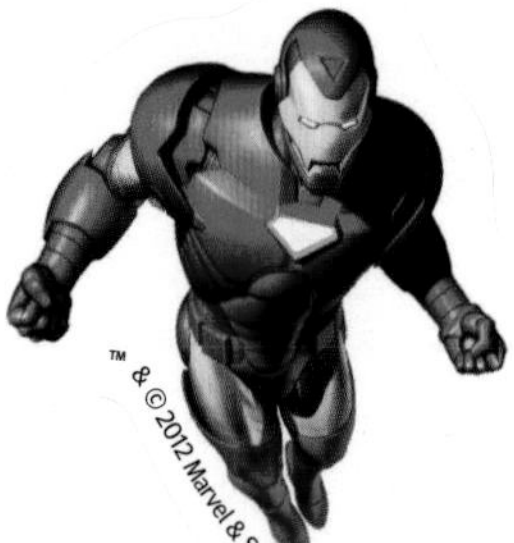

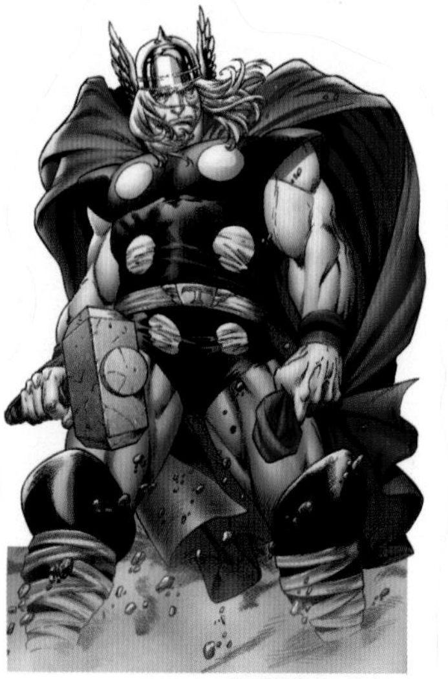

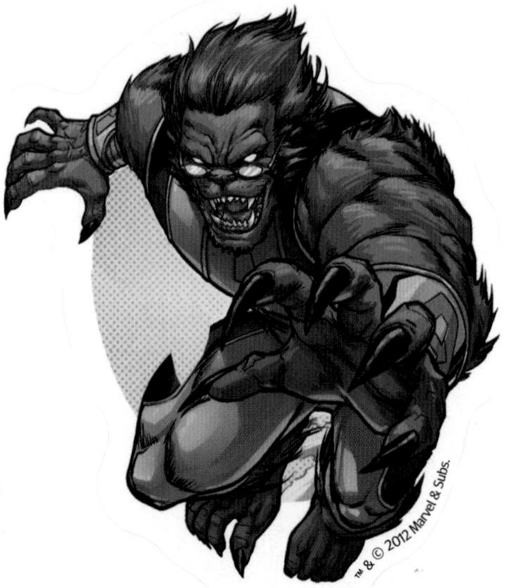

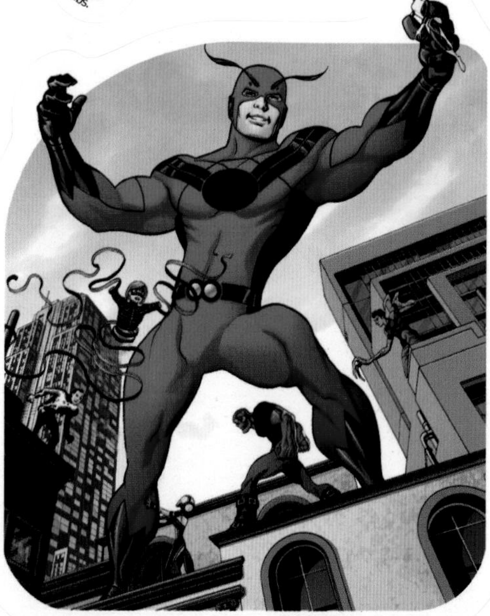

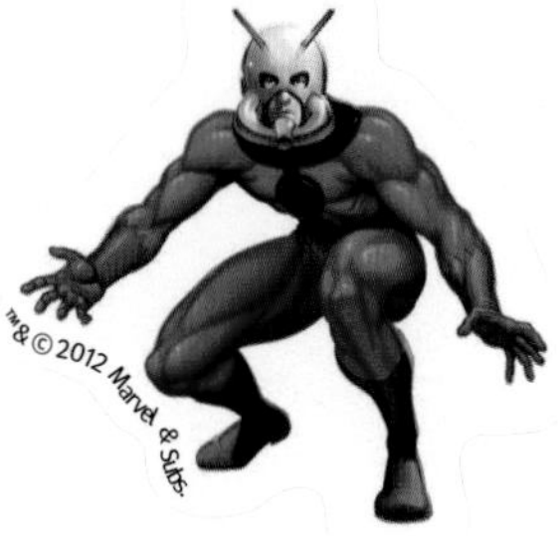

EXTRA STICKERS

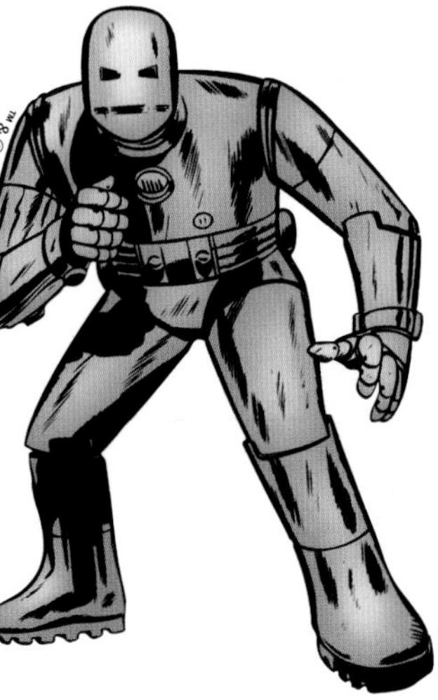

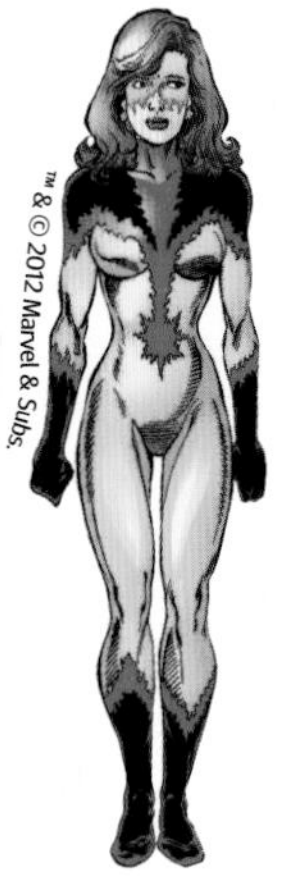

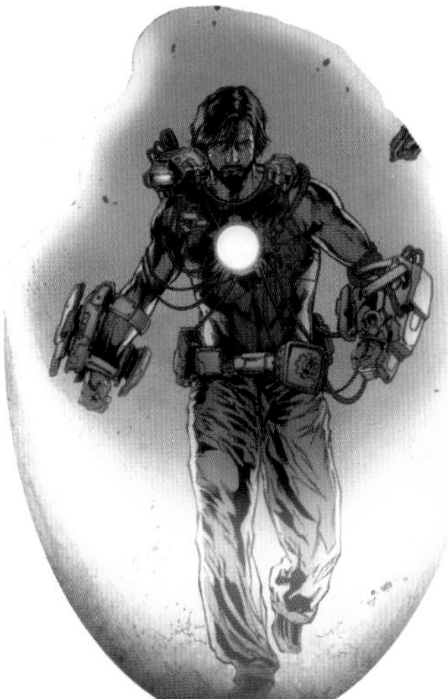

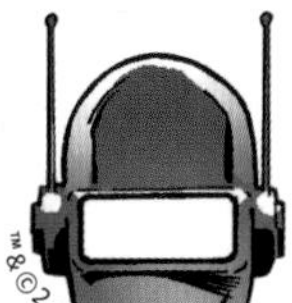

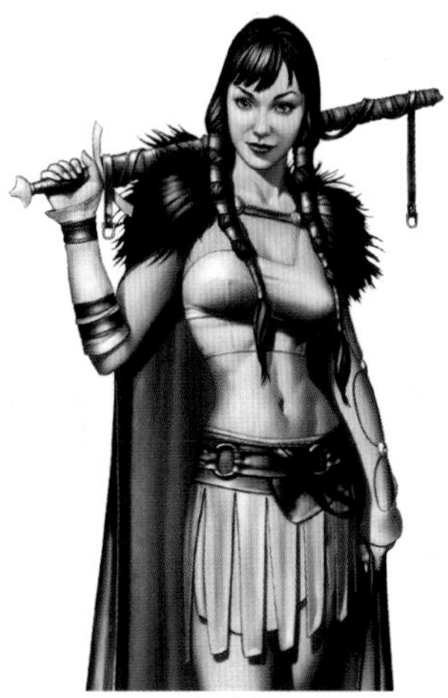

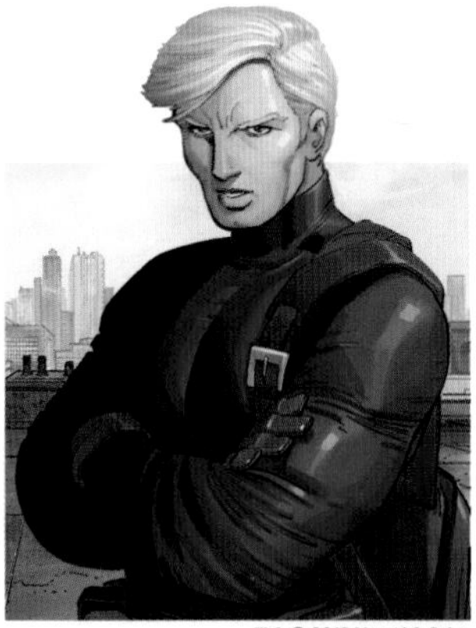

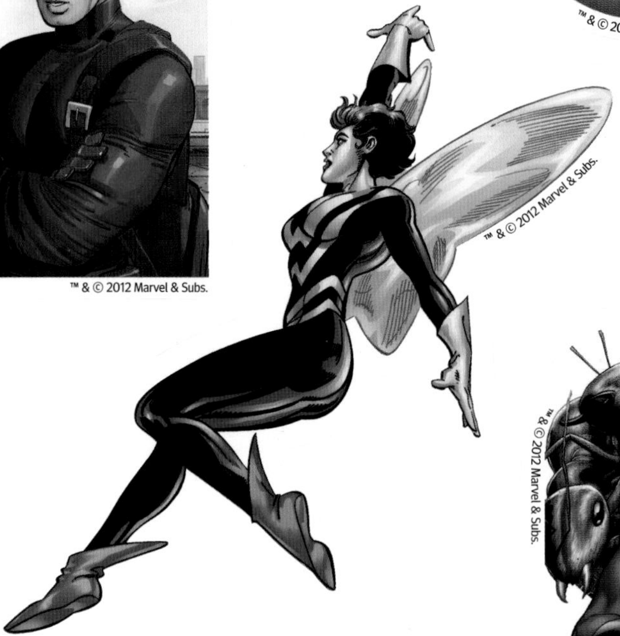

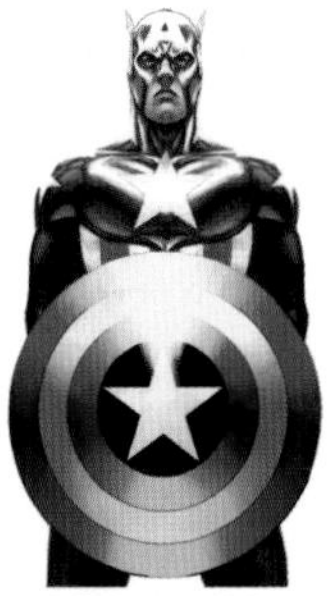

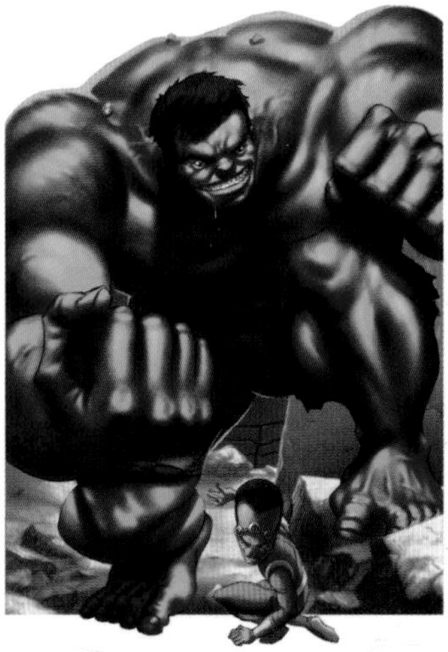

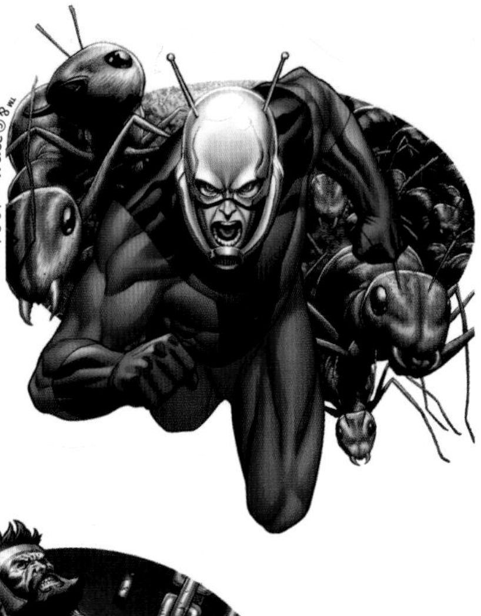

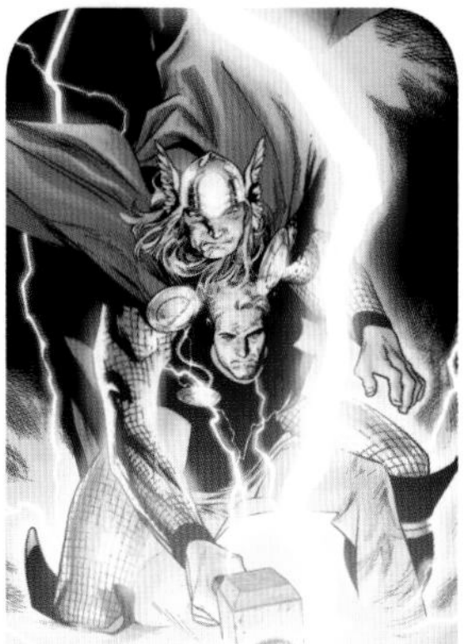

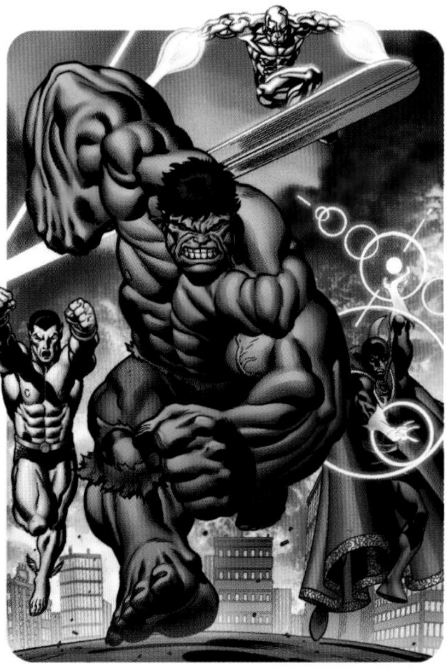

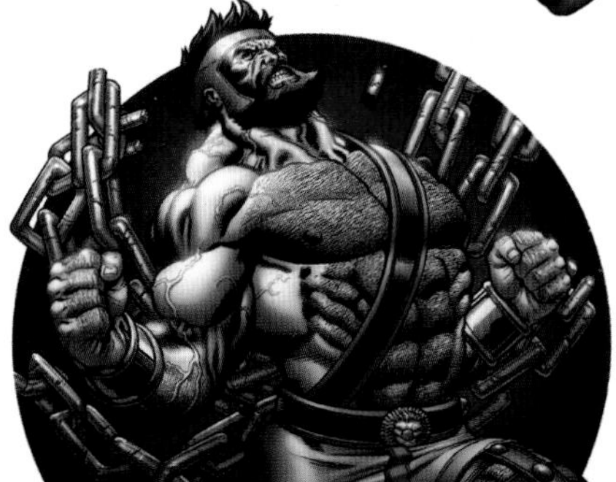

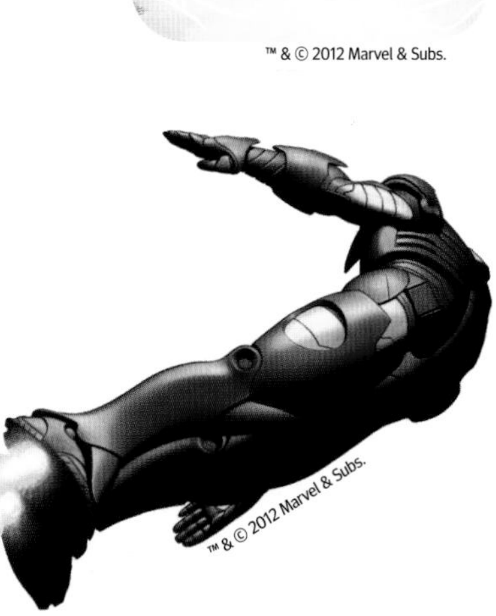

EXTRA STICKERS

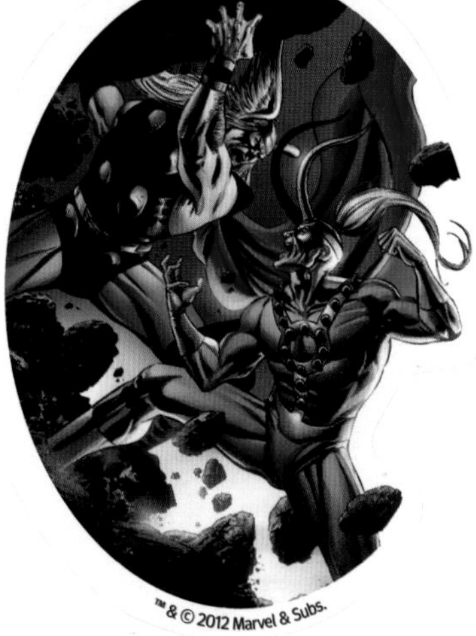
™ & © 2012 Marvel & Subs.

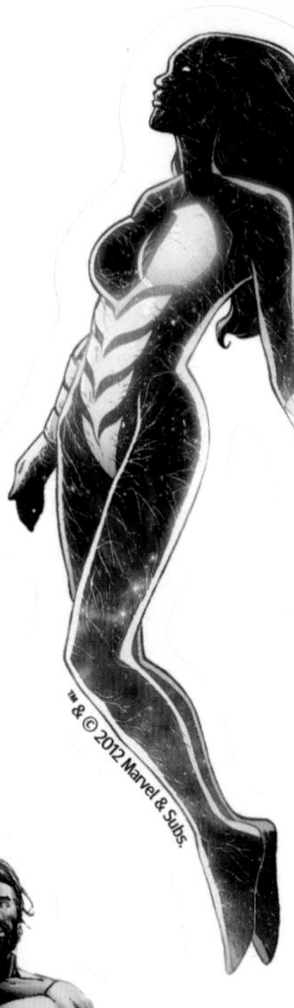
™ & © 2012 Marvel & Subs.

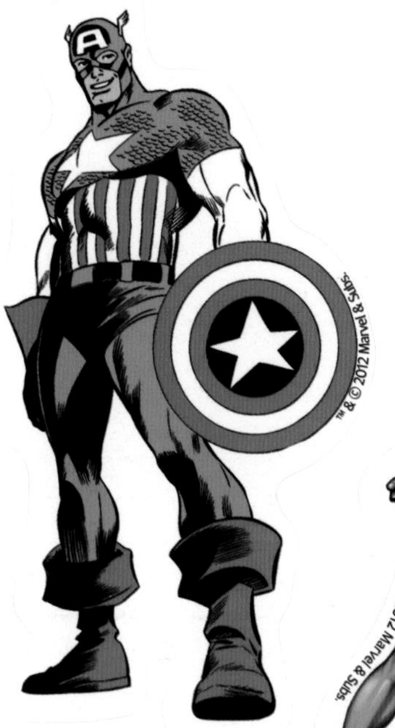
™ & © 2012 Marvel & Subs.

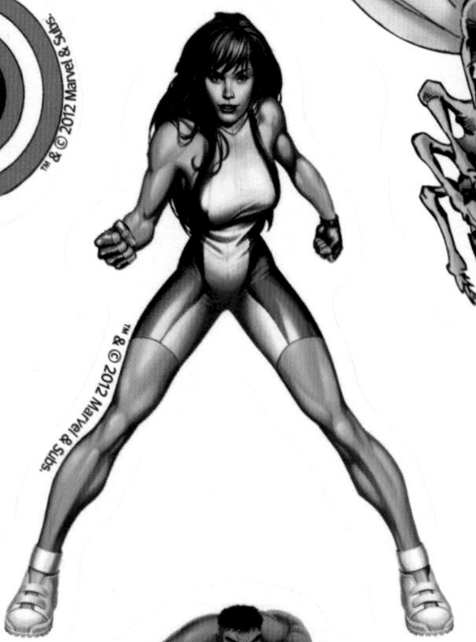
™ & © 2012 Marvel & Subs.

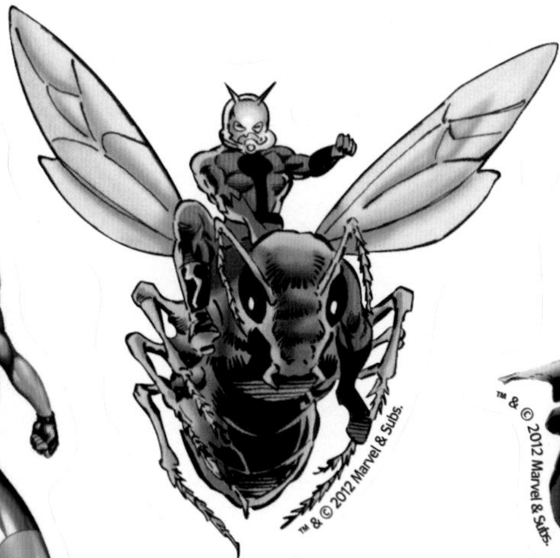
™ & © 2012 Marvel & Subs.

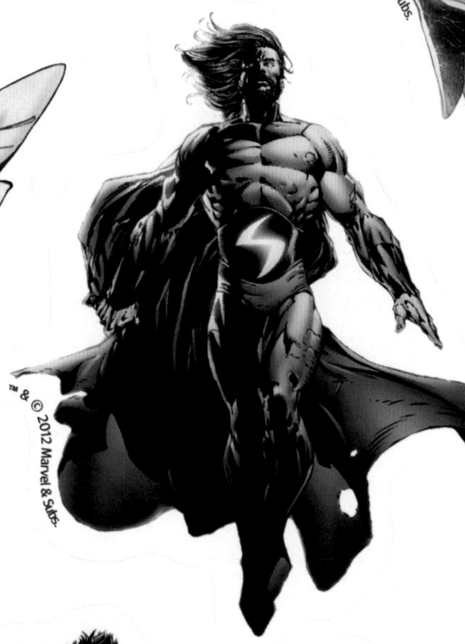
™ & © 2012 Marvel & Subs.

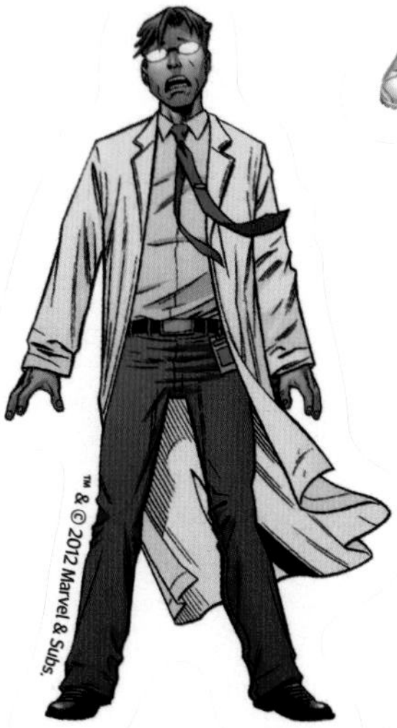
™ & © 2012 Marvel & Subs.

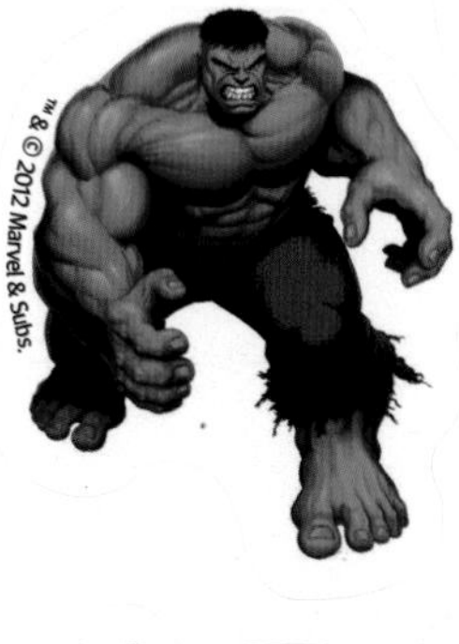
™ & © 2012 Marvel & Subs.

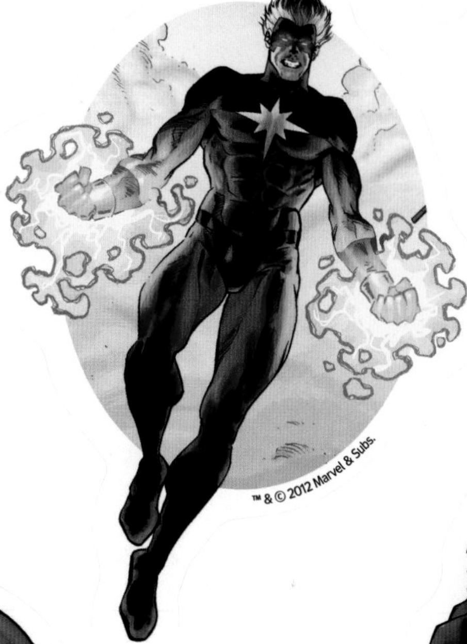
™ & © 2012 Marvel & Subs.

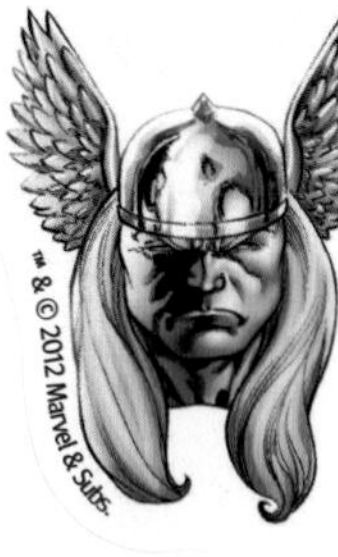
™ & © 2012 Marvel & Subs.

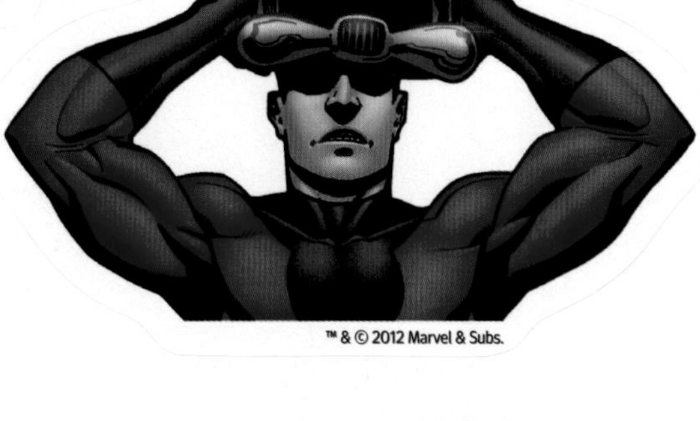
™ & © 2012 Marvel & Subs.

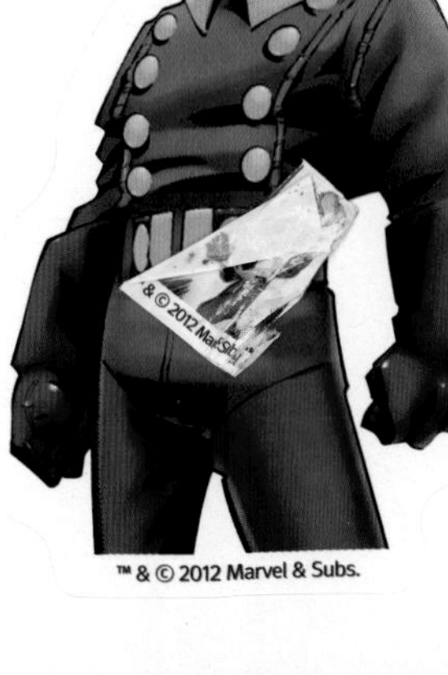
™ & © 2012 Marvel & Subs.

EXTRA STICKERS

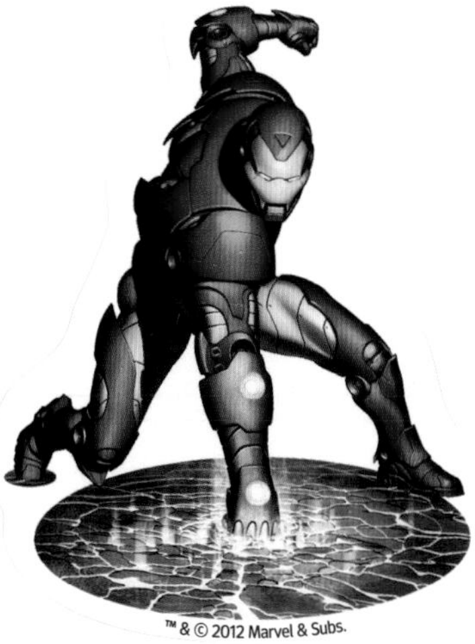

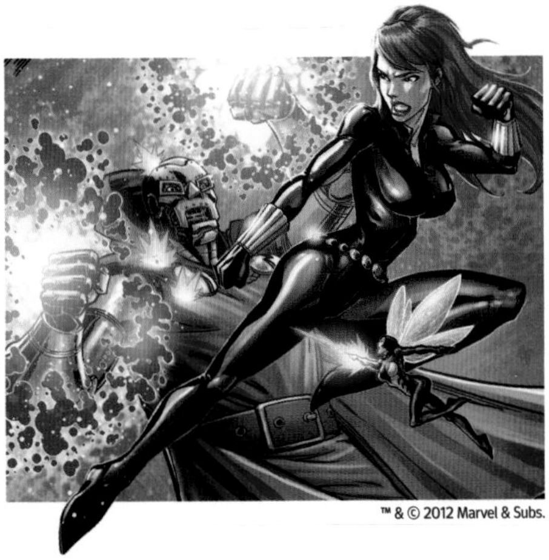

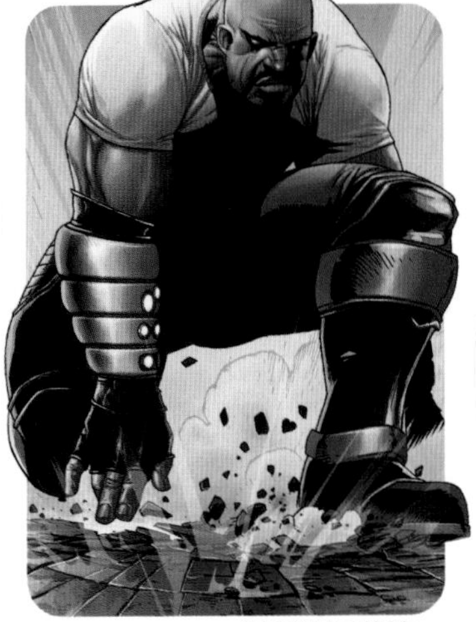

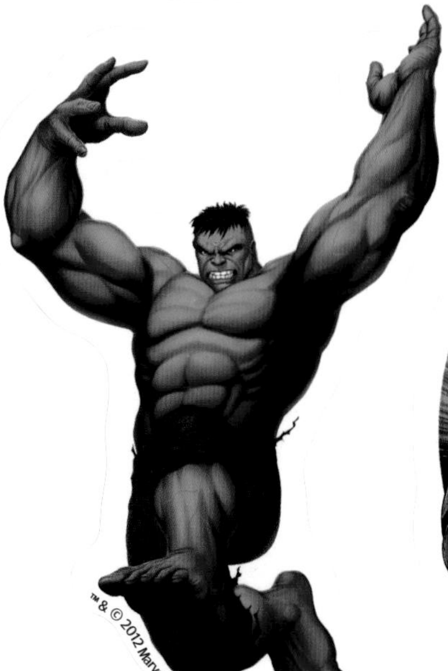

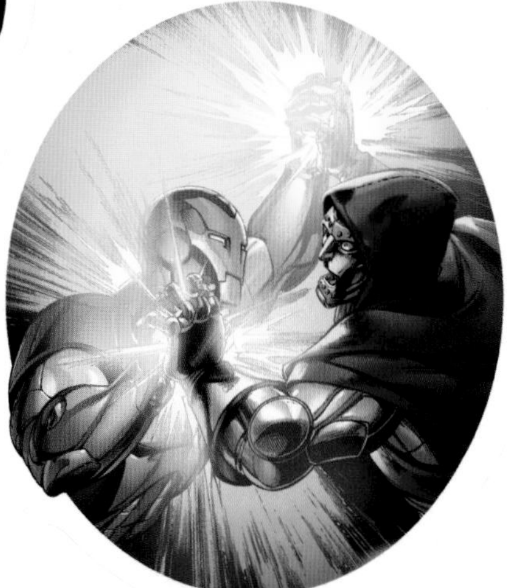

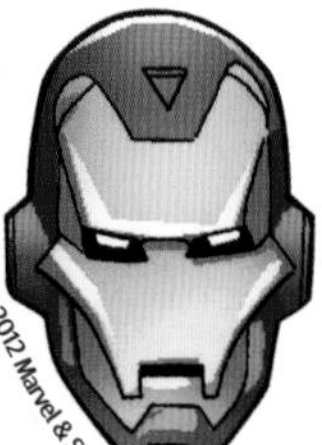

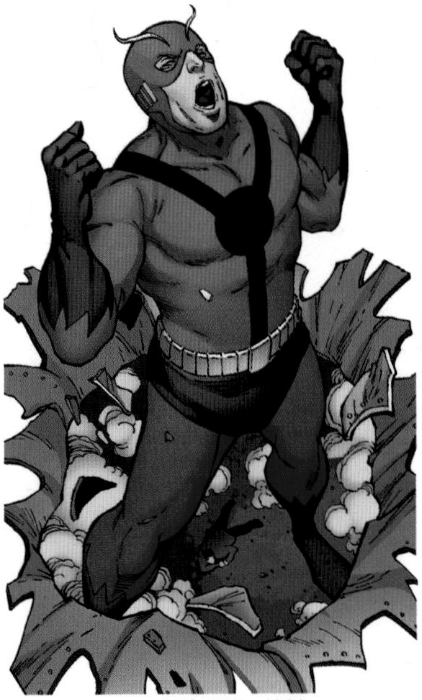

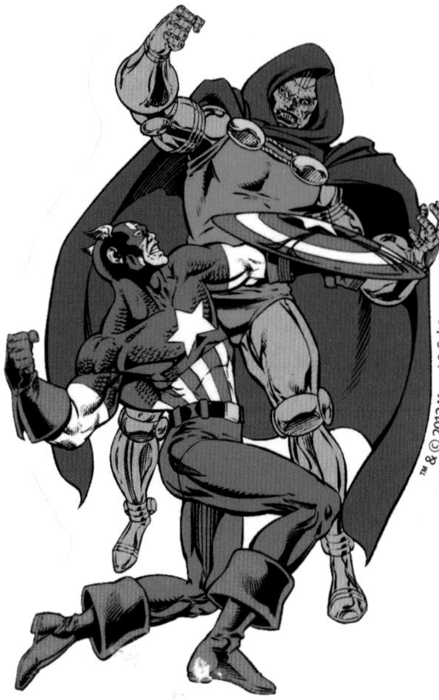

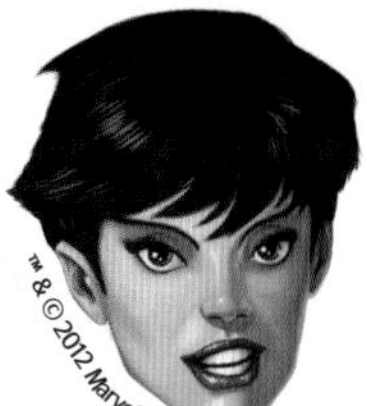

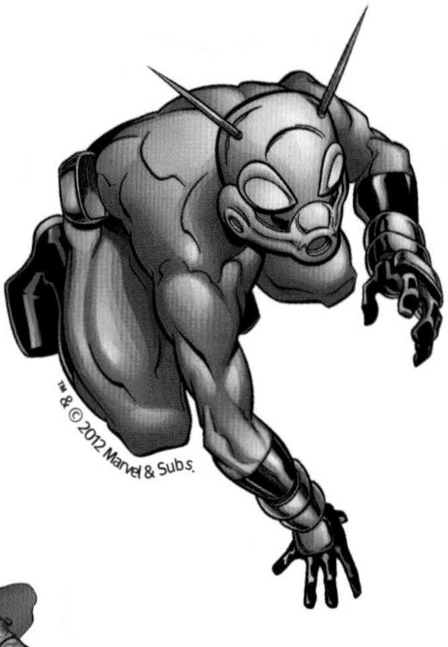

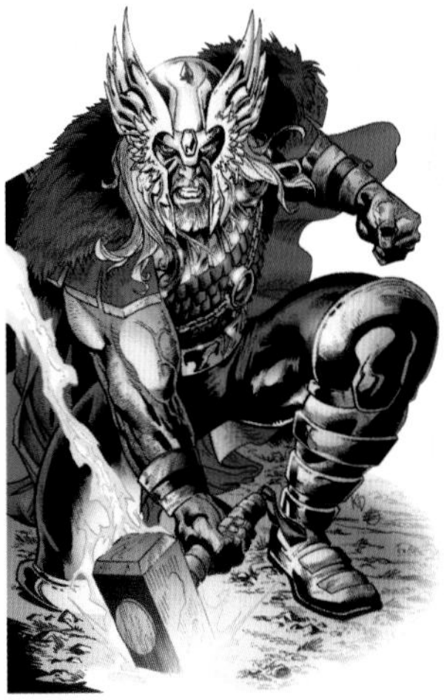

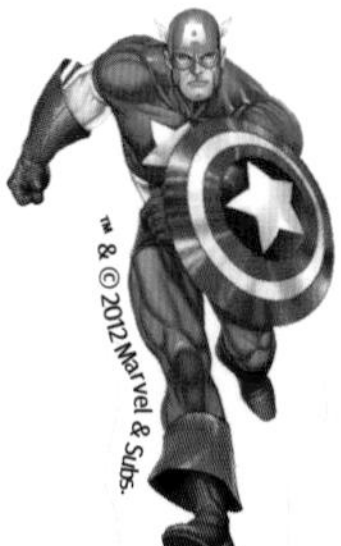

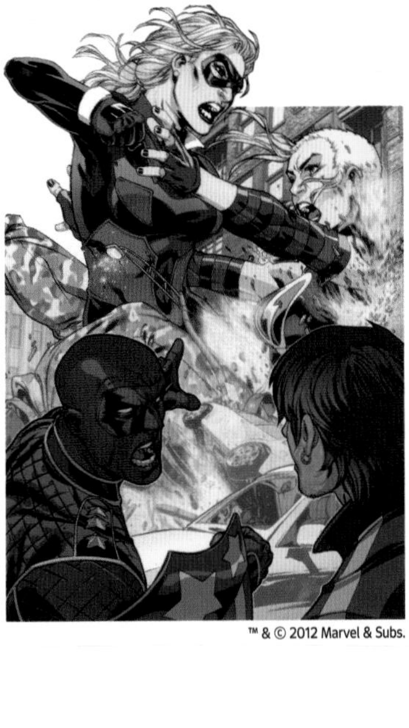

EXTRA STICKERS

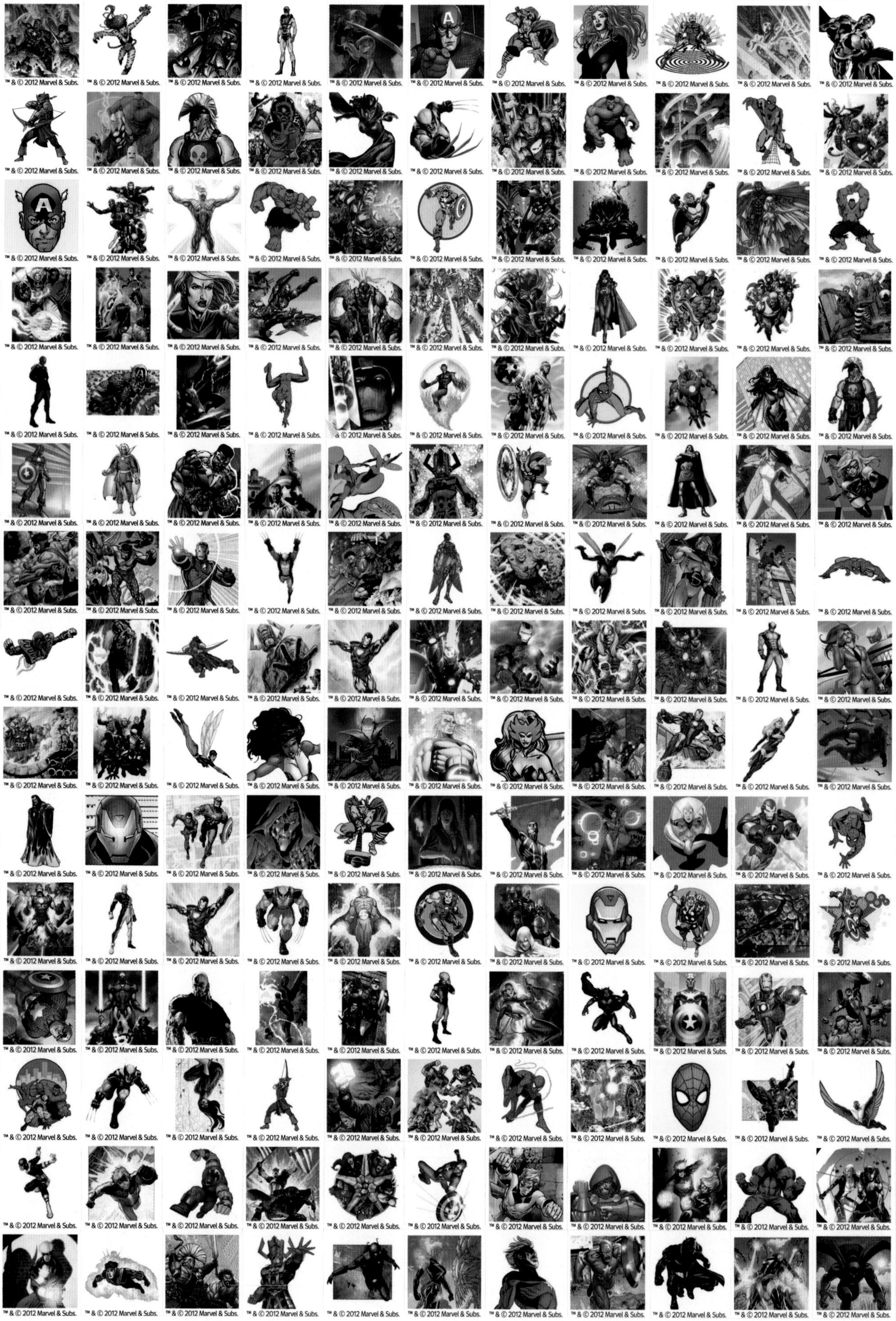
™ & © 2012 Marvel & Subs.

EXTRA STICKERS

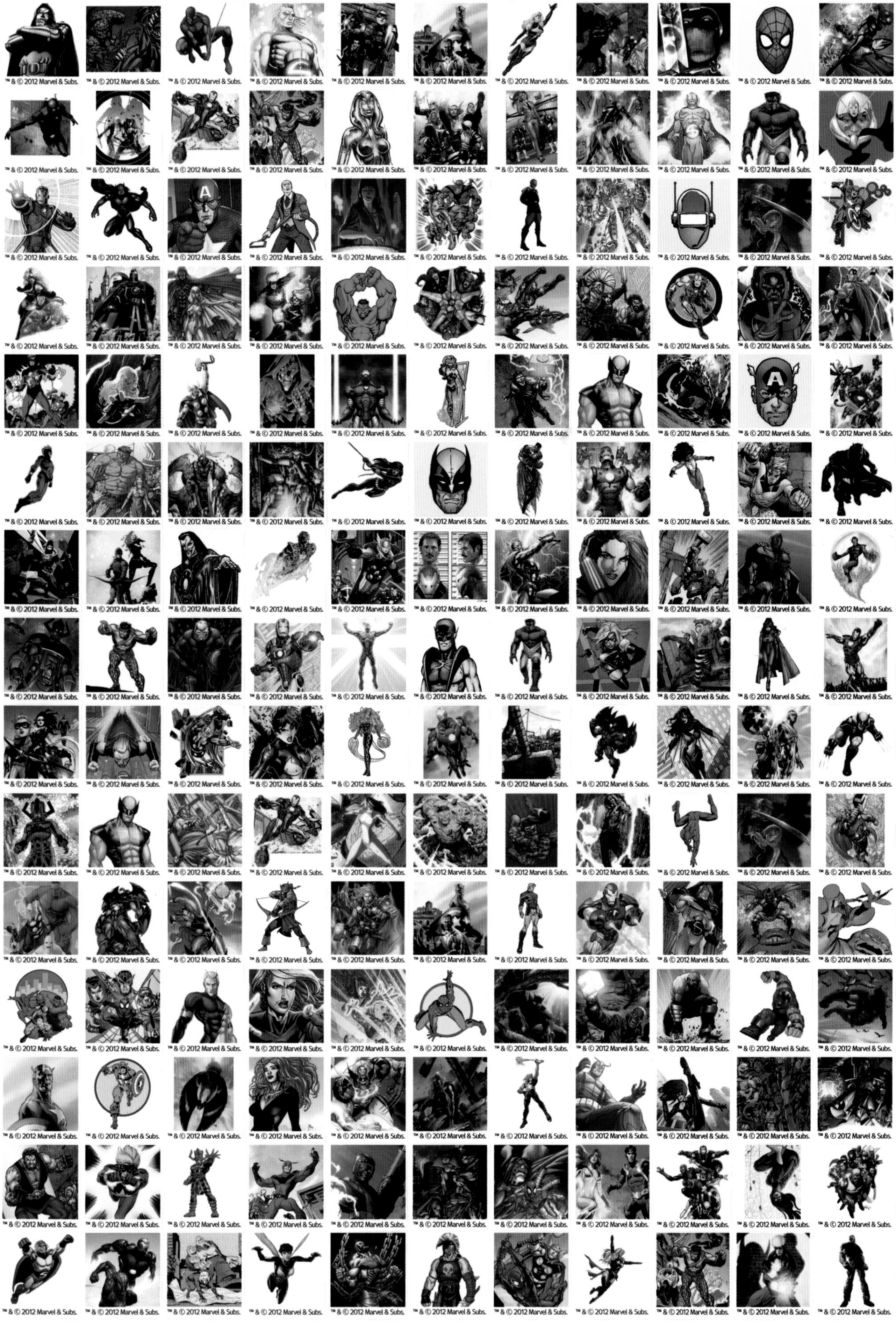
™ & © 2012 Marvel & Subs.